FLESH MADE
WORLD
DAULTON DICKEY

Published by Rooster Republic Press LLC
www.rooosterrepublicpress.com
roosterrepublicpress@gmail.com

Copyright © Daulton Dickey
Edited by Nicholas Day, Jeff O'Brien
Cover Design – Nicholas Day, D.F. Noble
Interior Design – D.F. Noble

Find our catalog at
www.roosterrepublicpress.com

For everyone suffering from depression. You're not alone.

For my father. I'm lost without you.

And for Alice. For putting up with my madness.

"My habits of thought have been so conditioned by innumerable torturous processes that today I find myself unable to place complete confidence in any notion I may have of the universe without first subjecting that notion to an abstract examination." —Louis Aragon, *Paris Peasant*

a.

The **bedroom looks** more or less as it did when Sarah's mother had returned from the hospital, like something out of a 70s Style magazine: khaki colored carpet—shag carpet, mind you—vanilla walls, a beige ceiling. A dresser stands beside the closet door. A bed towers in the center of the room, one of those velvet numbers. It looks old and worn, the bed, like it's been sitting beneath a pile of scrap metal for years.

As a child, Sarah loved to peel the sheets and blankets off and roll around on it. Complete with a velvet headboard, the bed attracted her; she loved how it felt, adored it, even.

It repulsed her after her mother died. And, as a teenager, it embarrassed her when, on a rare occasion, a friend, rarer still, showed up to the house and peered into the room. The headboard alone belonged in a museum, it was so old; and its

7

color, purple, caught the eye. It never failed to elicit a comment, usually about her father, which further embarrassed her.

Sarah shoves her fist into the mattress. It creaks. She recoils and blurts something like a scream but not quite a scream. More like a yelp. Touching the mattress had raised gooseflesh on her arms, which she now pulls to her chest and massages.

Her mother's absence lingers, but it's vague. It reminds Sarah of the feeling she experiences when she leaves her house and forgets something —but not certain if she has, in fact, forgotten something. And this evokes pretty much the same sensation, her mother's absence. Why does she linger? But then does she linger?

After a while, the sensation dims. It dims. The shadows of years gone by darken the signature of her existence.

And Sarah's father ... His absence is fucking oppressive. Like at any moment Sarah expects him to call from downstairs or to make an appearance or to ask why she's in his room. Like it doesn't even feel as if he's out of town or on vacation or something. It feels like he's there, right there, alive and well and in the house, maybe in the living room, maybe, or in the basement. And ... but ... she doesn't have access to him. Like he's there but she can't pinpoint his location; like she knows he's home but she can't figure out in which room he's doing whatever it is he does.

She opens the closet door—inside, it smells like dust—and fumbles for the twine dangling from the light fixture. She flails her arm and pinches her fingers. Then, still flailing her arm, she slaps the twine, catches and pulls it. Photons ping pong around the closet.

Clothes hang from wall to wall. Men's clothes. Some old, some new, some she's never seen. She slides her fingers across the sleeve of an old jacket. Goosebumps. The clothes retain his smell, his signature. Tears threaten to assault her. She clears her throat and closes her eyes and pops her neck, slaying the tears before they usurp her.

It's almost funny. Every suit, every shirt, every pair of pants—everything seems plucked out of the 1970s and 80s, like her father was maybe some secret sitcom star and had saved his wardrobe. As a teenager, of course, she didn't find it funny, even though his style wasn't as outdated.

Among blues and whites, and even a pink, among velvet and cardigan, a black suit sticks out. Does it look good? Seams are frayed and, at some points, gray dulls black, turning it more or less silver. So no: it doesn't look good. But then so what? Does it matter what he looks like when he's buried?

But even in death people tend to appear the way others expect them to appear.

—It's such bullshit, she says.

More faded clothes. More frayed seams. Did the man own a decent suit?

But does it matter? Does it really fucking matter? People will see him in this outfit—whichever suit she settles on—for at most a day, and they probably won't even remember the damn thing. Then, after a few hours, someone will lock him in a box, in darkness, until the clothes rot, until the tectonic plates shift and drift away, until the sun expands and devours the planet.

An eternity of the absence of experience is indifferent to the clothes someone forces onto a corpse, she knows, and yet a strange obligation roils her: he must, at the very least, appear presentable.

She bumps the closet door with her ass, closing it—her father had installed the door backward. Never the DIY type, he more or less shrugged it off. In fact, he claimed to prefer it. Whoever heard of an inward swinging closet door? he'd said. She hadn't, for one, so she picked on him whenever she saw or remembered it. He'd laugh or shrug it off or mutter something about getting around to it, a favorite phrase: "I'll get around to it later."

The thought brings a smile to her face.

The smile fades.

She drops to her knees and digs through boxes filled with bags of socks and new clothes. For some reason, her father had purchased these clothes and tossed them into a box and either forgot about them or chose not to wear them—tags, still affixed to at least half of them, advertise a clearance sale in red ink.

It makes her want to laugh. It makes her want to cry. It makes her want to choke him, this box, these clothes. For years he had joked about Sarah's mother, about how she'd hoarded knickknacks and books, clothes and even newspapers. And yet, on those occasions, he'd failed to disclose his at least minor proclivity for hoarding shit.

It's not surprising in hindsight. On the rare occasion he let something approximating sentimentalism slip, he'd produce an object Sarah hadn't seen. Like the time he showed her a spoon inherited from his mother-in-law. He coveted the damn thing. At some point—Sarah couldn't remember when—he even built a display case and hung it on the wall in the kitchen, beside the table, and betrayed anxiety when someone sat near it.

The world dims. Light grows again.

Sarah's sitting in the kitchen now, examining the spoon. In the display case. Her father, sitting on the other side of the table, eyeballs her, then the spoon, as he tears into a New York strip. Sarah picks a piece of lint from the corner and flicks it away. Her dad drops his fork, reaches out, belches a sort of visceral scream.

—Settle down, Sarah says, laughing. —There was lint.

—Where?

—Right there. On the corner.

—I'm thinking about building a sturdier case. Maybe putting some glass on it.

—That seems excessive.

—It's a valuable piece.

—It's a spoon.

—With Paul Revere's maker's mark.

—Are you shitting me?

—It's worth tens of thousands, he says. — Easily.

—Bullshit.

—Look it up.

Patina darkens it, gives it an almost marbled-copper coat. It's old, but otherwise undistinguished. Just a spoon. Nothing fancy or ornate. It seems mass produced, recent, like a piece from one of those "heirloom" sets sold door-to-door in the fifties.

—The mark's on the back, her father says. —I'm thinking about mounting it so you can see it, maybe include a picture or a brief history, or ...

First he smiles and then he frowns. First his eyelids narrow and then they open. Then he says something—it comes across as a moan—and water flows from his mouth. Bubbles churn on the surface of the water. They pop as the water slams into his neck and chest, and the word "Help" escapes from the bubbles as they pop. Visible—not sounds but symbols, as if typed: "Help"—the words float up, up, and crash into the ceiling.

As words coalesce around his head, Sarah's father's face turns pale and gray. His eyes and mouth droop. Then more bubbles, more symbols, more words: "Oh god, help." His face shifts, his skin bulges. Another yelp—another popped bubble—produces a groan. Slumping forward, he slams his face into the table. His arms fall to his sides.

Sarah scrambles to her feet, kicks over her chair, and, screaming ...

She's back in the closet now, squeezing a shirt. The walls seem closer; the closet, smaller. Dimmer now, the light casts everything in an almost sepia tone. The twine rattles against the light bulb as it sways back and forth, back and forth, crosshatching everything with shadows.

Then ...

Something moans.

Sarah drops the shirt and steps back. The door, pressing against her, feels like meat. Sounds in the bedroom—is it a moan?—shake the walls, the floor, the door. Boom. Boom. Boom. Her lungs stiffen. Her breath disintegrates. She's going to hyperventilate, she swears to fucking god. Boom. Boom. Boom. She sucks in air. Boom. Boom. Boom. It escapes her lungs. Boom. Boom ... And, fuck, is that a moan? a groan? Boom. She grasps the doorknob, fumbles with it as she tries to open the door. But her hand flies away from it, more or less of its own volition: the doorknob feels like raw meat—cold, wet, and slimy.

Boom.

She gasps. Inhales, inhales, exhales. She thrusts her arm toward the ceiling. Her fingernail snags the twine and the light powers down. The photons evaporate. She can't see them but she senses the walls—the fucking walls and the ceiling—closing in on her, pushing toward her, trying to crush her, and she ...

Boom.

Sounds from the other room.

Boom.

Sounds like thunder. Or gunshots.

Boom. Boom.

Her chest tightens. Her lungs stiffen. She gasps for air. Gasps. She's going to hyperventilate, she fucking swears it. Darkness envelops her. It squeezes and crushes her. She reaches behind her again and fumbles for the doorknob again, fumbles to ...

She arches her spine and, thrusting her ass outward, pops the hinges and flings open the door. Light pours into the closet. It blinds her. She stumbles; the back of her head smacks the floor as light pops in her eyes and ringing fills her ears.

Still lying on her back, she slams her eyelids closed and massages her forehead. Air fills her lungs again. She inhales and exhales without difficulty. But now her head hurts. Pain shoots through her back. And something, something like sadness maybe, courses through her. It detonates in her head and chest and flows through her veins; it hollows her stomach, replaces the marrow in her bones.

And ...

Tears roll down her face. They slip into her ear or race down her neck. And her stomach ... fuck ... her stomach ...

Then ...

That sound again: boom, boom, boom. It's neither thunder nor gunshots, neither moans nor groans.

It sounds like ...

Footsteps.

Footsteps?

In one motion she cranes her neck and opens her eyes and spins onto her stomach. A kid— Michelle?—traipses through the doorway. Sounds like moans and popping bubbles fill the room. A conversation: child and adult.

Sarah flies to her feet.

Her mother—ashen face, sunken eyes sparse hair—lies in bed and shifts to her side. Michelle —now only a child—holds her mother's hand.

That empty feeling, that sad and empty hollowness, returns. Sarah stands motionless. She's unable to move or to think while she watches her dead sister push an ice cube over her dead mother's lips, moistening them.

Her mother says something. Michelle laughs. But laughter doesn't leave her mouth—water does; it flows as though she'd chugged a glassful without swallowing, then opened her mouth; bubbles pop; and then laughter escapes the popped bubbles.

Triangles superimposed over Michelle's nose, mouth, and eyes shift, shift, shift. The triangles distort and mangle her face; but the creases in her cheeks imply smiles. All smiles. Yet Sarah infers sadness, fear. More popped bubbles convey laughter. More inferences: sadness and fear.

Then …

Water stops flowing. Laughter vanishes.

Sarah walks backward and stops when she senses a chair in the corner. She drops into it and curls her hands over the arms. Her stomach actually fucking ripples. Triangles shift; they're superimposed over her mother's face—connoting her eyes, nose, and mouth—and distort her features as they move. It nauseates Sarah. The face, that face … Pale and gray and sunken. It terrified Sarah as a child as it terrifies her now.

—Glub glub. Michelle says something but it's garbled.

—Glub, her mother says.

Sarah feels emptied. Exhausted. Her bones hollow, her head vacant, she rubs her temples.

—Glub glub?

She slides out of the chair and glides across the room.

—Glub.

Her mother's voice sends shockwaves through Sarah.

—Glub glub. Glub?

She seems so real, so present. In this room. Right now.

The triangles on her face shift. It's hard to discern, but she seems as though she's smiling. Her cheeks bulge. Certainly it's a smile. Right? Or maybe it's a grin or a grimace, or maybe it's her mother fucking with her. Always fucking with her. Haunting her, rendering her sleepless and helpless and terrified.

—Why are you always like this? Sarah says.

She drags her finger across her mother's cheek. The flesh ripples, the ripples trail Sarah's fingers, then the flesh tightens and reforms.

—Glub glub, glub?

Her mother's arms twitch. Twitch.

Then ...

That sound again: boom, boom, boom.

The walls and floor tremble. The bed vibrates. Sarah's mother groans as her body shakes. Convulsions seize her. She writhes and groans and kicks off the blanket. Pillows tumble to the floor, almost in slow-motion,

—Glub.

Still writhing, still groaning, she sits up and lunges forward. Her arms float in front of her. Her fingers snap at the air.

The lights flicker.

Boom. Boom. Boom.

Groaning, Sarah's mother turns her head, slowly, and she swings her arms, groping for Sarah. The flesh on her face peels and flakes away. Everything in Sarah's peripheral vision vanishes. She leaps back when her mother's arm and hand fly into her field of vision. Something inside orders her to run, all but screams it, but Sarah ...

The triangles over her mother's face stop shifting. Her flesh transforms from gray to black, as if cooked in time lapse. It withers and decomposes. The skin over her cheeks stretch and snap. Her cheekbones protrude. Blood runs down her face, her neck, her chest. The lights flicker. A sound like "boom" roars outside. And blood—glowing blood—drenches her, as if someone had dipped her into a vat of ichor. Her mouth sags. Her eyes grow, like they actually fucking grow, at least three times larger than average adult eyes. Bile-secreting fangs sprout from her gums. Black goo hangs from the tips.

—Glub. Glub.

She growls and lunges forward again, but only her upper body moves. The flesh on her neck bulges and tears, and blood squirts across the room. Growling, louder now, she swings her arms forward. She snaps at the air, trying to snag Sarah, to grab her. What the fuck does she have in mind?

Her growls deepen. Deepen. Then they transform into screeches. Bloodcurdling screeches, which don't resemble anything a human could produce; they sound closer to metal crushing metal than to anything humans produce.

—Is this how you remember me? she says. — This is how you remember me? as a living body, a mind, transitioning into a corpse? This is how you choose to remember your mother?

Tears stream down Sarah's face. Her mother lashes out at her again, grasps at her face by bending and contorting her fingers. Sarah leaps backward, too shocked to scream. Barely able to move, at least not consciously able to will movement, her leap doesn't push her too far away. On hitting the ground, she trips over something, a pair of boots maybe, and tumbles backward.

Lying on her back now, she spins onto her stomach and scrambles to her knees. But she stops; again, she can't will herself to move. She can't ...

Michelle, lying on the floor: This is Michelle as an adult, hands crossed at her chest. Not Michelle, the happy sister; this is Michelle the corpse, lying in a box, hours before they planted her, only a few months after her diagnosis. It had happened so fast—she was sick, then dying, then dead—and so Sarah didn't have time to process it, she didn't ... And that image, that fucking image of her sister lying in a box stuck in her brain, and ...

Sarah sits frozen in a sort of Lotus position. She tries to move but she can't. She tries to scream, to cry. Nothing comes out. Michelle's corpse groans. It groans. The sound triggers an outburst of emotion. Tears overtake Sarah. Something inside her tells her to stand. Something inside her tells her to run. Something inside her tells her to scream or to shout or to close her eyes and imagine a sunset on an island or on Mars or ...

The universe blinks off and on again.

Sarah's sitting on the floor in her kitchen, crying while she cradles Cynthia, her wife. Blood flows from canyons carved into Cynthia's forearms. Color drains from her face. Her eyes are open but she's either spaced out or more or less unconscious. Sarah screams into her cell phone, practically ordering the 911 operator to send a fucking fleet of ambulances, like now, like right this fucking goddamn minute, like what are you waiting for why aren't you and the blood oh god the blood how the fuck is this happening of the all the people all the fucking people she never not once suspected Cynthia of doing it and what the fuck is the holdup I'm going to lose her lose her goddamn it send the fucking ambulances now like right fucking now what's the problem motherfuckers do you fucking want her to die you fucking bureaucratic monsters

A woman without a face appears out of nowhere. She stands behind Sarah, touches her. Sarah doesn't need to look at her to verify to whom the hand belongs.

—Bracket your experience, the faceless woman says.

Standing in the bathroom now, studying her face in the mirror, Sarah's triangles shift. She's familiar with the shapes beneath the triangles, eyes, nose and mouth, contorting into a limp expression, as if she's too sad to emote. The shifting triangles turn her face into putty, making her expression harder to countenance.

The faceless woman hovers somewhere behind Sarah—outside the boundaries and her field of vision. Her presence is palpable, like the presence of an animal under a table; you know it's there but have no need or inclination to verify it.

Blue and gray light crawls through the room. It moves like molasses, as if someone had slowed the photons. Everything feels empty and gray. Dead. Such awareness drains her. Like Sarah remembers standing there, surveilling the mirror, her distorted reflection and her contorted face.

Her limbs felt both weighted and empty. The struggle of moving, of so much as raising an arm or curling or unfurling a finger, transformed into a Sisyphean chore.

—You're here but not here, the faceless woman says. —You're not conscious of this room; you're conscious of being conscious of this place, this time. Bracket that. Cut off the consciousness of being conscious and focus your intention solely on what's in front of you.

—What's the point? Sarah says. —Everything is broken.

—Do it.

In the mirror, Sarah's triangles shift. Her face resembles unfired clay stamped by a bare foot, then kneaded by a lobster: her eyes shift below her cheeks; her mouth slides to her temple; her nose droops, touching to her chin.

—I can't …

—Do. It.

She tries to focus. But on what? Where is she? In her father's bedroom. She'd fallen out of the closet and landed on the floor, so … But, no; now she's in the bathroom, at the sink. Or is she?

Where the hell is she?

She tries to break free, tries to orient herself, to see beyond the memories and the manifested ideations.

—What's the …

Then she sees it—the ceiling: the fucking ceiling in her father's bedroom. She's standing in the bathroom, but she sees the world as if she's lying on her back, staring at the ceiling. Light dances across the tiles. Bright light. Yet everything is blue and gray and dead.

In a flash it's gone. Now she's in the bathroom again, watching her face shift and contort. Her features move, shift, and blur. It's like watching an animated Picasso painting.

—What's the point? she says. —Everything's broken. Everything's dead.

—You've got to focus, the faceless woman says. —You've got to get out of here.

Haze envelops the bathroom. A smell, citrusy, like shampoo, triggers a memory.

—Bracket your experience. Bracket your awareness of your experience.

—This was my second attempt, Sarah says. —Do you remember?

—You've got to focus, Sarah.

Sarah scoops up a razor blade and slices into her forearms. Blood bubbles out of the wounds; it rolls down and across her arms. Even though her triangles shift, shift, shift, Sarah remembers her reflection: she's smiling. She's crying but smiling. Everything feels gray. Everything feels dead. Yet she's smiling. And she remembers kind of laughing, thinking, "it'll all be over; soon it will all be over."

The little things, the seemingly insignificant or inconsequential traces of a life once lived, are most haunting, Sarah realizes: a spoon—still showing streaks where lips squeegeed peanut butter—sits atop a jar of *Peter Pan*; a package of crackers, the sleeve twisted and folded to preserve the crispness of the remaining crackers; a note scribbled in ad hoc shorthand; an open magazine with ink circling an advertisement—all fragments of stories, once-banal behaviors or affectations, now teem with pathos. Viewed through the lens of death, these remains assume previously unheard of sentimentality.

Something to her right, just outside her periphery, snaps and pops. She senses, more than sees, space-time continuum warp, as if the fabric of the universe converges at a point in the corner of the room. It refracts light, warping everything around it.

She walks in measured steps. The floorboards creak. Overhead, the lights flicker and fill the room; it's unlike anything Sarah has encountered: white like the white on glow-in-the-dark stickers. White like the asterisks blooming behind her eyes, where something pulls and pokes and prods her, sending pain spiraling through her head.

The combination of the hyper-real light and the footsteps, and the throbbing tension stretching the flesh on her face, especially at the temples, makes everything feel meaningless and dead.

She crosses the room after what feels like hours, or even years, and reaches the filing cabinet, her father's notorious filing cabinet. He attended it for hours, meticulous in his chronology and categories.

For a split second, she squats in the chair beside the desk, but then she jumps to her feet. The chair is empty, yet her father's presence is palpable, and Sarah, maybe really for the first time, feels the extent of his absence.

Across the room, the warp in the space-time continuum bends and shimmers. Still refracting light, it warps the walls and the corner of the television. Sounds like gurgling, low-pitched whines flow from it.

Sarah glances at it, unable to force herself to gaze into it. Is it there, that warp, like actually there? Or is it ...

Her father's there but not there—both p and ¬p. He's sitting in the chair and either writing a note or pulling a spoon from his mouth, squeezing his lips to extract peanut butter from a spoon. Or perhaps he's spinning the chair forward as he scoops up the television remote.

But he's there, goddamn it. He's there, in the flesh. Sarah taps his arm. His flesh ripples.

And yet he's not there. The chair is empty and the room is quiet, and everything is silent and still, and everything is dead—and yet everything is alive. Colors spill from the room and the windows, from the world outside the windows, and yet everything feels gray.

Everything feels empty and gray.

And everything feels dead.

She had spoken to her father hours before his death. A head cold had muffled his voice. He'd cough whenever he'd laugh. Sarah had noted the cough and suffered premonitions of his death. A feeling of dread washed over her, a sensation similar to the fear she felt when she contemplated her death.

Or was that true? Had she thought about his death, or had she corrupted the memory?

—But that's not how things are, he'd said. — You know that as well as most people.

23

—It's not how things are that matter; it's how things could be. And you should know that.

—Possibilities are largely exercises of imagination.

—So says the man who once willed a wormhole into existence.

Silence, then her father had said,

—So then what's on the itinerary?

—It's not inconceivable, you know.

—I was watching television and ... Now television ... Perfect example: everything you watch, even the news, everything is an example of possible worlds. Whether you're watching a procedural drama, a so-called reality show, even commercials flogging tennis shoes, you're actually observing a possible-world scenario.

—Dad, how'd you do it?

—Nothing there is real. It may seem real. But nothing is real. Most things ... not everything, but most things ... are possible, he'd said, —and it's the confluence between the real and the imagined, between cameras capturing real people acting out imagined scenarios, that's so seductive and confusing, that lures you in and traps you.

—You've done it more than once, she'd said. — How did you do it?

—Exactly. And that's how, I think, advertisements are so alluring. The entertainment seduces you and primes you, convinces you that the possible is actual, and so the transition from commercial to program to commercial again ensnares you; it pulls you into the possible, so the possible is ... it just becomes real, and everything is twisted into one massive, confusing mess until we convince ourselves that the possible is real.

This was when she was nine and didn't know any better. She'd climb the tree out back and sit there for hours, on a web of hammock-like branches, and read. In all the years she'd sat in that tree, she'd never, not once, experienced anything like vertigo or fear.

Branches hanging over the fence draped onto the neighbor's lawn. She'd follow them with her eyes from time to time, but she only rarely ventured that far east. Instead, she'd sit near the trunk, cozying up against it, the book in her lap, only peeling her eyes away from it to glance at the sky.

Sitting in the tree to read became routine. Day in and day out, she'd go on adventures without so much as wiggling her butt. And every day, the neighbor's dog, a mutt expressing the genes of a Labrador, at least in the face, specifically the snout, would sit below the branches—and their tentacle-like shadows—and all but beg for attention.

Sarah would cough on occasion, clear her throat on occasion, and the dog would waggle its tail back and forth, back and forth, smacking a sign nailed to the fence in an alternating 1/4, 3/4 rhythm.

Sometimes it'd whine, sometimes it'd bark, but usually it refrained from making noises—except for the fence-smacking rhythm.

The day before Sarah's tenth birthday, after sitting in that tree for at least an hour, reading a collection of short stories about robots, she realized the dog wasn't present. On noting the dog's absence, she stopped focusing. She read and re-read the same paragraph a half dozen times. Before she'd made the connection, something had hung in the air; it seemed to coalesce around her; yet she hadn't discerned the source until she noticed the absence of the 1/4, 3/4 rhythm.

The nagging feeling—knowing the dog's absence without realizing it—stuck with her. It filled her head with vapor, with helium, and it emptied her. Flesh, bones, organs seemed to vanish. Heat followed chills. Hair stood upright; it cascaded up her spine and across her arms. As she felt the hair rise, she imagined video of dominoes falling, only the video played in reverse.

Grief.

She'd heard the word when her mother had died, but it hadn't meant anything to her, just a word adults had used to explain the tears and the ashen looks, or the sleepy film crowding their eyes. To her, it had sounded like nonsense, like a word you'd come across in a picture book.

Realizing the dog was gone, but only somehow and secretly suspecting it, defined the referent of the word "grief." That feeling inside, those sensations swelling as she glanced at the patch of grass and dirt below, signified what people called "grief": sadness mixed with emptiness.

But then how could she know what "grief" meant when someone else uttered it? How could she know this word pointed to the same feeling experienced by her father and sister, by her aunt and her uncle, when they told her they were grieving? How could she know what she had experienced, as she gazed at the ground, intersected with the sensations everyone tied to the word "grief."

This confused her.

Pretty much everything confused her—as a child and as an adult.

Like when, shortly after her nineteenth birthday, she watched the universe blink on and off while the world fell apart and repaired itself. Thunder rolled in reverse and rain flew from the ground to the sky. Buildings collapsed; others replaced them. Trees transformed into people, who walked backward. Every car and truck, even every airplane and cloud moved backward. Backward.

This had happened before, many times before, and it still confused her.

She remembers walking to the store to get a pack of cigarettes—still a secret habit—when the universe blinked off and on. The sidewalks, the buildings and the people and the cars reversed; they crumbled and disappeared. Some birds exploded. They sky flickered as clouds flaked away.

Birds cawed overhead. Something roared beneath the ground. The roaring jolted her and she stepped, then floated, backward.

Country had replaced city, and Sarah found herself standing beside a hill overlooking a valley. Flocks of birds flew over the horizon. Deer grazed beside a pond. The pond grew into a lake. Trees sprouted, grew, then towered overhead. A breeze detached leaves from branches and carried them downward, ever downward.

The world blinked in and out of existence again.

Sarah was in the city again, standing on the sidewalk, watching people and cars roll by. Clouds rolled overhead; airplanes soared. Thunder clapped and rain fell from the sky again.

She remembers feeling anxious, dazed—yet nonplussed. Like what she'd witnessed, the virtual-particle-like behavior of the world and time, seemed both authentic and not-authentic, like it somehow violated the law of non-contradiction, and yet it seemed more than possible, or even plausible: it made sense.

The experience had seemed like an authentic model produced by her brain, from information transmitted by her sense organs, but at the same time it seemed artificial, a hallucination, a model produced independent of, or only partly dependent on, the immediacy of the transmissions of her sense organs.

So was it real? Or was it a hallucination?

It confused her whenever it happened. And it was at least partly confusing because she couldn't always anticipate when it would happen.

Sometimes a chill curled her spine, sometimes her temples throbbed, sometimes her knees ached —and then sometimes the world blinked off and on without warning or the slightest provocation, at least as far as she could tell.

She sat on a chair beside a window overlooking a cemetery. Fetuses encased in sacks of bile replaced photons and dripped from light fixtures. They pulsed and glowed. Yet everything seemed dim. Dark, even. Everything seemed immersed in or obscured by shadows. She pulled the book from her lap and held it near her chest and read another page. The lighting sucked tears from her eyes, pulled her temples inward, as though it had injected a maelstrom into her skull. Setting the book aside, she closed her eyes and massaged her temples.

Outside, something howled. That goddamn dog, probably.

For the past month or so, a group of teenagers had haunted the cemetery. They'd gather around headstones and talk—loudly—for hours. Although Sarah hadn't bothered to investigate, she suspected they were either dispensing or consuming drugs—or both.

Their voices transmogrified into sound waves. The sound waves—visible, like rainbow colored ribbons—blasted into the windows in her apartment, shattering the glass, which blew inward. Shards flew around the room, which reflected the dripping fetuses, firing them in all direction.

The shards—each of the at least ten thousand fragments—transformed into moths or butterflies. They floated upward, upward, spiraling toward the ceiling.

Sarah watched them fly, mesmerized. Her head throbbed and her knees ached.

—Bracket it.

The butterflies merged with the dripping fetuses. Cocoons dropped to the floor and wiggled; they wiggled.

Then everything collapsed. Now she was outside, in a landscape she didn't recognize. The trees shook at the stars swirled.

Leaning against a tree, Sarah examined the horizon. The sun penetrated it. Streaks of matter glided across the sky. Like molecules in neurotransmitters, the matter broke apart and floated around. Some fit into receptor sites in the sky; others floated, floated, carried away by the wind.

Overhead, bulbous-looking splotches marred the blue.

As the matter piled into receptor sites an explosion tore through the atmosphere: clouds disintegrated. They tumbled to the ground. The atmosphere fell inward, and, to Sarah, it resembled what it must look like to sit inside a deflating balloon.

White eclipsed color. The explosion expanded outward.

Everything collapsed and tumbled down, down, down.

The world fell over her. It wrapped around her and snuggled and suffocated her.

Light vanished. Darkness reigned. Sounds terminated. The void nullified every sensation, every feeling and sense of experience; every indication of conscious life vanished; and she felt more like a doll or a mannequin than a person. An uneasy sensation, to say the least.

She vanished, and the emptiness, the totality of the absence of everything, of every possible sensation and experience, morphed into an event horizon.

Impossible to comprehend—or to describe—the complete and total absence of everything, the void, the darkness had more on less *become* her.

She wasn't even "she" anymore. "She" dissolved, evaporated, vanished.

Nothing.

Nothingness.

Void.

Then …

She was lying in a room in a hospital.

This was a decade before her father would die and two years after her sister had died.

Gauze covered sutured valleys she had carved into her forearms. Gaping wounds in the ceiling pulsed. Light spilled from the wounds. The pulsing spasms strobed, painting everything gray and white.

A groan: —Bracket it.

But whose groan? Hers?

Boils grew on the walls; they inflated and deflated like bladders. Sounds billowed from the windows and crawled beneath cracks in the doors: floating and swerving, they convulsed and popped, merged and transformed. Each color, she knew, or at least sensed, represented snatches of conversations or modern technological ambiance. Red and green = voice or footfalls; blue and yellow = doors closing or machines buzzing, beeping, or whirring.

Soon, colors filled the room. Some spun and some merged, transforming the air—the fucking air—into kaleidoscopes. Then ripples started near

31

the periphery and expanded toward the center of the room. Although she couldn't see it to verify it, Sarah somehow sensed the door had opened and closed. She squinted, tried to see through and beyond the colors, but the ripples intensified, muddling everything.

Cynthia broke through the haze and screwed her eyes upward. Tears streaked her cheeks. She sniffled, dropped into a chair beside the bed, and clutched Sarah's hand.

—How are you feeling?

Sarah sort of shrugged and twitched her neck, as if trying to use her shoulder to scratch her chin.

—I talked to your father, Cynthia said.

—...

—He's leaving the conference, flying down as soon as he can.

—Why?

—To be with you.

—But why would he fly? He doesn't need to fly.

—He says he has something for you, something he's bringing. Says you'll be "taken aback" when you see it. Those are his words: "taken aback."

—I know this, Sarah said. —I know all of it. I've been here before. Experienced this before.

—He assured me he'll take care of everything.

—Like I know everything you're going to say.

—I know. I know.

—"I tried to tell him, but he won't listen."

—I tried to tell him, but he won't listen.

—And yet nothing I say matters. Nothing I say now matters.

—But ... Exactly. That's ... I know, I said the same thing.

—Because what I'm saying now wasn't said then, so changing what I say won't change what you said.

—But ... Well, of course he's weird. What father isn't?

—And I just don't like being here. I don't know why I have to be here, Sarah said. —Why am I constantly thrust back into this room? into this situation?

—Things will get better.

Sarah remembered saying, "No they won't. How can things possibly get better?" And so, reliving this, she parroted herself:

—No they won't. How can things possibly get better?

And she remembered what happened next: Cynthia rubbed Sarah's arm and said,

—I'll always be here for you.

And it meant something then, what Cynthia had said. And it meant something later. Reliving this moment, Sarah knew how precious it was, how precious everything was—and is.

—I love you, she said.

Cynthia massaged her temples.

—I know when you'll die, Sarah said. —And it makes this worse.

Sarah knew when Cynthia would die because she'd experienced it. Several times, in fact.

—Six years, Sarah said. —If only I knew then ...

Knowing this and not knowing this, Sarah now and Sarah then covered her eyes and cried.

b.

Sarah **knocks and scrapes** her knuckles on the wood. After she knocks again, she checks her hand. Her knuckles are red but not bleeding. Fucking door. Fucking Marcus for not fixing the damn thing.

Boom. Scrape.

She tilts her head, focuses on the noise. It's like a thump but not quite a thump. Is it movement? Two or three seconds pass. The sounds vanish.

It probably isn't movement.

Chains scrape metal. A lock pops. The door opens wide enough for Marcus's left eye to slice through the shadows. Then it slams shut. More scraping and the door opens.

—I'm sorry about your father.

Marcus leans in for a hug. Sarah wraps her arms around him without touching him; she sort of leans, sort of stands on the balls of her feet.

They lock into a quasi-embrace, after which they step back and gaze into one another's eyes.

Eyelids heavy, Marcus smirks. His hair is messy; his beard, unkempt.

—You look terrible, Sarah says.

—I can't sleep. Please. Come in.

He limps as he walks, and so Sarah, for whatever reason, mimics him. They limp together and cross into a second doorway, landing in the living room.

Marcus makes his way to a chair and, on dropping into it, gestures to the couch. Sarah stands near the doorway, her eyes scanning the room. Cracks spiderweb the walls; piles of powdered plaster polka dot the floor.

—Want something to drink?

—Do you have an ashtray?

—Now that sounds like a horrid drink.

—Funny.

Marcus scoops up an ashtray—on the floor, beside the chair—and hands it to her.

Silence settles over the room. It chokes Sarah and fixes a deer-in-headlights-like expression on Marcus's face. Wide-eyed, mouth agape, he sort of grins. Or is it a grin? A grimace, maybe?

He glances around the room like he's encountering it for the first time. He flutters his eyebrows and twitches his lips, searching for words, probably, for something to say, possibly. Then he studies the room again, grinning or grimacing or whatever.

—Dad left a will, Sarah says.

—Doesn't surprise me.

—But I can't find it.

—That doesn't surprise me, either.

—I searched the house but ...

Marcus fixes an expression with eyes like inverted teardrops. He's either on the verge of crying or feigning empathy—but Sarah can't determine which is more likely. Marcus was strung out on painkillers the last time she saw him —the last few times, actually—and the opiates had masked his behavior; they had disguised his internal sensations and turned his face into a sort of kabuki-theater-esque performance; so now she's not sure how to read him.

—What? she says.

The air seems incapable of transmitting sound. Silence permeates the room, a deep and foreboding silence. It's three-dimensional and oppressive, and whenever Sarah hears anything— birds or cars or kids outside—she's half-convinced the noises are products of a brain not accustomed to the absence of sound.

It happens in a flash:

The room and the house, Marcus and Sarah and, yes, even light—all things disintegrate. Everything breaks apart and vanishes. Then a pinprick of light tears through the darkness. The white-light contains all primary colors, and these are additive colors, not subtractive, so they create images and hallucinations when they merge: some colors change, some return to a more or less white state, others collide and paint a kaleidoscopic mural teeming with snapshots of realized and imagined worlds.

Sarah hasn't become one with the void. She hasn't merged with the absence of everything; instead, she feels herself standing, feels the sensations of standing. Her kinesthetic senses inform her of the relation of her body parts to each other, and to the ground. And the information is unambiguous: she's standing.

The sensations come as a relief, but the visual absence of her body disturbs her. It's happened too many times to count, yet it fills her with a sense or a feeling of depression—or even dread.

—It's all part of the process, her father had said.

This was one year after her sister had died and eleven years before her father would die.

—But what does it mean? Sarah had asked.

—It doesn't mean anything.

They were sitting on a bench in a park overlooking a lake. Sarah rolled a cigarette while her father broke off chunks of bread and tossed them to the ground. Birds pecked at each other, occasionally wrestled, as they fought for food.

—Meaning isn't a thing, her father had said.

—I know. I know.

—It's not something magically connected to language. There's not some intangible umbilical cord linking the word "meaning" with a thing that obtains in the universe.

—I'm well aware of this.

—Yet you persist.

—It's sometimes just an expression. "What's the meaning of the life?" "What's the meaning of death?"

—I've never heard those used rhetorically.

—Okay, so those were bad examples.

—Language helps to structure thought, he'd said. —And thought helps to structure a person's model of reality. Therefore, language helps to structure models of reality. And models of reality are reality for most people.

—All right.

—Get into the habit of inquiring about meaning where none can exist and you'll fool yourself into thinking that "meaning" is a thing that obtains independently of people.

It took forever to roll her cigarette. She inhaled loudly when she finally lit it.

—I remember wanting to shake you, she says. —I remember wanting to maybe smack you and just talk about Michelle. Or mom. And I remember, at that moment, feeling insanely angry, infuriated even, about how sparsely or nonchalantly you'd talk about them, either of them, after they'd died. If you even talked about them at all.

Her father broke off a few more pieces of bread and scattered them.

Two birds darted toward the bread, their wings flapping.

She's in the car now, driving back to her apartment—or so she assumes. She doesn't remember leaving Marcus's house. She doesn't remember saying goodbye or walking outside or getting into her car. But now here she is.

The day is overcast; it was overcast when she'd pulled up to Marcus's house, which leads her to believe that she had, in fact, either just now or recently left.

She's trying to sleep but she can't sleep. She's trying to force herself out of bed but she can't will herself to her feet, or even to uncover herself. She wants to cry and yet she fights it.

What purpose would it serve?

Sarah woke her father. The clock read: 3:19.

—Daddy?

—Hmmm?

—Can I sleep with you?

—Hmmm.

She crawled into bed and under the covers. She dropped her head onto her father's pillow. It was wet. Tear-soaked, she knew, or at least suspected. He was lying on her mother's pillow now, and he twisted and contorted and kicked the blanket off, throwing it to the ground.

Sarah clutched her stomach and curled up. Her toes were cold.

—It's hard to go to sleep, she said.

—Just try.

Silence. Then:

—What happens when you die?

—Try to sleep, Sarah.

—Like, is it heaven or is it nothing?

But this idea, this concept of nothingness, evaded her. She remembers what it was like back then, to attempt to visualize nothingness: darkness, like a dreamless sleep. But the concept was still too remote and abstract for her, which didn't stop her from at least attempting to visualize it.

—Don't think about it.

—I want to cry. But I don't want to, too.

—Cry or fight the tears, he said. —No one will fault you.

—But which one will make me feel better?

—Crying or fighting tears are two sides of the same coin. Giving into it or resisting it only alters the behavior other people detect. Cry or fight it; either way you're shackling yourself inside the prison of grief.

Grief sounded awful. A prison? Who wanted that?

—Grief is something we all experience when we lose someone, he said. —Who knows if it does any good? It might. It might not. I don't know. But even if it doesn't, no one will think less of you or make fun of you for grieving.

—Okay.

—A child is supposed to grieve the loss of her mother.

—Okay.

—You are supposed to grieve the loss of your mother, Sarah.

—Daddy?

—Yeah.

—Is it okay to cry now? I feel like maybe I want to cry now.

Halloween night, oh so many years ago:

Sarah sat on the sofa, smoking a joint while listening to acid jazz. Disjointed, the music sputtered on and on; its sounds seemed to mimic a spaceship entering orbit and jumping into hyperspace. Audiences clapped. Then the speakers popped.

A swarm of bees invaded the room. But the bees weren't organic; they were metal. They crowded the room and congregated at the ceiling, and then they blasted through the window and vanished as another spaceship rocketed into hyperspace.

Clutching her phone, Sarah considered calling Cynthia. They'd locked themselves into an on-again-off-again pattern and were currently in a sort of gray area: they weren't dating but they didn't hate each other, either. They were actually kind of talking again but not yet to the level of fucking again.

But for whatever reason she couldn't force herself to dial Cynthia's number, so she dropped the phone and took a hit from her joint. Then she exhaled and leaned her head back and watched the smoke curl overhead and dissolve.

Blood sprouted on the ceiling; it hardened and formed domes, thousands of them. Millions, even. The ceiling resembled microphotography of papillae. Sarah imagined reaching out and touching a dome. She imagined penetrating it with her finger to feel a heart pulsing inside it.

The domes pulsed but they didn't pulse in sync. Blood dripped from some. Other domes exploded, spraying blood onto the walls and the floor.

Sarah, phone in one hand and joint in the other, slid off the couch and darted across the room. She stood in the kitchen doorway, watched blood fill the living room, forming a lake; she watched and felt the climate shift from air conditioned apartment to rainforest, only walls replaced trees and blood replaced rain. What the fuck was going on?

Then ...

A spaceship hummed. Thunder cracked. Blood rained from the ceiling and drenched the floor; it ran down the walls and pooled in the corners of the room.

—Where are you? she said. —I need you I need ... Where are you?

Knee deep, the blood spilled into the kitchen. It beat against the bathroom door. Suction sounds alerted her to blood draining into cupboards, cabinets, the bathroom. Even her bedroom.

Thunder cracked. Boom. Another spaceship jumped into hyperspace. Bippity-blee.

Waves curled over the surface of the lake. Blood-rain pockmarked it with ripples. Thunder. Boom. —Where are you? Please. Then a hand penetrated the surface of the lake. Blood coated it. A forearm and an elbow and a bicep emerged. Sarah's heart clattered. Thunder cracked. —Where are you? I need ... need you. A shoulder emerged from the lake. Then a neck and a head emerged. It belonged to a woman. Covered in blood, her hair matted, she was indistinguishable yet somehow identifiable: it was Michelle.

Her eyes were black and her flesh—though covered with blood—was rotted and sagging. She opened her mouth. Bile, thick as syrup, flowed from her mouth, sticking to, then dripping from, her lower lip.

It hit the lake of blood and dissolved.

Bubbles formed on the surface of the lake, and Sarah's sister's screams emanated from the blood as the bubbles burst.

Sarah's heart pounded. She dropped the phone and the joint and backed into the kitchen, but the lake had risen, and wading through it slowed her.

Michelle moaned, screamed, cried.

Sarah slogged through the kitchen, fleeing to the back door.

—Where are you? she said. —No. Please. No. Where are you?

Her heart pounded, pounded, pounded.

c.

Imagine an inverted triangle:

Vertex *a* points down, so vertices *b* and *c* are on top.

Then imagine a triangle below the inverted triangle:

The *a* vertices of both triangles intersect, creating a sort of polygonal hourglass.

Now imagine this polygonal hourglass represents the proportions of a human face: vertices *b* and *c* of the inverted triangle mark the eyes while vertex *a* marks the nose. Then, below it, the lips belong in the space just south of vertex *a* on the lower triangle while vertices *b* and *c* mark both sides of the chin.

Exempting the shape of the head, imagine perceiving these triangles whenever you glance at a human being—or even yourself in the mirror.

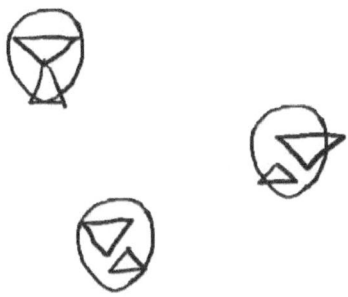

Now imagine days in which your perception of these triangles dominates a person's face, and imagine days in which your perception distorts these triangles, so on some days the lower triangle protrudes or pushes inward; on some days, the upper, inverted triangle shifts to the left or right. Imagine the potential combinations of the placement of the triangles, and how their placement—or displacement—alters a person's face. The upper triangle shifted to the left and the lower triangle shifted to the right distorts a person's face, so the jaw and cranium are nearly horizontal. Or imagine the upper triangle raised, so the eyes—vertices b and c—sit on top of the head, while the lower triangle folds inward, pulling the chin back- and upward.

Or imagine days in which the triangles shift to the left and to the right, out of sync, so the lower triangle shifts to the right as the upper triangle shifts to the left, and vice versa, thus creating the illusion of a face on the verge of twisting into a sort of meat cyclone.

These are a few examples of the combinations of the placement of the triangles.

These are a few examples of how Sarah perceives human beings.

Where are you?
No.
Please.
No.
Where are you?

Sarah floated in a lake of blood. She swam upward but couldn't find the surface. She twisted and swam downward but, still, she couldn't find the surface. Holding her breath, clenching her eyes, she spun to the side and swam. She swam.

Her diaphragm seized. Her lungs nearly burst. Her parasympathetic division jolted and howled, fought to wrest control. And so she tried to find the surface, tried to break free. But she couldn't find the surface. She couldn't break free.

Everything told her—ordered her—to breathe, to open her eyes and breathe. But she ignored the orders, she ignored the sensations and suppressed the impulses, and she swam. She swam.

Somewhere in the lake, somewhere in the darkness, somewhere in the world of muffled sounds, something dove at Sarah, latching onto her arm. Fingers curled around her wrist. Then the thing latching onto her propelled her through the lake of blood.

She emerged on top of a hospital overlooking a barren landscape. Blood-red sand filled a valley below, like something out of a Bosch painting. Naked people and meat monsters twisted and writhed, locked into orgies, forcing each other into either dominant or submissive roles.

Somewhere, out in the distance, a building shaped like a head with an asshole protruding from the base of its skull loomed. The asshole farted; skinless people tumbled out of it; they writhed on the bleeding sand.

Sarah was sitting on the edge of the roof. Her feet were dangling over the side. Her hair and skin and clothes were dry; there wasn't a trace of blood on her.

Her breathing slowed. Her head hurt. The image of her sister, her rotting sister, for fuck's sake, stuck with her. It haunted her. She wanted to scream, or vomit. Or both.

—You sounded awful. The voice grew behind her. —I thought maybe it was the phone. Are you all right?

Sarah slid away from the edge.

Hands clenched behind his back, a man ambled toward her. His face contorted and shimmered.

The man's face resembled putty. Sarah tried to perceive it as it might have been. She pictured a man in his mid-30s, a man with a beard and blue eyes. She couldn't see them, but she sensed blue eyes. Comparing the ideation to the real proved impossible, however, because his triangles wouldn't stop shifting. His face was a blob of flesh: it twisted and flipped. Twisted. Flipped.

—Things are getting worse, she said. —I can't ... There's got to be a way to control it.

—You can't control it. You know that.

—I can't deal with this, all this. It's too much.

—Even for you?

—Especially for me.

The man sauntered to the edge of the roof. He glanced over his shoulder, at Sarah, and said,

—Tell me what you see.

—We're on the roof of a building, a hospital, I think, overlooking some sick, sadistic hell.

—Where on the roof?

—The edge. You're about to fall off.

The man raised his right foot, as if to step off the building.

—And what do you suppose would happen if I took another step?

—We're at least a hundred feet off the ...

He stepped forward, seemed to hover in the air. Hands still clenched behind his back, he twisted toward her and said,

—You may see the roof of a building, but I see a clearing. I'm standing in grass. The dew glistens. He pointed. —And over there is a forest. There's a deer. He pointed to his left. —And over there, near that tree, is my father, in his thirties maybe, it's hard to tell, holding a rifle, setting the deer in its sights.

Sarah followed his finger. She didn't see a deer or a hunter, she didn't see a clearing or a forest—she saw a hellish landscape: people and monsters writhing and fucking, scissors with feet cutting people in half, Marquis de Sade sodomizing a mirror image of himself. And then there was the man with a shimmering face, hovering in the air near the roof.

—You still don't see it, the man said.

—I told you what I see.

—And I told you what I see.

—"And ne'er the twain shall meet."

—And ne'er the twain shall meet.

—I knew you were going to say that.

—And I knew you were going to say that. We both know what the other will say. So where do we go from here?

—But the conversation is never the same, she said. —The way some are. Sometimes I can change what I said ...

—But it doesn't change people's responses, does it? he said. —Yet you do it anyway. Hoping to ... What? Encode the revised conversation? Turn every memory into something "meaningful" or "profound"?

—I just ... I sometimes have to say things differently. I need to ...

—But does it change anything? he said. —Anything external to you? Does it change the behavior of other people? Does it change their memories of conversations? Does it change what they think of you? Or thought of you?

—No, she said. —I don't know.

Still hovering, the man extended his arm. The triangles on his face shifted, shifted, shifted. The illusion nauseated Sarah.

—Come, he said, curling his fingers inward, unfurling them, and curling them again.

—I can't.

—Why not?

—Because what I see is real.

—Is it?

—To me, it is, she said. —But you ... Why can't I see your face?

—We've had this conversation before, he said. —And I've answered that question before.

—So answer it again.

—I will when I see you again.

—When will that be?

—When you need me. Or when I need you.

—But I need you now.

—No you don't.

He spun and strolled away.

—Wait, Sarah said. —How do I know you're not a figment of my imagination?

The man stopped. But he didn't turn to her.

—We've had this conversation, too.

—But how do I know? she said. —I think you might be a figment of my imagination.

Before he swung his hands out, before he flew away, the man pointed to his head and said,

—And I've asked you before: What if you're a figment of mine?

d.

Death brings phone calls. Some are official. Most are social. A relative here, a friend there. Everyone calls to offer condolences or apologies. Some people call to express regret. Some people call to say nothing at all, really, other than to make an appearance, so to speak, to fill an obligation they suspect they're forced to fulfill.

Of all the calls, those are the worst. A cousin calls, or an old friend, and they dance around the issue. Then they mention death in a sort of backhanded way while shooting the breeze. Part of her feels relieved at having to avoid talking about her father's death. But part of her feels annoyed, too. Sometimes she feels like shouting. I'm mourning, she wants to say; stop spewing gibberish and leave me the fuck alone.

But then ... Were the conversations pointless? Or were the people implicitly addressing the issue?

It's always strange. What's she supposed to say when someone offers their condolences? Thank you? It seems inappropriate somehow. You say thank you when someone passes a side dish. You say thank you when a stranger opens a door for you. You don't—or shouldn't—say thank you when someone trades a phrase concerning the death of a loved one.

—Hello? Is this Jamie Carrington?

—Yes.

—This is Sarah Goodwin. John Goodwin's daughter.

—I'm sorry about your father, dear. He was a great man.

—Thank you. It's been difficult.

—I lost both my parents a few years back. Oh, five now. Jesus, has it been that long? Believe me, I know what it's like. So what can I do for you?

—I'm going to the funeral home in the morning to make arrangements, and I can't seem to find his address book. Is it in the office?

—I can call Janet over there and ask her.

—You're not ...

—I haven't worked with him for three years.

—Oh.

—I was offered a job I couldn't refuse.

—I'm sorry to bother you, then.

—Don't worry, honey. Why don't you give me your number and I'll get in touch with Janet and call you back?

The phone didn't stop ringing in the hours and days following Michelle's death, either. Sarah, for reasons still not clear, was put in charge of her sister's phone, so she was inundated by two ringing phones for several days.

She remembers leaning against her car in the parking lot of the funeral home, smoking a cigarette while listening to both phones ring. Christ, how they annoyed her. Ring x ∞. The phones were in the car—the windows were up and the doors were closed—and, still, the chirping rattled her. She considered grabbing them and throwing them across the street.

Then, while lighting her third consecutive cigarette, the ringing got to her, and so she wandered away from the car and the chirping phones and crossed the street. The ringing drifted, but it was low, almost a whisper. Grinning, thinking about smashing those fucking things, she sat on the curb and studied the funeral home. Brown colored bricks, windows covered with gold tint, it seemed as if someone had torn the building from the 1970s.

A group crossed the street at a nearby crosswalk. A toddler waddled after her mother. Arms flailing, she stumbled and tripped. Sarah lunged forward, to cushion the child's fall, but something stopped her, something not dissimilar from intuition. So she pulled her arms to her chest and took another hit from the cigarette.

The girl's face reddened. She opened her mouth. Sarah braced herself. But the girl held her mouth open without making a sound. Her mother glanced at her and laughed. She said something and laughed again. The girl watched her mother, eyebrows curled, baffled. Still red-faced, she twisted the corners of her mouth. Upward. Then she cackled. Her mother said something something—her voice crackled and popped, muddling the words—and she carried her daughter across the street.

A man with an unkempt beard was standing in front of the funeral home when Sarah settled her eyes on it again. He lit a cigarette, watching her the way a predator eyeballs prey.

Instantly uncomfortable—how fucking creepy was that?—she glanced at the ground and pulled her cigarettes and lighter from her pocket. But something tickled the back of her head. Something... He was there. Still there. She didn't have to glance at the man to know he was still watching her.

His eyes penetrated her flesh.

She paced up and down, down and up, the sidewalk. The man's eyes drilled into her. She could feel it. What a creepy bastard. Stopping to pat her pockets, to search for something, to do anything, feign distraction, she glanced at the man. Furtively. Then she spun again and nearly bumped into ...

She actually oh god how embarrassing she actually fucking yelped.

... the man, who was standing beside her—but not standing. It seemed as if he were levitating, or ... Sarah glanced at his feet: they were planted on the ground.

His arms bulged near his armpits and his head wobbled, as if it were too heavy for his neck.

At some point during spinning and nearly bumping into the man, Sarah had dropped her lighter. Now the man bent over and picked it up. He handled it with care, as if it were a priceless artifact, and then he dropped it into her palm. Nodding, Sarah lit her cigarette and slipped the lighter back into her pocket.

Then a feeling seized her, a fight-or-flight-type sensation. Every muscle tensed and tightened, and something in her brain screamed 'run, run, run.' Something about the man ... His face ... His triangles shifted and ... but he seemed familiar somehow, yet strange, and ... 'Run, run, run'—but she didn't run. She smoked her cigarette and examined him.

—I'm sorry about your loss, the man said.

—Thank you.

She didn't mean to say it. She didn't mean to say anything. But then her stupid brain and her stupid mouth went ahead and uttered the one stupid phrase she couldn't stand. At least not in this context.

—Your sister was a good woman.

The man's face—his presence—didn't trigger a memory. If Sarah knew him, if she'd met him before, then she hadn't encoded the meeting, or his face.

—My name's Daulton, he said, extending his hand.

—Right, she said. —How are you?

—It's always awkward, isn't it? To bump into someone who knows your name and yet you have no idea who he is?

—It ... yes. She laughed. —I'm sorry, I ...

—I should be the one to apologize. Sneaking up on you the way I did.

—I didn't even see you cross the street.

—That's because I didn't.

—No? she said. —You carrying a personal teleport?

—The world is a model, he said. —I constructed it and reconstructed it when you looked away. Reconstructed it and placed us both right here, on the same side of the street.

Two words popped into her head: "my" and "god." Images of psychopaths and serial killers followed.

—I know what you're thinking ...

—I doubt it, she said, laughing.

—You're thinking I'm crazy. Trying to connect me to psychopaths and serial killers. It's understandable, believe me. But tell me: why would you, an atheist, think "my god" after engaging with someone you believe is insane? You, of all people, should know better.

Sarah realized she was backing away from the man. She made herself stop. She made herself focus on him. Then, without looking, she realized she was holding her cigarette pack, compressing it. Crushing it.

—You've been through this before, the man said. —When your mother passed. And you'll get through this, too.

The man's face shimmered. The triangles shifted from left to right, right to left, and they traded places, so the inverted triangle replaced the upright triangle. His eyes hung on either side of his chin and his mouth replaced the tip of his nose, and it wiggled.

—This is all ...

—Too much? he said.

The triangles spun again, returned to their original positions again. They shimmered and shifted from left to right, right to left, and so on.

Her stomach swirled.

—The feeling will pass, the man said.

—I think maybe I should go to the hospital, maybe.

—You're fine. You know it as well as I do.

—I can't ... Your face ...

—It's all part of the process.

—But what does it mean?

—It doesn't mean anything. Meaning isn't a thing.

—I know. I know.

—It's not something magically connected to language. There's not some intangible umbilical cord linking the word "meaning" with a thing that obtains in the universe.

Her cigarette fell to the ground. Ember popped and rained on the sidewalk.

—It's familiar, isn't it? The man said. —This conversation?

His face jettisoned all thoughts, emptying Sarah's mind.

—You will have that conversation with your father. About a year from now. Strange, though, that you remember a conversation you haven't had yet. Don't you find that strange?

At some point, her father had arrived at the funeral home, his car parked beside Sarah's car.

—He's inside, the man said. —In the office. Staring blankly at the funeral director while she offers him a cup of coffee.

—How do you ... I don't ...

—Your father refuses to make any decisions without you. He's as crushed and as fucked up as you are.

The city exploded: everything blew apart and disintegrated, brick by brick, atom by atom.

The universe blinked off.

She was lying in bed with Cynthia when the universe blinked on again. Cynthia was naked, smoking a cigarette. Sarah was sitting up, scanning Cynthia's chest and neck.

—I'd say take a picture, Cynthia said, —but I know you have plenty.

Sarah's head pulsed and throbbed, pulsed and throbbed. She rubbed her temples as she lay beside Cynthia.

—That's like, what, the fourth one this week?

—I told you it's fine.

—You shouldn't get migraines so frequently.

—I probably just need glasses. Bifocals, maybe. These glazzies endure considerable strain.

Sarah closed her eyes and listened to the hum of the refrigerator in the next room. Cynthia kissed her temples, her forehead, her eyebrows. A thought tugged her eyelids open, but the thought vanished when she focused on Cynthia.

—You're gorgeous, Sarah said.

—Liar.

—Am not.

Cynthia lay down again and planted her hand on Sarah's thigh. Then she laughed. —God, she said, —I got into the dumbest argument with Roger today.

—You two ... Jesus ... What was it this time?

—How empty so much etiquette is.

—Example, please.

—I'm sitting at my desk and I ask him for a Kleenex. So he hands me one and I blow my nose. Then a minute later, I look up, and he's giving me like this evil eye. And so I say, "What?" "It wouldn't kill you to say 'thank you'"? he says. But his tone isn't joke-y; it's shitty, like he's fighting the temptation to punch me.

—You should've said, "thank you."

—For what? It doesn't mean anything. Just a gesture I'm supposed to make. And what good is it to say it when he's expecting it?

—But it does mean something. It's an acknowledgement, Sarah said. —He didn't have to hand it to you.

—No, he didn't. But he did. The whole scene is just this weird conditioning thing. I'm conditioned to blow my nose into something. If I don't have immediate access to it, then I'm conditioned to ask for it. Given the situation, work, Roger's more or less conditioned to reply. Then I'm conditioned to say "thank you," and he's conditioned to respond. But then I don't say it and so his whole system is disrupted. That's why he got so visibly angry.

—I thought you rejected behaviorism.

—I reject it as the be-all-end-all, Cynthia said. —But I don't reject it as a concept. Conditioning does work. And I think much of our day-to-day activities are the result of conditioning.

—But so what'd you argue about? Didn't you say you got into an argument with him?

—It was over that. He tried to act as though not saying "thank you" was an implicit admission of disdain for him, or something. Like my not saying "thank you" somehow reflected some weird negative opinion I might've had of him.

—But you don't like him.

—I didn't refrain from saying it because I don't like him. When do I ever say it? It's one of those weird social quirks I tend to avoid.

—Thanking someone is a weird social quirk?

—If it's meaningless, yes.

—But it's not meaningless.

—Of course it is, especially in that situation. Professional decorum dictates that, in the work environment, especially when you work in close proximity to other people, you don't blow snot and phlegm around the room. Which is why I asked for Kleenex in the first place. Then he only handed it to me because decorum also dictates that you don't return paperwork to clients covered with snot. He did it as much for him, to save face, as for me.

—That's nonsense, Sarah said. —So what about at the store? when someone, a perfect stranger, holds the door open for you? Thanking that person is meaningless, too?

—Yes. I mean, think about it. Say we're strangers. And say I'm leaving a store as you're entering. You hold the door open for me and I glance at you without saying anything. What would you think?

—Honestly?

—No, fib. Of course, honestly.

—I'd probably think you were a bitch.

—But see ... That's my point. You expect me to say "thank you" because you've been conditioned to expect it. And if I did say "thank you" for holding the door for me, it's only because I've been conditioned to say it. I mean, what's the point? What does saying it accomplish?

—It's acknowledging this little act of kindness. Showing gratitude for it.

—But why do you have to verbalize it? Now when you held that hypothetical door open for me, I glanced at you in lieu of saying thank you. Glancing at you is a form of acknowledgement. Say I even offered a smile to express my gratitude. Assuming there is meaning outside of the conditioned responses, then what difference does it make whether I glance and smile or say thank you?

—There's a big difference.

—No there's not. Spoken language and gestures are basically the same: they're both forms of communication. The only difference is the subjective state of the recipient. To a person who expects a response, only the expected response

61

will suffice. Or maybe something that exceeds the expected response.

—Humans aren't robots, Sarah said. —We're not machines programmed to behave in relation to other robots.

—Of course we are. Haven't you heard the terms "enculturation" or "socialization"? That's what we do. That's all we do. We train or condition other people to behave in certain ways. And they in turn train us.

—But what about free will? Free will? Free free will?

The universe blinked off and on again.

Overnight, flesh had replaced the plaster and the paint on the walls. It had replaced the wood on the floor, the doors, and the trim. It resembled human flesh—porous, with clusters of hair, like the hair on a person's knuckles—only with the color of muscle and fatty tissue, like it had evolved overnight, the flesh, and indoors, in the mid-Western autumn, hence above the equator and away from the iron-fist of the sun, and so evolution had selected against pigmentation. Sweat flowed from the pores and drenched the meat-covered floor—but the sweat resembled snot and phlegm, and so the walls and the floor seemed ill somehow.

Lying in bed, the only thing not overgrown with flesh, Sarah massaged the pillow beside her,

Cynthia's pillow. It still smelled like her, still vaguely smelled like perfume and sour-apple-scented shampoo. In a sense, the smell was Cynthia. And she remained, at least a part of her remained, as long as her smell lingered.

And it seeped into the walls, that smell. And the walls pulsed, convulsed and contorted. Somewhere, the flesh emitted a groan. Or a moan. Somewhere, the flesh made sounds like weeping.

Sarah had more or less lain in bed since the funeral. She had left the house only two or three times—she couldn't remember which—and that was more or less to assuage someone, to convince someone she was somehow functional, able to eat. But then she stopped pretending. She stopped bothering to pretend. If someone called or knocked on the door, then she'd lie still, as if motionlessness = invisibility.

Her father had once told her the motionless of ennui is a subset of the fear of death. This maxim popped into her head whenever someone knocked on the door, and for some reason it both comforted and terrified her.

But then ...

The flesh on the walls moaned and groaned and wept.

Cynthia's smell lingered. It floated upward and coated the walls. It floated into Sarah's nostrils, slamming into the cilia and transmogrifying into electrical impulses, which rocketed to her brain, assaulting hundreds of millions of dendrites. The dendrites communicated with other neurons via axons, neurotransmitters, synaptic gaps, and the resulting storm of activity enabled her brain to retrieve a memory, to reconstruct it using previously preserved, and current, information:

—I want to thank you. I never truly thanked you. For being you. And for being with me. For saving me.

She and Cynthia were floating in ichor in a cave. Flesh covered the walls. Theoretically dark, the cave benefitted from some kind of hypothetical light, which illuminated Cynthia's face and chest.

Cynthia was lying down and Sarah was leaning over her, partly on top of her, and so Sarah assumed—but unable to confirm—the hypothetical light, mostly behind and above, drenched her in shadows.

—Bracket your experience.

The shadows spilled onto Cynthia. The silhouette of Sarah's profile darkened the left side of her wife's face.

—Bracket it, a voice said. —Step outside yourself and bracket your experience.

For a moment, and from the right angle, their faces merged in the shadows, and they transformed into a sort of corporeal statue of Janus.

—I can't do this, Cynthia said.

—Please don't make me do this, Sarah said.

Janus smiled and frowned. Janus laughed and cried. Janus looked to the future and gazed into the past.

—I don't think I can live without you.

—Not ... Please don't ...

—I don't want you to leave me. Not with these ...

—You can't go. Not now. I won't let you.

Here's the thing about hospitals: they didn't always make people better. Sometimes, they made people worse—or so it seemed. Like sick people went to the hospital to improve their health. Everyone swore by them. "Go to the hospital. Go to the hospital." But the hospital had returned Sarah's mother with eyes sinking into gray flesh and only a few strands of hair sprouting from her head.

As she stood in the doorway, peering at her mother, Sarah dictated a mental note to herself: never, ever go to that hospital.

Her father had sent her up to the room—"Just go visit her"—and, as she studied her mother's sunken face, she resented him. Well, she wasn't certain those sensations = resentment, but she suspected they did. But then ...

And so here's why she resented her father:

He had more or less commanded her to visit a room occupied by a gray-skinned skeleton. Although the skeleton-person resembled Sarah's mother, the resemblance wasn't concrete; like it was probably easy to glance at her and not recognize her at all if you hadn't like seen or spoken to her in a really long time.

As she stared at the person resembling her mother, Sarah couldn't with absolute certainty determine whether or not this person = her mother.

Instead, this person was like a skeleton. And gray. And old somehow—and her mother wasn't like old lady old. This person ... yeah; like this person was like what happened when you stared into your reflection in a mirror in a dark room: after a while, you feel your eyes trying to adjust, and you watch yourself become old and gray and skeleton-like.

That's probably what happened to this person: like maybe the world was a giant mirror and she had stared at it too long or too hard, maybe.

—Hey.

The woman's voice jolted Sarah. It didn't sound like her mother at all. It didn't sound like it belonged to a human at all. It sounded like someone had held a deep breath and died, and then a person pushed down on the dead woman's chest while someone else dragged a violin bow across the dead woman's vocal cords.

—Come here, sweetie.

A person-shaped hole in the space-time continuum warped the light beside the bed. It mumbled.

The woman who resembled Sarah's mother tried to smile, but her lips stuck to her teeth as she made a face like a screaming ghost.

—You sure look pretty. That dress is gorgeous.

—Thank you.

Sarah wanted to run away, she wanted to scream, but she didn't do anything; instead, she stared at this woman.

She just stared at her.

—Come to mommy, sweetie.

—...

—What's wrong, Sarah?

—...

—Mommy's sick. Mommy's been sick, that's all.

—Did you eat something bad?

—No, honey.

—Is it a cold? or like the flu or something?

—It's much, much worse.

—Are you getting better now? Is that why the hospital let you come home?

The woman curled the meat above her eyes. She closed her mouth, pinching her lips, sucking them inward, and cried. She cried.

Sarah watched the skeleton-woman bawl like a little kid. She studied the woman's face. It seemed seem to melt and dissolve. Then Sarah peed. She peed. She felt her panties absorb the urine and she heard pee drip onto the carpet—plop, plop, plop.

Then …

She ran out of the room, screaming and crying.

Drifting out of the bedroom, sobs bubbled from the throat of the skeleton-woman who resembled her mother.

e.

She's in the present and in the past, locked somewhere in a sort of temporal tesseract—or just outside it:

She's in a car on a highway, locked in a traffic jam.

And she's on a cruise ship with her sister. They're on the dance floor, shaking it to a lounge lizard performing big band renditions of King Diamond.

The car is an older model, with a cigarette lighter, and she depresses the lighter then waits for it to pop as she navigates the radio, searching for of something worth listening to, for something to drown out the noise.

Noise tumbles from a speaker near the singer, static like from a blown speaker. The singer, dressed in a metallic gold suit, croons something about dead grandmothers. He flails his arms and legs, performing some strange variation of the Charleston. Several people, including Sarah and Michelle, laugh.

The lighter pops. Sarah lights her cigarette. A song begins in the interim, a loud and obnoxious metal song. She usually loathes metal, but something compels her to turn it up. Cigarette smoke tumbles out of her mouth and slips through the window, vanishing.

Facing each other, doing the Charleston, Sarah and Michelle laugh. They've each had about three drinks too many. Michelle improvises a sort of electroshock therapy dance move: arms akimbo, she shakes her limbs, torso, and head.

The traffic lurches forward. Sarah mutters, — About fucking time, and taps the gas pedal.

At the back of the room, near a vaguely looking Turkish doorway, a man with a bruised face slips into the ballroom.

The traffic stops and lurches, stops and lurches.

Michelle, still dancing, cackles like a child. Sarah focuses on the bruised man, practically feels the sympathetic division of her autonomic nervous system jolt to life. Something's wrong.

The man argues with a woman. Something is definitely not right.

Traffic spreads out. About goddamn time. The metal music—is that King Diamond?—sprays sound waves around the cabin; they rattle her ears, rock her temporal lobe.

Michelle frowns and stops dancing, too. She spins, searching for whatever arrested her sister's attention.

A horn blows. Then ... a sound like steel falling from the sky.

The woman and the bruised man argue. The woman shouts something and slaps him.

More horns. More sounds like steel falling from the sky.

In a flash, so fast it's almost imperceptible: the bruised man reaches inside his jacket and withdraws a revolver.

A horn blows, a long tremolo.

A woman screams. Then a man screams.

Sounds like steel falling from the sky.

He fires two shots into the woman's chest. Michelle backs into Sarah, slams into her chest, and screams. People scatter. Others trip or dive for cover. The bruised man puts the gun in his mouth and pulls the trigger.

In a flash, so fast it's almost imperceptible: a car jumps the median; it flies through the air and slams into Sarah's car, landing on top of it. The undercarriage blots the sun. The passenger-side tire penetrates Sarah's windshield.

Blood is everywhere.

Glass is everywhere.

People scream. Some race to the woman's body. Some race to the doorway. Michelle tugs Sarah's arm, screams, —Come on come on come on. But Sarah can't move. Something inside won't grant permission.

Tires screech. Feet slap the concrete. Someone knocks on the rear window, shouting, —Miss, can you hear me? me? can you ...

—... hear me?
—What?
Sarah was glancing out the window. Watching people walk by, honing in on their faces or fictionalizing their life stories, she'd tuned her father out a few minutes earlier.
—You didn't hear a word I just said.
—Of course, I did.
—Then what'd I say?
—You were talking about the universe.

—What about it?

—...

—Is everything all right?

—It is, she said.

—You seem aloof.

Silverware clattered. People chatted. A waitress carried a tray past their table, delivering food to an elderly couple. Nearby, a baby whined. Bruises covered her father's face.

—I haven't been sleeping.

—I'm willing to wager it's your anxiety. It's physiological as well as psychological, you know. And as much caffeine as you consume, you're probably keeping your heart rate close to permanently increased, which only exacerbates your anxiety.

—Caffeine keeps me awake.

—This might be one of those vicious cycles you hear about. Caffeine might trigger anxiety attacks, which prevents you from sleeping, so you consume it to stay awake because you haven't been sleeping. Follow me? Try avoiding it. At least for a week or so? To gauge the response.

—But at best it'd be correlational, she said. — Say I do sleep better. But then how would I know the caffeine was the problem? Correlation, as you are well aware, doesn't prove causation. In fact, I'm kind of surprised that you, of all people, would even suggest such a thing.

—Then call it a potential folk remedy.

Outside, near the window, a man wearing a bowler hat held up an apple, which seemed to replace his face. Sarah twisted her neck and jutted her head to the side, to see around the apple, but she couldn't see the man's face. He lowered the apple and something like electricity frayed Sarah's nerves. The triangles on his face shifted, shifted, shifted. One side of the inverted triangle collapsed, so vertices *b* and *a* nearly touched: the man's right eye pressed against the tip of his nose. The lower triangle twisted and pushed to the left, so his chin and lips, even his lower jaw, seemed warped as displaced, set midway between his shoulder and ear.

—Do you see that ...

The room was empty. Her father's seat was empty. Everyone was gone. The restaurant was desolate.

—Bracket it.

The lights dimmed, then faded, and the room sounded like what she imagined a vacuum might sound like—so devoid of sound that its soundlessness more or less forced her brain to invent sounds. A cackle here. Footsteps there. A clattering of silverware or change hitting a table. Somewhere, either outside or between the walls, a bird chirped.

—You're here but not here. The voice boomed, rising from the ground, falling from the sky, as if emitted by the earth.

Through the window she noticed—or, rather, sensed—absence.

She glided through the door and onto the sidewalk. No people, no cars, no movement— nothing. The city was empty.

—Cut off the consciousness of being conscious and focus your intention solely on what's in front of you, the voice said.

Sarah crossed the street. Then she walked down the sidewalk and crossed another street. Not even a bird flew through the sky.

She stopped in the middle of the street and spun.

—Hello? she said.

A man—it sounded like a man, definitely a voice with a lower register, at least lower than hers—sobbed.

—Hello?

More sobs.

Running now, she chased the sound, following it up a street and through an alley.

Daulton was sitting on a cinder-block-wall. His elbows resting on his knees, his face resting in his hands, he cried.

—What's going on? Sarah said.

Daulton blinked rapidly, as if trying to expel hair or dirt.

—I don't know if I can do this anymore, he said.

—Do what?

—This. All of it.

He spread out his arm and traced the horizon with his hand, as if introducing Sarah to the city. Sobbing, he leaned forward and covered his face.

—What's wrong? she said.

—My father died tonight.

—I'm sorry.

—It's awkward, I know. Responding to something like that.

—What happened?

—Fatal cardiac arrhythmia and myocardial infarction. Or so the coroner said. He couldn't be certain without an autopsy, but given dad's medical history, those are the likely culprits. I feel like a fool for crying. It doesn't make me feel better, he said. —It makes me feel worse. So I don't know why I'm doing it.

—Crying or fighting tears are two sides of the same coin. Giving into it or resisting it only alters the behavior other people detect. Cry or fight it; either way you're shackling yourself inside the prison of grief.

—I just talked to him today. I can't ...

—I know, Sarah said. —I understand.

Daulton stared at her. Or so she assumed—at some point, his triangles had started shifting.

—I know you do, he said.

—I feel like I'm fucking cursed. I encounter death pretty much everywhere I turn.

This was when Sarah was twenty four.

She was sitting in her psychiatrist's office. The woman stared at her, mouth agape, like a fucking monkey or something, trying to discern the pattern of a fly slamming into a closed window. Sarah hated that expression, that dumbfounded-mouth-agape gaze, and she seriously, for some reason, considered smacking it off that uppity bitch's face.

—Didn't you say a few weeks ago you don't believe in curses?

—No. I don't think so. I don't know, Sarah said. —Maybe. But then who knows? Sometimes I'm not sure what I think or know, what I believe or hold to be true. Like sometimes I think someone's the fucking author of my goddamn life and I don't know what to think or believe or whatever until this asshole gets around to writing it.

—Indeterminacy might be an expression of an underlying cause.

—Meaning ...?

—Are you familiar with learned helplessness?

Sarah shook her head.

—Some years back, a group of scientists conducted a series of experiments on dogs. Trying to understand a cognitive basis for, or variation of, operant conditioning.

—Okay.

—They put a dog in a box, divided by a partial wall. The researchers put electrodes on the floor, on both sides of the wall, and when a tone sounded, the electrodes administered a shock. As you'd expect, after a few cycles the tone sounded and the dog jumped over the wall, into the next cubicle. But it received a shock on that side, too. Then it jumped back over the wall and received another shock. After more cycles, the dog eventually stopped jumping altogether. The tone would sound and it'd just sit there and receive a shock.

—Jesus.

—They weren't harmful: intense vibrations, not raw electricity.

—So the point is ... What? Sarah said. —The dog failed to escape the shock so it stopped trying?

—We observe the same behavior in patients with depression. If you feel as though you're in a situation from which you must escape, and yet you've tried and repeatedly failed, then you might learn to become helpless. You might learn to sit there and take it, so to speak, even if it's possible to become proactive, to change the situation.

 —But what if I can't change the situation?

 —Then try to change your approach to it.

f.

The man at the microphone told another joke, some inane drivel about his wife. Yeah, he was one of those comedians, the kind Andy Kaufman had parodied decades earlier, the more or less "take my wife; no, please, take her" comedian. And so when he ended his set, a gasp, a breathy celebration, exploded from the audience.

Then the emcee jogged to the stage and said,

—Give a hand for Mike, everyone.

A scattering of applause.

—Next up, the emcee said, —is Cynthia. He checked a piece of paper. —No last name? Just Cynthia? She's a one-name persona, I guess. Like a Madonna. Or a Liberace. Or a Hitler.

A few laughs.

Sarah clenched Cynthia's hand. Smiling, Cynthia stood and kissed Sarah's cheek and strolled to the stage. She moved clumsily, swinging her arms while tightening the muscles in her legs, stiffening her gait.

She shook the emcee's hand. He popped the microphone into the mic stand and strolled off stage. Cynthia pulled the mic from the stand, waving as the audience applauded.

—Fuck you very much, she said.

Laughter.

Actual fucking joy filled Sarah. Crowded in a room the size of a convenience station, the audience chattered and giggled. Everyone smiled. Everyone applauded. Sure, it was open mic night, when anyone could get on stage, and even though it was a joke, a gag—Cynthia's decision to go on stage—Sarah felt proud in a weird way, like the applause for Cynthia was somehow indirectly meant for Sarah—like at least a part of it, maybe a small percentage of it, was meant for her.

In unison, the triangles Sarah's brain superimposed over the faces of everyone shifted. The room dimmed and brightened, dimmed and brightened. Onstage, Cynthia waved again. Her face opened and flipped and expanded, as if someone had stretched her flesh over the petals of a closed flower, then recorded time-lapsed footage of the flower blooming.

—I really don't know why I'm here, Cynthia said, into the microphone. —I'm still getting over my sister's death. She just died. Of cancer.

A few people laughed. Then the room fell silent.

Sarah ate it up. This was part of the plan, part of the joke: go onstage at a comedy club and say the most appalling things imaginable.

—It's funny, too, how sallow she looked, Cynthia said. —Don't you hate it when people are dying of cancer and they're all like, "I'm a living skeleton. Woe is me. The time is near. Don't cry for me. I love you all."

A few people laughed. Sarah felt like bursting. This was back when she smoked pot more or less religiously and so of course Cynthia's shtick was funnier than it probably actually was.

—So I was at the gynecologists the other day, Cynthia said, —just getting a routine pap smear, and the doctor said, somewhat sullenly, "I'm afraid you might have a tumor." And I thought to myself, "Will asking him out right now make this situation less awkward, or more?"

A few people laughed. Two women, near the stage, glided toward the exit. Three people passed them, carrying what smelled like cotton candy and elephant ears.

Sarah cackled and applauded. Something grew beside her; it seemed to bloom from shadows. She glanced, first by shooting her eyes to the side, then by turning her head: Daulton was sitting at her table, smoking a cigarette. His triangles shifted. And although they rendered his face equivalent to paint mixed together and spun with a stick, Sarah sensed a smile.

—I was watching a World War II documentary the other night, Cynthia said, —and it occurred to me: Hitler was kind of hot. I know it's an un-P.C thing to say, but I think if I were alive back then, I'd probably try to fuck him. I've never fucked a one-ball man before. And I'm willing to bet he was a fantastic lay, all screaming in that crazy German of his and slapping your ass while his hair flops around. And you know ... you know how I know he was a good lay? Two words: Eva Braun. Here was a woman who so loved Hitler's cock that she couldn't bear to go on without it. That must've been one tasty appendage.

A few more people laughed. Most didn't make a sound.

—So where are you right now? Daulton said.

—Zingers.

—The comedy club?

—Cynthia went onstage from time to time. Just to fuck with people.

—Fuck with them how? Like tell bad jokes?

—Uncomfortable, deeply offensive jokes.

—Now that's funny.

—We'd talked about it forever, and I remember feeling so embarrassed and yet envious while she was up there. Then: —But I thought you couldn't see what I see.

—You can talk to her, you know, Daulton said.

—I can talk at her. There's a difference.

—You can say anything you want. I don't usually recommend it, but ... it might help.

—What's the point? She can't respond to what I have to say.

—Still, it might help.

—It hasn't yet.

—Maybe you haven't said the right things. Or enough of them.

—What I want to say to her, the conversation I'd love to have, the questions I'd love to ask wouldn't yield anything meaningful. Because what I want to address hasn't occurred yet. So how can she have answers?

The room shifted. The walls melted. Daulton and Sarah were seated at the table from the comedy club, only the table was now beside an elephant ear vendor at the county fair. Throngs of people crowded the food vendors. Screams rose and fell in the distance—people enjoying rides. Overhead, clouds threatened to merge and blot out the sun.

—I love elephant ears, Daulton said. —Do you want one?

—No thanks.

Daulton wandered to the elephant ear vendor.

Sarah drilled the tip of her shoe into the grass. Dirt specked her shoe. People crossed in front of her. She glanced at them without really paying attention to them. Then she dug her shoe farther into the grass and ...

Now this thought occurred to her: they look familiar.

She searched for them among the crowd. Scanned the fairgrounds from right to left. She stood and elevated herself onto the balls of her feet. But they'd vanished. Or perhaps they hadn't crossed her path at all. Perhaps she'd imagined it. But then ... Of course she'd imagined it.

Or had she? Was it possible?

They crossed her path again, like they were stuck in a film someone had just rewound. Two women, younger, early twenties. Holding hands, they grinned and talked.

Sarah's heart pounded, pounded, pounded.

The women were Cynthia and Sarah. This was when Sarah had chopped off her hair and bleached the remainder. Fuck, to others she must've looked like an idiot, or a junkie artist or something. What was she thinking? She looked like a freak. But not Cynthia: she was as beautiful as always. Long black hair framed a pale but not anemic face.

Cynthia said something—it was garbled—and they swung by a cotton candy booth. She fucking loved cotton candy. A man wearing a bucket hat handed each a spool of cotton candy, then he waved away their money. Cynthia attempted to more or less force the cash on him, but he refused it. Sarah remembers feeling annoyed at that, for some reason.

—I wish more people were like you, Cynthia said.

Cynthia's tone conveyed sincerity, which was something of a rarity with her.

They headed for a bench but stopped in the middle of the crowd. Cynthia took a bite from Sarah's cotton candy spool and Sarah took a bite from Cynthia's. Then they kissed. Sarah remembers the kiss: sugary and sweet.

But how obnoxious they seemed now, like teenagers on their first date.

—Something catch your eye? Daulton sat beside Sarah and dug into an elephant ear.

—Cynthia and me.

—Ah, I see.

—I still don't understand how this works. Like tell me what you see. Right now.

—Over there, by the face-painting booth, I see my family. My sisters and me. My mom. My dad.

Sarah didn't see a family. She didn't see a face-painting booth at all.

—But how are we ...

—Our brains are different. You know that. And but does it matter? In this moment, right now, do you care?

—It feels so real, Sarah said. —Like I can reach out and touch it.

A man stopped near the table to tie his shoe. Daulton slapped the man's face. He stumbled forward, smacking his cheek on the leg of a nearby table. Jumping to his feet, he gazed at Daulton, stared past him, as if he couldn't see him. Daulton shouted, —Boo, and the man bolted.

Daulton laughed.

—You know you can touch anything you'd like, he said. —Feeling it, on the other hand, gets tricky.

Younger Sarah and Cynthia sat on a bench near the elephant ear vendor, eating cotton candy. Cynthia said something. Younger Sarah laughed.

—Can I touch her? Sarah said.

—You might make you jealous. Daulton laughed. —But you know the answer to that.

—Could I have a conversation with her? A real one?

—You can talk to her any time you'd like. You know this, Sarah.

—But will it mean something?

—What is this "meaning" you speak of?

—Christ, you sound like my father.

Sounds of people chattering and laughing, screaming, crying, singing drowned out Sarah's voice. She cleared her throat and repeated herself. But Daulton, moving on, flicked his wrist and said,

—It's too broad, "meaning." Define it in context and I'll try to give you a useful answer.

—I guess what I meant to say is: will it be real?

—Define "real."

—As in, actually happen.

—If you go over there, right now, and talk to her, then you can absolutely say it happened.

—But will it mean something?

—Define "mean something."

—Goddamn it. Sarah slapped the table. —You and your goddamn questions.

—The ambiguity of natural language is frustrating, isn't it?

—It's not language, she said. —It's you.

—Sit down, Daulton said.

—Then give me a straight fucking answer.

—You ask "will talking to her be meaningful." I say the act of speaking to someone you've lost, after you lost her, is meaningful. But the sense of "meaningful" as I'm using it is clearly different from the sense in which you're using it. And, to be honest, I'm not quite certain how you're using it. You say, "Will it be real?" You see her, don't you?

Younger Sarah lit a cigarette as Cynthia peeled an egg-sized piece of cotton candy from the spool. She folded it into her mouth and pierced her lips. She preferred to let it dissolve, a preference she passed on to Sarah.

Her triangles shifted, shifted, but white sparkled: her teeth. She was smiling.

—Although I can't see what you're seeing, Daulton said, —I'm willing to wager that, if you follow me, the other Sarah will disappear. Now concentrate. Think about getting rid of the you over there.

Daulton snapped his fingers. Younger Sarah disappeared.

—I'm assuming you have an 'in' now, Daulton said. —So go talk to her.

Sarah studied his shifting face.

—Are you joking?

—Concentrate. Think about what you want. Right now. In this moment.

Daulton snapped his fingers again. All sounds —all voices, all music, all ambient noise— vanished.

—Did you get what you wanted?

She nodded.

—So go talk to her, he said.

Cynthia was smiling, moving her lips, still talking to the Sarah who was no longer there. She laughed and dropped her hand beside her, massaging an absent thigh.

Sarah was stoned out of her mind back then, but she remembers this—but not the conversation. It was stored somewhere, lost among shriveled dendrites, probably.

She dropped onto the bench beside Cynthia. Like a glitch in a video game, Cynthia's hand vanished into Sarah's leg. It drifted upward, upward, stopping after it floated up, through the flesh and over the denim.

And Sarah felt—she actually fucking felt— Cynthia's hand on her thigh. Its warmth sent tremors through Sarah; tears streamed down her cheeks.

—... and so certain, you know?

—I still can't believe this is possible.

—And she acts so fucking holier than thou, Cynthia said. —I think that's what I've always found so repulsive about her.

—The way you touch me. How it feels. And the way you smell. I swear, I can actually smell you.

—And like we're not exempt from her one-woman crusade, either. To right the wrongs. That's her deal. But go ahead and ask her: what wrongs are you righting? And you get a look like you're Adolph Eichmann stepping off the plane in Jerusalem.

—How long's it been? Sarah said. —A year? A decade? It feels like a fucking lifetime already.

—I find the whole pseudo-feminist thing so baroque anyway. Instead of fighting for equality, wouldn't trying to filter out the concept of gender be a more respectable goal? I mean, if you eliminate the concept of gender, then wouldn't equality be the default?

—I can't say I remember this day so well. Like did we have this conversation about Hillary here, at this fair, or was it somewhere else? Wherever this conversation happened, is this even an accurate reconstruction of it?

—No, Cynthia said. —On that, we're in agreement: our species would absolutely find some other, non-gender means of categorizing or criticizing or condemning people. So, yeah, it's probably an unrealistic goal. But isn't it at the very least admirable?

—Why aren't you with me now, goddamn it? Why the fuck did you do it? At least break through and tell me that, answer that one question. Please.

—Right. Exactly. And so the way she acts generates endless conflict, which in turn inspires some people to generalize, like all women are, deep down inside, angry man-hating feminists. And that bullshit mentality is already far too prevalent for my taste. Like all feminists hate men. Such shit.

—You were the happy one. The better-put-together one, at any rate. We both expected that ending for me. At least I did. But you ... nothing indicated such a fucking ending for you. You could've offered hints, clues. Goddamn it, you could've fucking primed me for it.

—And I should, too, Cynthia said. —Writing her off would solve so many problems, at least as far as anxiety and frustration go.

—I miss you so fucking much, Cyn. It's sometimes unbearable, how much I miss you.

—But ... I don't know. We grew up together, you know? I've always had this weird, little sister attachment to her.

The triangles superimposed over Cynthia's face collided and transformed into an unfolding, never ending Sierpinski triangle: Cynthia's face morphed into a gelatinous blob with thousands of presumed eyeballs and mouths, thousands of presumed noses and chins. Her face grew and expanded as the Sierpinski triangles unfolded. Everywhere, everywhere, flesh unspooled, unraveled. Her head exceeded the weight capacity of her neck; it dropped down, down, down, splitting her sternum. Blood sprayed in all directions. As the weight of the unfolding triangles tore into her sternum, ripping each rib on its descent to the ground, pieces of bone and chunks of flesh fell into her lap, yet she continued to talk.

Blood sprayed. Flesh unspooled. Triangles unfolded. And Cynthia kept talking about Hillary, complaining about her friend's misguided weltanschauung.

—Fuck oh fuck oh fuck oh fuck oh fuck ... Sarah covered her ears, closed her eyes, and screamed.

She screamed.

Complaining about Hillary, Cynthia's voice sputtered and faded. Faded. Faded.

Darkness.

The utter and absolute absence of light.

Sarah couldn't see her body.

Her kinesthetic sense alone informed her of its existence. But did the absolute absence of light create a phantom-limb-like sensation? Like did she even have a body, or was the proprioception itself a hallucination?

In such a mind-altering absence of light, her brain, her neurons, her fucking consciousness seemed intermingled with the darkness. Were the two inseparable? Was it even possible to disentangle them?

In such darkness she felt so intertwined with the void that it, in a literal sense, wove itself into the fibers of her conscious state, like she and the void were one. Like the void seemed inside her—

if such a concept made sense—and replaced the myelin sheath on every axon on every neuron, allowing her to experience such absolute darkness. But could she even call this state "experience?" Like was it even possible to "experience" such darkness? Like would it be possible to float into a black hole and linger inside the event horizon and exist in a state which allowed for "experience," or would the experience itself be too traumatic to yield "experience?"

g.

—You're equivocating, her father said.

—What's that mean again?

This was when Sarah was maybe twenty-five. She and her father were in a park overlooking Lake Michigan. It was early in the day, midway between morning and afternoon, and the sun was backlighting the too-blue yet empty sky.

Not even a trace of clouds muted the tapestry overhead.

—You are funny, my dear.

They sat on an elevated platform maybe a dozen yards from the lake. Rows of concrete tables and benches lined the platform. Black and white checkerboard tiles covered the tables, allowing for games of chess or checkers.

—I learned from the master, she said. —Your move.

Sarah's pieces outnumbered his—her black to his white—but past experience prevented her from feeling anything resembling hubris. Her father needed only one mistake to dominate the board. And, if past experience augured the present, then the birds flying overhead signaled doom.

—If the sense of a word is different in each premise, then the argument is not sound. You're using the sense of the word 'love' differently in each premise. Your argument, therefore, is not sound.

Laughing, Sarah said,

—You really need to learn to talk shit. It can be so invigorating.

—I'm capable of "talking shit."

Sarah laughed again.

—It sounds strange even hearing you say that. "Talking shit."

Her father touched his queen while examining the board. He removed his finger from it and scanned the board again. His eyes met Sarah's eyes.

—You already touched it, she said, —but I'll be nice.

He snagged her rook with his knight, then he flashed a grin and, nodding, twirled his hand.

Sarah leaned her elbows onto the table. Studying the board, she played out possible scenarios. She envisioned eight possible moves over two full turns. Every move benefitted her somehow, which raised flags. In her experience, when imagining moves, the situation rarely converged with her expectations of it. So she scanned the board again. She imagined eight possible moves again. She doubted herself again and wondered what she'd overlooked. What move would or could he make to upset her plans?

—Sarah.

—Shush. I didn't rush you.

—What would you say to someone who experienced something so profound that it altered his way of viewing the universe?

—I'd ask what drugs they were on and could I have some, please?

Her father wasn't smiling.

—What do you mean, she said, —like a religious experience?

—Not religious. Maybe numinous?

—But aren't those the same thing?

—Then numinous in a secular sense, he said. —Profound.

—What exactly are we talking about here?

—I don't know how to describe it.

—I'm confident you ...

—I was watching television, eating peanut butter, for some reason the sensation of eating peanut butter, the way I salivate and how my masseter tightens, almost tingles before I take a bite ...

—Dad, Sarah said, —what are you talking about?

—Everything in my periphery turned bright, as if an explosion had occurred. Then the white turned blue, almost neon blue.

—My god, dad. Have you gone to the doctor? When the fuck did this happen? And why the hell didn't you call me?

—I don't ... It wasn't an anomaly, I don't think. I don't think it was a neurophysiological malfunction, either.

—For fuck's sake, she said, —what if it was a stroke? She stood and felt his forehead for some reason.

—It wasn't a stroke.

—I think sometimes people can have strokes, like mini-strokes or something, and not know it. I can't believe you haven't seen a doctor.

—It wasn't a stroke.

—And why the fuck didn't you call me?

—Sarah. His tone betrayed anger, which caught her attention. —Listen to me, please: everything ... I saw the world as we construct it, in the various ways we can construct it. I saw ... I was staring at the television and I was simultaneously staring at trillions of photons scattering, and I was simultaneously staring at electrical impulses as well as the word "television," a black word, hovering in prisms of light. The words "entertainment stand" surrounded "television." Photons scattered. Electrical impulses fired. And I saw the television, the television as you or I would ordinarily perceive it.

—This is insane. I'm taking you to the hospital. Right fucking now.

—I focused on the words hovering in the prism. Strings of letters cycled through a box composed of the word "television." Looking down I saw: "floor." Looking up I saw: "ceiling." And I also saw photons and electrical impulses, and I saw the floor and the ceiling ... as I'd usually see them. It was as if ... as if I saw all possibilities of seeing or expressing these things, and they, the possibilities, were superimposed over each other. In layers.

Sarah smacked the top of the table. She scrambled to her feet, collected her cigarettes, and grabbed her father's arm.

—We're going to the hospital, she said. —Now.

—I think I willed it, he said. —And I think I can do it again.

h.

That she left you with regret, that she left you confused, that she left you at all; that she was lying there but not "lying" there; that she was now little more than meat, meat resembling your sister; that the mechanical impulses flying through idiosyncratic arrangements of neurons, with idiosyncratic connections, had ceased firing; that these neurons, arranged as they were, had created a system of patterns you'd called your sister no longer fired; that this meat resembled your sister, and for many years was your sister; and that this meat lying in a box in a room filled with people lacked the neural activity to trigger those patterns, putting webs of activity into motion, constituting Michelle is what you find most disturbing as you stand in front of the coffin.

People chatted and people talked. Some cried and some laughed. The lighting faded or the lighting was dim—who knows? You remember it was dim but it probably wasn't dim.

Standing in front of the coffin, beside your father, unable to so much as glance at him because glancing at him, seeing his face, an undoubtedly destroyed face, would probably cause you to collapse. And while standing in front of the coffin, while gazing at the meat resembling your sister, you wonder if you're perhaps stuck in a dream, a lucid dream, the kind you'd read about or heard about but hadn't experienced.

Were you dreaming?

Probably.

Standing in front of the coffin manufactured a sensation which violated one of the fundamental laws of logic. The situation felt both p and ¬p. But then how could a situation feel both p and ¬p? It couldn't. It was logically impossible.

So yet there you were: standing in front of a coffin, gazing at meat resembling your sister. It felt both real and not real—both p and ¬p. It felt not real in the sense that it felt imagined, like a thought filtered into the occipital lobe and then distributed through the association areas before regrouping in the frontal lobe.

For all situations such as real and imagined, it was not the case that some situations were both real and imagined; this case was not real; therefore, this situation was imagined.

But you weren't consciously imagining it, were you? No. Probably not. If you were consciously imagining the situation, then you'd be aware of it, and if you were imagining the situation but not consciously imagining the situation, then you were dreaming it; you weren't consciously imaging the situation; therefore, you were dreaming it.

Were you dreaming it?

Her mother's funeral, her sister's funeral, her wife's funeral—she'd only ever remember them the way she'd remember certain dreams. Sometimes a dream impressed itself on her and she'd think about it over the course of a day or a week, but she'd only rarely remember dreams as visual images. If she were lucky, she'd remember an image here or an image there, but she'd not remember a continuous stream of images; instead, she'd remember the feelings or sensations a dream imprinted, and she'd dwell on them, reviving them whenever the dream cycled through her head.

Like dreams, at the funerals she'd spent less time, it seemed, encoding visual stimuli than recording the sensations those stimuli elicited. She assumed the stress and the anxiety, the trauma, had more or less prevented her from somehow accessing those memories, like maybe she'd also encoded something like a failsafe to push out memories in fragments, to prevent a possible déjà-vu-like summoning of emotions and sensations.

When Sarah had articulated this theory to her father, he'd suggested that maybe, under moments of high stress, such as a funeral, the sympathetic division was more likely to wrest control from the parasympathetic division, and so the modulation of her involuntary actions and responses differed. This, he'd speculated, maybe affected the process of encoding information as memories, like maybe since the sympathetic division was in charge, then maybe its ancillary processes dominated the encoding process, and so she'd encoded less visual stimuli and information and more chaos, tension, anxiety.

These were, of course, only speculations. They were only possibilities. In the circumstances, the sad, grim circumstances of, say, a funeral, everything appeared as a dream because everything was, in a sense, a dream. The ability to consciously focus her attention: the only difference between obtaining in a dream and obtaining in a conscious state. In the former, her attention guided her. In the latter, she could, at times, guide her attention.

But, no...

Was that right? Or was it the other way around?

—I can't process my father's death, Daulton said. —Something inside me shuts down whenever I think about it, and so it lingers in this weird sort of intellectual purgatory, half present and half repressed.

—I know what you mean, Sarah said. —You want to dwell on it and yet at the same time you don't want to think about it.

—I keep trying to picture how I must appear to other people. Last night, my wife, she said to me,

"You know, it's okay to cry." I do know that. And part of me wants to collapse in tears. But then another part resists it, and so I feel like a rope tugged from both ends: the force is the same on either side and so the rope doesn't move. Yet I feel the tension. I understand it.

—I sometimes think to myself ... I find myself thinking, "Is it a disgrace, somehow dishonoring his memory, that I'm exerting so much effort to avoid thinking about him?" I feel guilty about it. He was my fucking father, a man I absolutely adored, and but at the same time I can't bring myself to so much as think about him.

—That's the problem. Right now it's too new. The wound is too fresh.

—Right, Sarah said.

—You alter a memory every time you retrieve it, Daulton said. —You sort of reconceptualize it in a framework suitable to your current state, to the state in which you're retrieving it, as opposed to the conditions that obtained when you'd encoded it.

—And of course therein lies the problem.

—Therein lies the problem.

—So what you're saying is ... If I may be allowed to draw some inferences ...

—Infer away.

—If you retrieve a memory when you're in mourning, then you'll experience that memory as sad or tragic.

—Exactly. And what's worse is ... When you retrieve a memory and unpack it, you don't put it away untouched. You then re-encode it, sort of update it, and you encode the altered memory. So whenever you retrieve a memory, you change it until you retrieve it again, and then you change it again. Eventually it gets so corrupted that the bits representing the original are mostly replaced by subsequent retrievals.

—So if you retrieve a memory of your father, especially now, then you'll alter it forever? Making a previously un-sad memory sad, or even tragic?

—And then that's the memory. So then five years down the road, for example, when something triggers that memory, and when you retrieve it, you'll experience the sadness, the grief, the mourning, sensations that probably weren't attached to the original situation you'd encoded.

—So thinking about your father so soon after his death in a way destroys your memories of him?

—The process corrupts them. Absolutely, Daulton said. —I want to keep memories of my father as close to the events I'd encoded as possible. Because if I retrieve them too often, I replace them bit by, bit by bit, so eventually the father I reconstruct from this information isn't my father at all; it's me, what I'm feeling or experiencing, reconstructed as my father.

—That's terrifying, Sarah said.

Then that goddamn dog barked. Again.

Those goddamn teenagers were at the cemetery again, no doubt doing or dealing drugs again. The dog barked. Someone laughed. Bark. Laugh. Bark bark. Laugh. Then more noise: music. Why didn't someone call the cops on those assholes? Why hadn't Sarah called the cops on them?

She was sitting in the chair by the window trying to read a book, a Barthelme novel about fathers, but something outside, some noise or note, shattered her focus, and so she found herself reading and re-reading the same fucking paragraph. Over and over. With short chapters and easy prose, the book was, on its surface, easy to read, but it required attention and thought, both annihilated by those goddamn kids and their goddamn dog.

Why hadn't she called the cops?

But then calling the cops would create problems. Calling the cops could create vendetta-type scenarios in which the teenagers would want to exact revenge. But ... so, no: she wouldn't call the cops.

She played music, trying to drown out the noise. But the music created another noise problem. So apparently reading wasn't in the cards. The universe, it seemed, had, for billions of years, set into motion a series of events culminating in this night, a night in which noise, noise, noise prevented her from reading.

She paced in front of the chair. She closed her eyes and envisioned the room, tried to remember every object, every crack in the paint—everything. Memorizing the room was useful. The Greeks and Romans used a technique whereby they'd memorize a room, then visualize it and add information they wanted to remember. Afterward, they'd visually roam through the room and retrieve the information. They called it the method of loci.

She thought about calling her father to inquire about the method, but she didn't feel like talking to him. Maybe just talk long enough to ask one question, one simple question: how do you will the wormhole into existence?

And was it even a wormhole? Was "wormhole" a misnomer?

Probably.

Eyes still closed, she spun in circles, trying to envision the room. She recalled the couch and sensed it, she recalled the bookshelves beside the door and sensed them, she recalled the crack in the ceiling, an almost lower-case y-shaped crack; she tried to visualize everything with an intensity rivaling the information received by her eyes. If only she could open her eyes, snag the information, and reproduce it with accuracy, with clarity—that might break the spell, the constant failure to reproduce everything as it was. Not as she imagined.

—What the hell're you doing?

Cynthia and Marcus were standing near the door, gazing at her as if she were a circus animal.

—Those fucking teenagers are driving me crazy.

—I keep telling you to ignore them.

—I can't.

—You want me to go out there, Marcus said, —scream at them?

—No.

—I want to, Sarah said, —but it'll only make things worse.

—But you've got to deal with it.

Marcus settled on the couch, cracked open a beer.

—So what's on the agenda? he said.

—I don't know, Sarah said, —I thought we were going to dinner.

—I didn't know there was an agenda.

—That's it? Just dinner?

—Money's tight. We can't go around hobnobbing with people who can afford to sustain themselves.

—That's right, Sarah said. —Who do you think we are?

Marcus said something and Cynthia laughed. A sensation like crushing metal flowed through Sarah. She felt hollowed. The world flattened—transformed from three-dimensions to two-dimensions. Everything appeared gray and empty. Everything appeared lifeless. Artificial. Dead.

As Marcus and Cynthia talked and joked, as Cynthia borrowed Marcus's cigarette and lit her cigarette, Sarah sat on a footstool near the chair, spacing out as she stared at the floor. That gray, empty, dead feeling pushed down on her.

It crushed her.

She didn't know it at the time, but that marked the beginning. That's how it began: the emptiness culminated in a third attempt.

Here's what it felt like, that "awful combination," Sarah's words, "of anxiety and emptiness":

Anxiety infiltrated her perception, her ability to construct and to reconstruct images. Life, then, seemed like an old movie. The act of seeing transformed: light, and the information it transmitted, appeared to hit eyeballs encased in eyeballs covered with grime. And the world assumed an almost sepia tone.

All people experience something called perceptual expectancy. In a nutshell: people tend to see what they expect to see. So at the height of her anxiety and depression, and for whatever reason, something in Sarah's brain, some synaptic knobs failing to release neurotransmitters, maybe, or molecules in neurotransmitters failing to fit into receptor sites, possibly, everything she saw looked empty and dead, depressed or tragic. So when she passed a couple on the street, and even though both man and woman laughed, Sarah blocked their happiness because she didn't expect to see happiness; instead, she focused on their body language and assumed the end of a relationship; and from there she extrapolated a possible world scenario in which the man, heartbroken, put the barrel of a gun into his mouth and pulled the trigger.

Depression consumed her—and, when she described it, she meant it: "consumed." Worse, it felt like cancer. Or what she imagined cancer might feel like. That's how she described it to Cynthia one evening. But then she'd dismissed the simile almost immediately. Intuitively, cancer didn't work as a simile.

So she tried another approach:

Picture your nervous system, fitted with millions of bundles of axons. Then imagine corrosive acid and hundreds of thousands of volts of electricity coursing through those bundles. Imagine existing in a state of feeling—always—on the verge of screaming. That's how she felt. There seemed—to her, anyway—two types of screams, a visceral scream and a voluntary scream. A voluntary scream was when an amusement park ride elicited a response. A visceral scream was the product of pure terror. A visceral scream was how you might respond while lying in bed in a dark room contemplating death —not simply contemplating it but actually fantasizing about it. When you're afraid of death and you fantasize about it, to the extent of trying to visualize it, so to speak, or of trying to imagine what it will be like, that eternal absence of experience, sometimes a visceral scream takes hold of you and you produce a guttural-like moan, a vocalized translation of pure terror. Now imagine a depressed person, a person existing—from day to day, from moment to moment, even —in a state milliseconds prior to releasing a visceral scream. And imagine expecting emptiness and sadness and death; imagine anticipating it always; whenever you see someone, whenever you meet someone, whenever you so much as even consider stepping outside, you expect the worst: you expect humiliation or sadness or even death. And that's the thing, the thing she tried to explain to everyone—depression was, to her at least, a sort of perpetual experience, and anticipation, of death. Like life, for her, consisted of a series of moments in which she began to experience death without the terminus of the patterns of sensations humans called "experience."

And so, as day bled into night and as days bled into weeks, the perpetual anxiety attacks and the continuous, death-like experiences launched her onto the top floor of a hypothetical high-rise. In this imagined room, she felt, with each psychic twitch, a sort of nudging toward an open window. Every negative or emotionally-charged sensation nudged her forward, ever forward. Then, as weeks bled into months, she transformed the hypothetical high-rise into an actual razor blade, and one morning she took the blade to her forearms and carved the meat. Something like a relief valve blowing open pushed blood out of her veins and onto her arms and the floor. Within seconds, she tumbled to the ground, concentrating on the tiles, on how cool they felt against her cheek. And then she waited. She waited for the terminus of experience. And then she smiled. She closed her eyes and smiled.

i.

—You going to eat that? Michelle said.

—Not now.

—Sorry. It looked good.

—Give me that artichoke heart and we're even.

—Done.

—How can they ruin artichokes?

—Nu-uh. No givebacks.

—I don't want it.

—Just keep it on your plate.

—Fine.

—Do you remember what mom was like right before she died?

—Where'd that come from?

—I can't remember what she was like. I remember visiting her in the hospital but I don't really remember anything after that.

—You were what? thirteen? Trauma like that ... we have defenses against it.

—But don't you find it strange that I blocked it ... And why didn't I block the hospital, too, then?

—These aren't really questions I can answer.

—But what does that do for closure? Having blocked so much?

—It seems to me, and I haven't given this much thought, but intuitively it feels as though closure is an artificial thing. Like in set theory how sets aren't actually things that obtain in, for lack of a better word, "reality." I think closure is at best an analytic tool and at worst a platitude.

—So then why do you think I don't remember anything after the hospital?

—You probably encoded it, but, for whatever reason, your ...

—How well do you remember it?

—I remember some things better than others. Like, I remember dad, I remember mom, but I don't really remember you being there.

—So what exactly do you remember?

—The day she came home. How terrifying she looked.

—You know, I could be mistaken but ... I remember you pissed yourself.

—That's right. God. So you must've been there.

—But, like, I completely blocked mom. I remember you peeing yourself and racing out of the room. But I don't remember her. What'd she look like?

—You seriously don't remember?

—I seriously don't remember.

Meat again. Flesh again. Everything rising and collapsing again. Everything dead and swimming to life again. Swimming, swimming in a night-sea journey, to a place of simultaneous death and rebirth, Sarah's floating in a sea of haze. Mist. Fog. Night shatters. Day replaces it.

Lying, eyes closed, she senses people, loved ones maybe. She doesn't see or hear anything. But she senses conversations, reminiscences:

Do you remember that dog, that damn dog? how she had a real love-hate relationship with it? How it taunted her probably as much if not more than she taunted it? And how strangely heartbroken she was when it died? Well, it was so close on the heels of her mother's death and so she might've used it as a vehicle for her grief. She didn't grieve for her mother, at least not outwardly, I don't think. I always thought it was bizarre. Disturbing, to tell you the truth. How stoic she seemed. She was old enough to at least understand how to properly use "death" in the context of a conversation and yet she seemed too young, really, to grasp what was going on. It was too abstract for her. It can be too abstract for kids sometimes. Yet somehow that dog did it; it triggered an awareness or something, and, remember, the tears? How they flowed.

Is this real? It's like a lack of experience. Not really an absence of experience but a lack of it. She tries to consider the situation, but thoughts hang in spaces between the ticks of a clock. All thoughts feel trapped or imprisoned, like everything she can possibly even attempt to think falls victim to *presque vu*.

And so is this real? Is she even thinking this right now? How can she even think if all thoughts are shackled and locked inside an impenetrable prison-like skull?

—It's not a thought, really, so much as a feeling, Sarah said. —But not even a feeling. That, too, implies connection, if that makes sense. I don't know. It's like the experience exceeded the reach of language. I literally can't describe it.

—It's what Wittgenstein called the limitation of language, Daulton said.

They were sitting at a booth beneath a frozen waterfall. Inside a cave. Beside them, a wall decorated with red and black handprints; around them, the walls glistened. Somewhere inside but not nearby, an animal howled, a wolf, maybe. The cave retained the fair weather of spring—although, to Sarah's knowledge, the nation had just celebrated the anniversary of its independence.

The triangles on Daulton's face shifted—again and again. His flesh imploded and spread outward. It nauseated Sarah. She glanced at the table, at her hands, and avoided so much as even glancing in the general area Daulton occupied.

—Here ya go, sweetie.

A person-sized insect carried a tray to the table. It set a plate in front of Daulton and a plate in front of Sarah. Gold light shimmered on Daulton's plate. A wad of meat, at least as large as Sarah's head, twitched on her plate; it pulsed and throbbed, as if filled with a dozen or so randomly inserted bladders.

She plastered a less-than-authentic smile on her face and said, to the insect,

—It looks delicious.

—Enjoy it, now. And holler if ya need anything. The insect didn't really speak; instead, it more or less projected its voice into Sarah's head.

Daulton stabbed a fork into the light plate. He brought it to his face, presumably toward his mouth. Lozenges of light fell from the fork and dropped onto the table.

—It looks good, Daulton said. Chewing the light, he jabbed the fork toward Sarah's plate.

—I've always wanted to try it, she said, without touching her silverware.

—Everything okay?

—To be honest, it doesn't look the least bit appetizing.

—What's wrong with it?

—It's just ...

—What do you see?

—What do you see?

—I asked first, Daulton said.

—I see a ball of meat. And it's pulsing.

—Sounds delicious.

—Want to trade?

—Why? What does mine look like?

—Light, she said. —Gold light.

Daulton's face shifted, twisted, twirled.

—Where are we? he said.

—In a cave.

—A cave?

—Yeah.

—Describe it.

—There are handprints on the wall, Sarah said.
—Overhead there's a frozen waterfall. Or a glass sculpture. I can't tell which. What do you see?

—A 50s-style diner. The waitress looks like my wife.

—Doesn't look like anyone's wife to me.

—So then what's she look like?

—Gregor Samsa.

The wad of meat on her plate pulsed. Pores secreted slime. A wound on its side bloomed like a flower and squirted blood. Sarah dodged the blood, slid the plate to the edge of the table.

—Why are we here?

—Why are any of us here?

—It's not an existential question, she said. —I mean, why are we here? in this specific place?

—Things aren't going well for me, Daulton said. —My mind is ... Everything is breaking apart.

—I know the feeling.

—Listen, he said, —I think ... whatever this is, I think it's a sign of maybe instability.

—What are you talking about?

—You, Sarah; I'm talking about you.

—Well, I know I'm unstable.

—Sarah, he said, —and I want you to listen closely: you are a figment of my imagination.

—Then I think we're at something of an impasse. Because I'm almost certain that you're a figment of my imagination.

The space beside her mother's bed bent and folded inward, as if a person-shaped tear had

113

opened in the space-time continuum. Sarah saw it indirectly, in her periphery, and, for whatever reason, she couldn't will herself to inspect it. Like maybe something in her brain prevented the action. And this put her in a sort of bind: she couldn't turn her head or avert her attention, but at the same time she wanted to turn her head. She wanted to avert her attention because her mother had, it seemed, lost more weight—pretty much overnight. Now she looked even more like a skeleton. In fact, she looked like a mummified corpse. Her flesh, dried out, like beef jerky, more or less stretched over her skeleton. Her lips, thin now, stuck to her teeth. Her eyelids wavered, locked into a position midway between opened and closed. And an odor filled the room, an odor unlike anything Sarah had encountered. Musky yet sweet.

Her mother was awake but she didn't seem awake, like she was floating in and out of another world, maybe. Sarah watched her, occasionally spoke to her. At times her mother mumbled. At other times, she didn't respond.

—Dad wants to know if you want some water.

Her mother mumbled. It sounded like, "nothing."

—Dad wants to know if you want anything.

The tear in the space-time continuum emitted sound.

—That's all right, honey, her mother said to the tear.

Goosebumps grew on Sarah's arms. She tried to turn her head, couldn't. She tried to spin and run, couldn't. She tried to open her mouth, to speak, but her lips wouldn't move, so she sort of gurgled.

—I want to tell you girls something, her mother said. —I want you to make sure, always make sure, that your father is all right. He sometimes ... sometimes he forgets to do stuff, little things, and sometimes he even forgets to eat. So you, both of you, must promise mommy that you'll look after him, make sure to remind him when he forgets things.

The tear in the space-time continuum emitted sound.

—No, honey.

—But you'll help him remember stuff, too, right? Sarah said.

—I'll try, baby. But I can't promise to be around forever.

—Why not?

The tear in the space-time continuum emitted sound again. Sarah tried to turn her head again. She tried to spin and run again.

—Just promise me, her mother said.

This was when Sarah was twenty—three years before her sister would die and twelve years after her mother had died. She was on a bus to Indiana. A failed suicide attempt had induced an extended leave of absence. Her father all but demanded she leave Massachusetts, on punishment of estrangement or pain. She didn't want to leave, but at the same time she didn't want to stay. And yet, for some reason, her desires didn't violate the law of non-contradiction.

—There's no excluded middle, she said.

A man in the seat in front of her swiveled his head, offering a look as though he expected her to shit in her hand and fling it across the cabin. Sarah lowered her eyes, curled inward; she wanted to disappear.

Outside, the world had vanished. Only the absence of everything obtained. The void was too black for night. At first, Sarah had dismissed the absence as a property of the tinted windows, but then she remembered, maybe two minutes earlier, watching a car keep pace with the bus. She remembered how the passenger-side window had reflected light: it seemed to beam asterisks at her.

Now ... nothing.

A sensation like 160,000-volts of electricity jolted her. Everything—every limb, every digit, even every nerve—felt tingly and asleep. She knew the feeling, had encountered it too frequently to misdiagnose it. So she grabbed her Moleskine notebook, flipped it to the first page, and started reading—a convenient distraction.

This was back when she wrote, when she secretly and vaguely harbored fantasies of becoming her generation's Sylvia Plath, though limited to prose.

The story was something she'd knocked out over summer break. It was about a man and his wife, who'd discovered a way to skip in and out of something like parallel dimensions—although it was mostly about the man, or at least told from his point of view. In trying to process a miscarriage his wife had suffered some years back, the man had discovered a way to alter his perception of reality, in effect creating many possible worlds inside the actual world. Then, while flirting with these possible worlds, the man's father died, and the possible worlds blossomed into more or less infinite subsets within the set called reality, which then itself became a subset of a larger set, itself a subset of yet another set. The logic of the story overcame Russell's Paradox without referring to Types—by more or less ignoring the issue altogether. And so while locked in this never-ending loop of jumping from subset to subset, the man, at some point, had non-consciously invented a doppelgänger—female, for reasons the story didn't elucidated. This female doppelgänger had a life of her own, a real life. A life that felt real to her at any rate. At times their lives intersected. At other times, their lives didn't intersect. The latter proved most disturbing: the disjoint set of A (the man) and B (his female doppelgänger) created the illusion of two separate and distinct lives, and so eventually both lives felt real to A and to B. Like neither ended when the other slept. Neither stopped nor vanished when the other managed to distract himself or herself. So then eventually each suspected the other was a fictional character: to the man, the female was a non-conscious invention; and to the female, the man was a non-conscious invention. And yet to each, the other seemed real. To each, the other *was* real: to the woman, the man was real. To the man, the woman was real. Sometimes they'd switch. Her reality—the subset in which she roamed—transformed into his reality—the subset into which he roamed—and so eventually each suspected the other of not existing. But at the same time each suspected the other of existing.

It confused everyone. No one understood it.

0.

Fearing this, I closed my Moleskine notebook, crawled into bed, wrapped my arm around my wife, and went to sleep.

1.

The world is the totality of things, not of facts.

A fact is a concept. A concept is a human—linguistic—construction. Therefore, a fact is a human—linguistic—construction.

To view the world, or at least to attempt to view the world, free of the superimposition of human constructions, we must remove the lens or filter of "fact."

Think of it this way (and here I'll make an assumption and leave you to prove it):

W = the World, T = Things, F = Facts

W = TF

W = T$\underline{F}$

F

Therefore,

$$\frac{W}{F} = T$$

To see the world as it is, we must divide it by facts, thus freeing it from facts.

And, of course, this is easier said than done.

Our experience of "reality" is a product of our brains. Our brains require concepts and frameworks to make sense of the information deluging it. Through such processes, our brains "create" "states" we call "experience." So then how can we view the world without imposing our concepts or frameworks on it?

That, my friends, is the million dollar question.

A distinct "popping" sound fills the cabin of the minivan as I read something I just wrote. I hadn't realized I was popping my knuckles until I stopped writing. Now it annoys me, the popping sound, and so I stop. Now, conscious of the action, I want to pop my knuckles again. So I light another cigarette and glance out the window—a convenient distraction.

Teenagers and adults lug their bags to and from the parking lot. Most of them—both men and women—are dressed as if they'd expected to wind up at a nightclub: expensive or scant clothing, makeup or sunglasses, well-groomed hair or, in the case of men, beards or goatees. Buildings tower behind them, khaki-colored, seemingly plucked from the 1960s.

I finish my cigarette and drop it into a pop can. It hisses and sizzles. Smoke spirals out of the can and fades. Now the cabin smells like wet ashes and burnt cigarette filters.

The clock on my phone reads "11:17." Class doesn't start until 12:30.

—Fuck, I say. Then wonder why, at 34, I decided to go to college.

At home:

My wife, Alice, is in the other room. I'm in the living room pilfering information from my psych textbook, which is what college kids call "psychology," apparently—"psych." I'd heard about four kids say it in class, and, on hearing it, I'd tried to explode their faces with my mind.

It should go without saying that my success rate never exceeded zero.

And now I say it, for fuck's sake.

In the other room, the craft room, the sewing machine plays a staccato rhythm. It stops and starts. Stops and starts. I visualize sneaking up behind Alice, wrapping my arms around her, sucking on her neck. Then I visualize a giant O hovering over the ceiling: it seems to divide the world; space spills into the room. The blackness of the absence of everything rolls from the O the way liquid tumbles from a container.

Alice is contrasting the object she's making to a schematic. I don't see this but I suspect it's the case; the sewing machine is now silent. So I stand and cross the room, on my way to the kitchen, and I peek into the sewing room, more or less confirming my suspicions—she's glancing down and to her left, studying the contents of a book.

—What's wrong? I say.

—I think I just made a mistake.

—Can it be fixed?

—I don't know.

—What do you want to do for dinner?

—I don't know.

Her tone betrays something—anger or annoyance, maybe.

—Everything all right? I say.

—My head hurts.

—Like a migraine?

—I don't ... My temples are pulsing, like they're going to explode.

We're lying in bed, talking.

We're kissing.

We're lying in darkness now, trying to sleep. She's as restless as I am, apparently. She rolls and settles onto her back and then she rolls onto her stomach and then onto her side. Her breathing slows, speeds up again.

We're lying in bed, pretending to sleep but not sleeping. The controlled metronome of her breath tells me she's awake—it's more chaotic, not controlled, when she sleeps.

We're in the van, on the way to school.

We're walking to class, kissing and then diverging. She heads to her class and I head to my class. Overhead, the sky is purple. I visualize and anticipate something awful, like a tornado.

I hit the "up" arrow on a panel beside an elevator. A woman joins me—seemingly from out of nowhere.

Something jolts me. Something about her ... She's like a colorless blob.

—Glub.

Her face shifts and twists; the meat spins and twirls.

—Glub glub, she says. Instead of words, water flows from her mouth.

—Good morning, I say.

I want to run. I want to turn and run outside, away from her, but something inside me, like a voice but not a voice, compels me to stay. Something inside me compels me to follow her into the elevator.

This is one of those 1960s-era service elevators with doors on the wall opposite the main doors, which close behind me as I step inside. The woman spins to face me. She has no backside: her face, her breasts, her knees are on both sides of her body, so she presents a face, and then another face, when she spins.

The triangles on her face shift and spin, shift and spin. Water rolls off her, drenches her chest.

—Follow me, she says, —Follow follow me.

The service doors open. The woman waddles into the next room, which isn't a room at all: it's a cave with flesh-like walls. Blood drips from the ceiling, pools in pockets of flesh at our feet. Sounds like flushing water roar all around us. And the walls ... the walls contract inward and expand, inward and expand.

—I've got to get to class, I say.

—Glub, glub.

—I'm sorry but I don't ...

—If A is a subset of B, and B is a subset of C, then it follows that A is a subset of C, which makes C the superset of A.

—Okay.

—But what about intersections and unions? she says. —You don't consider intersections and unions.

—I don't understand.

—Of course not, she says. —A $\cap$ (B $\cup$ C) is equivalent to (A $\cap$ B) $\cup$ (A $\cap$ C).But have you ever wondered if x is an element of A, B, and C, and if y is an element of A, B, and C, then how can you even so much as pretend to define them differently?

—But then have I defined them?

She pulls a pen knife from her pocket and carves this into the wall: $\forall x \, \forall y \, [x = y \rightarrow \forall z (x \in z \leftrightarrow x \in z)]$. Then she says,

—You need to sit down and really think about this. You need to define the variables, Daulton.

2.

Alice's **eyes struck me** immediately. Large and green, they framed her face, so she resembled a doll and a burlesque starlet. We were sitting across from each other, ignoring everyone around us. The waitress skipped past our table, stopping to chat with a group behind us.

This was when I was twenty-eight.

Alice said something. I sort of nodded. Captivated by her eyes, those green eyes, amazed by how fucking almost unrealistically green they seemed, I sort of nodded again when I sensed she had finished speaking.

—You weren't listening, were you?

—Are you wearing contacts?

She opened her eyes wider, fluttered her eyelids. A performance. —No.

—I've never seen eyes as green as yours. It's almost, I don't know, like something out of a painting.

—You get major points for looking into my eyes, she said.

—I can't help it, they're ... pretty fucking amazing.

This phrase popped into my head: Dreams of green flesh.

I repeated it as I watched my cousin lift his child to the coffin.

This was when I was fifteen. I was standing in a cemetery in Missouri, goggling my grandmother's corpse. She was lying in her coffin, minutes before they planted her. My cousin lifted his son, who kissed her cheek. I wanted to punch him. I wanted to threaten him until I could somehow unsee my grandmother, whose flesh seemed green, almost scaly, vaguely reptilian.

Dreams of green flesh.

My older sister stood near me. Eyes on grandma, she clutched her stomach and cried, red-faced. Shadows darkened grandma's face. The mortician closed the lid. Staring at my cousin, watching him walk away, my sister said,

—Fucking asshole.

She followed my family to the car.

Rain thumped the ground, the coffin, me. It found, and maintained, a staccato beat.

I more or less floated toward grandma's coffin, brushing my finger over it. On her headstone, beside her name—my grandfather's name: Dalton Dickey. Although the first name lacked a "u," it was close enough to jolt me. One day, a headstone somewhere would bear the name, "u" intact.

Dreams of green flesh.

Jogging to our van, I fought, and defeated, the urge to cry. Dad stood beside it, blank-faced, like he'd already cried and flat-out refused to do it again.

Lying in a hole in the ground near a tree, holding a rifle, Dad waited, Zen-like, for deer. He dragged his eyes from right to left, surveying the landscape.

This was when he was in his early thirties, maybe. He'd been there for hours and hadn't seen so much as a single deer.

Then ...

A deer—about a hundred or so yards away.

Dad raised his rifle, sighted the deer.

—You still don't see it, I said.

Sarah's triangles shifted.

—I told you what I see, she said.

She imagined herself atop a hospital.

—And I told you what I see.

—"And ne'er the twain shall meet."

—And ne'er the twain shall meet.

—I knew you were going to say that.

—And I knew you were going to say that. We both know what the other will say. So where do we go from here?

—But the conversation is never the same, she said. —The way some are. Sometimes I can change what I said ...

—But it doesn't change people's responses, does it?

She shook her head. The motion turned her face to putty: her eyes flung to the left side of her face while her mouth slid to the right.

—Yet you do it anyway, I said. —Hoping to ... What? Encode the revised conversations, turn every memory into something "meaningful" or "profound"?

—I sometimes have to say things differently.

—But does it change anything? Anything external to you? Does it change the behavior of other people? Does it change their memories of conversations, or the way they think of you?

—No. I don't know.

Branches snapped beneath my feet. Sarah lowered her face. The angle of the triangles implied an upward gaze. The illusion nauseated me, something I hadn't experienced in years.

—Come, I said, curling my finger, motioning for her to follow me.

—I can't.

—Why not?

—Because what I see is real.

—Is it?

—To me, it is. But you ... Why can't I see your face?

—We've had this conversation before, I said. —And I've answered it before.

—So answer it again.

—I will when I see you again.

—When will that be?

—When you need me. Or when I need you.

—I need you now.

—No you don't.

Dad fired a round. Then he scrambled out of the hole in the ground and ran. The deer stumbled forward, collapsed. Dad yelled something—celebratory, probably—and ran faster.

—Wait, Sarah said. —How do I know you're not a figment of my imagination?

I stopped, but I didn't turn around.

—We've had this conversation, too.

—But how do I know? she said. —I think you might be a figment of my imagination.

—And I've asked you before: What if you're a figment of mine?

Dad stopped near the deer; he raised his rifle without firing another round. I ran to him. Laughing, he dropped to his knees and pulled a Bowie knife from his belt.

—Good shot, I said.

He slit the deer's throat, he jabbed the blade into the deer's belly, carved an incision the length of its body. Then he stopped. He froze. Everything froze. The background vanished as the absence of everything bled into our surroundings. Trees and stumps, clouds and birds blurred and faded away.

Dad's triangles froze midway between shifting. His face resembled a sort of triangular iteration of a Necker cube.

—You must've regaled me with your hunting exploits a thousand times, I said. —And yet whenever you got to this part, I almost always tuned out. How someone like you could have, at one point, shot and then gutted a deer boggled my mind. It still does.

He unfroze and made the motions of cutting a deer, extracting its entrails. The absence of everything had deleted the deer, so dad made the motions without gutting anything.

—I couldn't picture it then, I said, —and I find it difficult to imagine now.

3.

Picture the universe in absolute darkness: all light has vanished. This is not an attempt to describe nothingness. Objects—planets, meteors, people, et cetera—remain, but light has vanished. Without light, colors vanish. Without light and without colors the universe is black, dark, colorless. It is, for all intents and purposes, empty.

Now imagine this darkness occurring for a second, only for one second. Light returns again and rescues the universe from absolute darkness. Now imagine I'm blind. Pretend I've been blind since birth, so I've never experienced sight. Now try to describe the transition from darkness to light. Try to describe light. Remember, I'm blind so you can't use metaphors, similes, or analogies.

This is what Ludwig Wittgenstein called the limitations of language. There are things we know intuitively, even intimately, yet the nature of language prevents us from describing them. From sharing them.

Attempting to describe my transition from state to state, from subset to subset, exposes the limitations of language: I simply cannot do it. Describing it is literally impossible. So then reverting to the earlier Wittgenstein, the Wittgenstein of the Tractatus, *I could attempt to reveal the nature of my transitions by using language to mirror the internal structures of my transitions, thus showing what I want to tell you. Assuming the early Wittgenstein was right, this scenario presents another problem: how do I use these tools to convey the structures of something like an experience of my transitions?*

Alice and her stepfather waited for a response. I hadn't realized they were waiting until the silence penetrated me. Moments earlier, a conversation had filled the air. Now silence reigned.

Reaching for bits still lodged in my echoic memory, I tried to piece together the end of their conversation, trying to infer a possible question, a question to which I could offer an answer. But I only retrieved scraps: something about dinner, or something.

—I didn't think it was a hard question, Alice's stepfather said, laughing.

—What was that last part again?

—How much Italian beef do you think he should make? Alice said.

—Jesus. I don't know. I've never had to feed so many people.

We were sitting on a patio behind her stepfather's house. Alice sat in a lawn chair to my right; her stepfather sat to her right. I imagined viewing it from above: we formed a sort of crescent.

—How much do you think we'll need? Alice asked her stepfather.

—Do we have a head count?

Something flittered in the corner of my eye.

To my left, a mirror image: Alice's stepfather sat to my left; Alice sat to his left. Behind her, another Alice sat beside another stepfather.

A dozen sets whose elements included {Alice, Alice's stepfather} materialized around us. Each spoke in clipped sentences. Each overlapped the other as we tried to plan the reception. Everyone spoke at once, their voices growing louder, louder, louder.

The smell of burning leaves wafted toward us. Overhead, an airplane rumbled. Beside me, around me, the sets {Alice, stepfather} chatted and laughed. They'd ask me a question every now and then. Every now and then, I'd sort of nod, not certain what to say, or whom to address.

The sets multiplied. Eventually, fifty or sixty sets—one hundred to one hundred and twenty Alices and stepfathers—crowded the patio, spilling into the backyard. Everyone spoke. Everyone laughed. Triangles shifted; faces morphed and imploded.

Then ...

A man near the back of the crowd stood out— gold among silver. Levitating, he floated over the heads of every set {Alice, stepfather}. He seemed intent on meeting me—I inferred this from his face; although his features were indiscernible, he never stopped facing me.

Then ...

The chattering and laughing stopped, the airplane disappeared, even the smell and smoke of burning leaves dissipated. Everything else stayed in place, though not frozen—every Alice, every stepfather moved, talked, nodded; their triangles shifted, shifted, shifted—as the man floated toward me.

I tried to stand but I couldn't move. I tried to avert my eyes but something refused to allow it. So I sat there, watching the man float toward me. His outfit resembled a cassock. Like he was a hellish priest or something. He floated toward me. He floated. His feet, aimed down, skimmed the heads of every Alice and stepfather he flew over.

I tried to close my eyes, I tried to run away or scream, I tried to call Alice, to shout at her—but nothing worked. Part of me wanted to watch. Part of me didn't want to flee.

The man landed beside Alice's stepfather, about three feet from me. Again, I tried to stand, again I tried to close my eyes, again I tried to scream.

—Do you know who I am? he sounded like a moaning corpse.

—...

—Do you. Know. Who I am?

I shook my head.

—But then does it matter?

—Probably not, I said.

—Everything's broken. You broke everything, and now you're stuck.

—Stuck where?

—Here. In this. Everything is broken, you stupid motherfucker.

—What do you mean "everything's broken?"

—The process. You can't figure out a way to undo it. So you're stuck.

—Here?

—Everywhere. You've fucked everything. Now there's no way to orient yourself.

—But how did this happen? And when?

—It's happening now. Right now. The Möbius Strip that is your experience is locking into place as we speak. And you know how it happened; how else could it have? You were so eager to alter everything, so fucking eager, that you didn't consider a fail-safe. Fucking moron.

—But there's got to be a way.

—Trust me on this: there is no way.

—But what if ... I could use Alice, I said, pointing to her. —Maybe she can orient me.

—You'll try. But it won't work. Because you'll never know which situation you'll trigger next.

Like light slicing through darkness:

A fist flew into my periphery.

A grunt chased it. Something hit my cheek, something cold and sharp.

My left knee buckled. I collapsed, smacking my face on the concrete. Someone screamed "motherfucker." Someone else laughed.

Everything shimmered and faded. Fog— alcohol-induced. I scrambled to my feet, tried to stand, but my knee buckled again. Then something else hit my face, a brick maybe, or ...

Try this:

Try lying in bed in the dark and clearing your mind. Try achieving a Zen-like state of emptying your mind. Completely. Then, when you've succeeded, when the absence of thought mirrors the absence of light, try conjuring up a memory, any memory. Try willing the reconstruction of a memory without thinking about, or seeing, anything.

Did you succeed?

We need retrieval cues to trigger memories. Various sounds, various situations, various emotional states, even various surroundings act as cues. These mostly occur non-consciously, and so we rarely consciously will the reconstruction of a memory. And we probably never will the reconstruction without the aid of some form of stimuli.

So then, my friends, and here's another million dollar question: how can we manipulate the reconstruction process if we're never certain which memory is in the process of being reconstructed?

4.

Resisting the urge to dwell on Dad's death creates a sort of Schrödinger's Cat-type scenario: lying in bed, fighting and momentarily defeating the urge to think about his death, I create something like a limbo in which he is both dead and not dead—both p and ¬p.

Alice sleeps beside me. I envy her. I've tried to sleep since I returned from the hospital, but my brain won't allow it. Iconic and echoic memory haunts me. It prevents me from sleeping. Whenever I close my eyes I see my mother and my sisters in the conference room. I see my nieces and my brother-in-law. Tears and sobs. Crying, my mother repeats, "Oh, man, I can't believe it. I just can't believe it," over and over. She leans forward, red-faced. My sisters cry. Emotions threatening to wrest control, and yet I somehow defeated them; somehow I refrained from crying, as if part of shut down, a trait dad bequeathed me.

He rarely cried. In fact, I only witnessed it three times: 1), at his mother's funeral; 2), at his older brother's funeral; 3), when my mother had a grand mal seizure. Usually, stoic, he froze and sobbed when he cried. He fought it and sobbed harder, as if he didn't know how to behave, as if he felt like a fool.

—So what do you like to do? Sarah said. —For fun?

—I'll have you know I'm married.

—I'm not hitting on you.

—Good. Because I don't want to explicitly reject you.

—No offense, but your face nauseates me, which more or less prevents me from finding you attractive.

—Gee, thanks.

—You know what I mean.

—You've crushed my self-esteem, I said. —I don't think I'll ever recover.

—So what do I look like right now?

—Imagine a Picasso. Hopped up on crystal meth. Only it's animated.

—That's pretty much what I see.

—Can you make out my eyes?

—Sometimes.

—Yours are a blur. At best.

—Why can't I see your face? she said. —Why does it shift and mutate like that?

—You ever encounter an optical illusion you couldn't quite comprehend? You see it, it's fucking mind-blowing, and yet you don't understanding, not so much what you're seeing, but how you're seeing it?

—I think so.

—I think that's what's going on.

—But that doesn't really answer my question.

—I'm a tourist here, myself, I said.

—I thought ... But you have answers.

—The nearest I can tell is that our perception isn't constantly shifting, and plus we're constantly popping in and out, so to speak, so I think the whole shifting triangles thing is probably a result of our volatile perceptions plus ... you know ... the nature of memories and all that.

—So there's no way to stop it?

—Like I said, the nausea eventually passes.

—But there's no way to stop it?

—Ever read Husserl?

—Who?

—Edmund Husserl. Look into him. I think, at least in theory, he might help. He has this notion of what he calls "bracketing"; I sometimes wonder if we can exploit that.

No matter how hard he tried, Dad couldn't make the peanut butter mushier. He jabbed the business end of a spoon in and out of the jar, in and out. For reasons we couldn't comprehend, he only bought crunchy peanut butter, then he tried to liquefy it.

Licking the spoon, he said something, which I missed it. The sound from the peanut butter jar distracted me. It reminded me of something I did as a child: I'd pinch my cheek, repeatedly, pushing it against and away from my teeth, producing a squishing sound. My sisters hated it. So, of course, I did it whenever they ate.

Onscreen, two plastic-looking women tried to persuade me to purchase shower gel. If you were to judge their behavior, it apparently triggered orgasms.

More liquid suction sounds.

—Blah something blah.

Dad's face shifted, shifted. He jabbed the spoon in and out of the jar.

—Blah blah.

Scrunching my eyebrows, trying to convey my annoyance. He jabbed the spoon into the jar again, stirring it. I tried to stop him telepathically, hoping to compel him to drop the fucking spoon already. But he jabbed and spun. Spun and jabbed. The telepathy routine had clearly failed.

On the wall behind him hung a mirror, in the mirror a man crouched—a man I couldn't recognize. The walls to my left and right bubbled, faded. People-shaped holes warped the space-time continuum; they shimmered, emitting something resembling a shriek.

—Something something blah they did that, Dad said.

On the television: Kenny took a spear to the face. Stan and Kyle expressed outrage as a dozen or so rats scurried onscreen and carried Kenny away, bit by bit.

The man in the mirror wielded a knife. A fucking knife. His triangles shifted, shifted, yet he seemed familiar. I couldn't place him, couldn't retrieve a memory, but I knew him.

Light danced across the blade, spiraling out of the mirror and crossing the room. It drifting in the air, like a float in a parade.

Then ...

A voice boomed, a voice from nowhere and everywhere: —There's nothing to be ashamed of there's nothing nothing don't be embarrassed to be ashamed of happens sometimes it.

Veins perforated the blade and hilt; they wound around the man's hand. He jabbed the knife in the air and the veins popped.

Blood covered the blade.

—You'll overcome it, the voice said. —Eventually you'll nothing to be ashamed. Everything nothing now and so

Dad laughed. —This show is so stupid.

—Yet you always watch it.

—It's idiotic.

—But you laughed.

—So, he said. —It's still stupid.

—But a comedy is supposed to make you laugh. You laughed. Doesn't that mean it did its job?

The credits ran. As if responding to a memory, to something triggered, Dad laughed and said,

—It's so stupid.

I'm standing in the doorway to the living room. Alice massages my shoulder. I try to step forward, into the living room proper, but my knees feel welded together, my feet feel bolted to the floor. Alice leans into me without moving forward. Is she experiencing similar problems?

Mom wheels to the center of the room. She's in a wheelchair. Dad's wheelchair. She pushes the brake lever and sort of stares off into space, seeming to focus on a spot near the ceiling. My younger sister slides behind Mom, massages her shoulders, rubs her back. Mom tenses. She lets out a sort of groan and cups her face, crying.

Objects clutter Dad's desk. They call to me, demand my attention, but something inside refuses to swivel my neck. Something inside me refuses to examine the desk, or the objects cluttering it. Seeing it out of the corner of my eyes, I'm conscious of it. But I refuse to make it the sole object of my consciousness.

—Maybe we ...

The muscles in Alice's face droop. Her eyelids frame red eyes: she's wearing that same deer-in-headlights expression so common since Dad's death, that I-still-can't-believe-this-happened-and-I-have-no-idea-what-to-do-now look.

—Something.

—Something yeah blah ha.

My older sister responds. Laughter chases her response, the kind of laughter connoting uncertainty, or meant to diffuse tension.

Still sobbing, Mom turns on the television, mutes it. Jimmy Stewart and John Wayne engage in conversation. The movie, nearing its end, fast approaches one of Dad's favorite scenes.

My eyes burn. I glance at the desk—at the clutter atop it. Alice screws her mouth to the side, dimpling her cheek, and grabs my hand.

Mom watches Stewart and Wayne with that spaced-out look she's perfected. Her mood nullifies every possible expression. She glances at the screen more or less dead-eyed. John Wayne's triangles shift. Stewart struts out of frame. Heaving, mom cups her mouth and doubles over and cries.

My sister massages Mom's shoulders again. As Mom cries, my sister says something and laughs. No one else does. She lights a cigarette and curls her arms over her stomach, her hands over her sides. Tears roll down her cheeks.

I float across the room. Eyeballing mom, I'm not even conscious of walking; I don't feel my legs moving, even; I don't feel my shoes tap the floor. I massage her shoulders when I reach her, trying to say something—anything; but nothing comes out.

Mom cried when I touched her. Now she's crying as I massage her.

—I'm sorry, she says.

—Don't apologize. You're expected to cry.

—Is there anything I can get you? Alice says. —Something to drink, maybe?

—I still can't believe it, Mom says.

—Do you need your medicine? My sister says.

Mom says, "yeah." My sister retrieves a pill bottle from a roll-top desk.

—I don't know what we're supposed to do, Mom says. —There's so much to do and I don't even ... He handled ... And ... I just can't believe it. I can't believe he's gone.

Thunder groaned. Blood rained.

Lacerations perforated the sky. Blood and entrails falling from the wound smashed into the ground. A bus-sized heart tumbled from the sky and plowed into a building. The building collapsed; the floors pancaked. Dust and debris curled out and upward. A pacemaker followed the heart; it slammed into the remains of the building, and everything exploded.

Bodies rolled out of the wound in the sky. They pelted the earth. Covered in blood and bile, they resembled my father—but in various stages: young and old, slim and heavy, decayed and skeletal.

Some smacked buildings on the way to the ground. Some piled in the streets. Others hit buses and street vendors, walls, other corpses. Some corpses collided and dissolved, erupting into fountains of blood.

Yet people ignored or overlooked them.

Men and women walked up and down the sidewalks, cars clotted the street, buses roared, airplanes screamed overhead. If anyone noticed the chaos, they either didn't mind it or they had more or less accepted it as routine.

One woman, a brunette with purple streaks in her hair, played with a phone as she strolled down the sidewalk. She glanced up long enough to sidestep a corpse after it had slammed into the ground.

—Glub glub. A woman skirted past me, holding a vinyl bag over her head like an umbrella. Water flowed down her neck and chest when she spoke. Her triangles shifted and coalesced.

Tires screeched. Two cars collided. Glass shattered. A man screamed. Then ... screeching, followed by an explosion. The two cars merged into a chunk of flesh and steel; they melted. Orange like molten steel, they dissolved into an acid-like liquid. The acid pooled in the streets, formed into a sort of blob, and melted a hole into the asphalt. A car drove over the hole; corpses fell into it.

A man groaned. A woman screamed. Somewhere, children cackled. Somewhere, something roared—a low, guttural sound. The sky rippled; a swath of it protruded, then tore open. More corpses fell from the sky. It rained blood, bile, entrails, and bones.

Reports echoed as the roar—that guttural roar —sounded throughout the city.

Like waves rippling a lake, the street rolled. Another roar. More screams. More corpses fell from the sky.

Roaring and screeching, a skyscraper-sized serpent exploded from the hole in the street and rocketed through the air.

Fire drifted from its eyes and mouth. Corpses fell from the sky. It blasted streams of fire at them, turning them into clouds of ashes, which blanketed the city. Flying upward, upward, ever upward, the serpent torched every corpse it encountered. Ashes rained down, down, down, covering me and everyone surrounding me.

I ran to a nearby building, took cover beneath an awning. Three or four people huddled beside me. Two rubbed their hands; the third stuck his tongue out, ashes drifting into his mouth.

Blood, ashes, and bone fragments flicked the vinyl overhead.

—Glub, glub.

—Glub, glub, glub.

Another man and woman sought shelter under the awning. Their triangles shifted, shifted.

Water rolled off their lips and chins. Bubbles popped, releasing words:

—Glub, glub, glub.

—Glub, glub.

Ashes covered cars, the street, the sidewalks. A man, dressed in black, standing on a rock across the street, glowered at me—presumably: his triangles shifted, but something about the shape of his face, like melted wax, and the way he looked at me, the way he pointed his face toward me, implied a not-too-friendly gaze.

The ashes fell around him but they didn't seem to land on him.

Something inside me shouted, 'run.' I ducked out from under the awning, jogged down the sidewalk. Ashes pelted me. It dissolved the way snow does on a warm winter day. I tried to block it, the ash, as I ran, but I couldn't block it because, for some reason, it reminded me of my father, and so touching it or smacking it unsettled me.

Turning a corner, I sprinted into a cavity-like alley. Skyscrapers towered on either side of me. Shadows twisted and swirled. I ran faster, faster. Something shouted. Something screamed. A woman sobbed. She sounded like my mother. Another woman, who sounded like my wife, cried. —Daulton, Daulton. No no no, she said.

The sobs and cries meshed with ash falling from the sky. Building facades flaked away. Bricks and steel crumbled, revealing meat structures beneath them. Red and yellow, like uncooked beef, the meat pulsed.

The man in black stood at the intersection. Cars crisscrossed around him. Screaming metal, screeching tires: the cars cascaded, as if slamming into invisible beams, and disintegrated. My mother sobbed, my wife cried—their voices boomed across the sky. I glanced around. Where were they? What the fuck was going on?

As cars disintegrated, as buildings transformed into lumps of meat, as ash fell from the sky, the man in black levitated above the street. Everything behind him shimmered, like the air around a flame.

Emerging from another alley, I entered a neighborhood where buildings were still buildings; not meat. I scanned for the man in black. Men, women, children followed their daily routines, crossing streets, filling sidewalks, dodging falling corpses. The man in black was absent. I searched again, lighting a cigarette. Either I had evaded him, or he was well concealed.

As ashes fell, the wind flicked the flame on my lighter. I turned my back, cupped the lighter. The cigarette fell from my lips, the lighter slipped from my hand when I glanced into a mirrored window beside me. In the mirror I saw my reflection: the man in black. In unison, he and I picked up our lighters and cigarettes. We lit them. Smoke flowed from our mouths.

I touched the window.

He touched the window.

I took a drag from my cigarette.

He took a drag from his cigarette.

—Everything is broken, he said.

His triangles weren't shifting, so I saw him clearly. Hair longer than shoulder length—where mine was short—his beard unkempt—where mine was trimmed—he was me, but an older iteration of me.

—What is this? I said. —What the fuck's going on?

—Everything is broken.

Although his mouth moved, I heard his voice in my head, like a whispering brain voice.

—What do you mean it's broken? I said.

—This ... Where you're at? This is reality for you now.

—I can't control it?

Laughing, he said, —You never could. At least not completely. And you're now powerless over what little you could control.

—Then how are you here? Now? I said. —Aren't I controlling this?

—What part of "powerless" don't you comprehend?

—But how ...

—Where are you now? He said. —What year is it? And why these images of your father? —Is it my father?

—Daulton, he said, —and listen closely: dad is dead.

His words bounced around my brain. I understood each word, I understood them in the context of the sentence, but, overall, the sense alluded me. He was speaking nonsense, utter nonsense.

I laughed.

—I was over there earlier, I said. —He's alive and well. As grumpy as ever.

—For me, he's dead.

The sense of his sentence unfolded inside my brain, nauseating me.

—What the fuck are you talking about? What happened? When does this happen?

—Of what value is this knowledge? He said. — You can't do anything with it.

—You're lying. Obviously, I'm sleeping. This is a light REM sleep. I'm clearly worried about him, just not consciously aware that I'm worried.

—He's dead.

—How the fuck would you know?

Through the mirrored glass I saw a building crumble. A ten-story heart replaced it.

Corpses fell from the sky. Each and every one of them resembled my father.

—But ...

Warped space hovered beside me, a person-shaped hole torn into the space-time continuum.

Then it hit me.

Oh fuck oh fuck.

Then it hit me:

—This is Chicago, I said. —We're in Chicago. I remember ... this is when Alice and I spent the weekend here.

The tear in the space-time continuum emitted sounds similar to mumbled words.

—But is it? my reflection said.

More corpses fell from the sky. The serpent chased them, scorched them. Ashes drifted to the ground.

—He gets cremated, doesn't he?

My reflection nodded.

—How can I frame this memory through the agony of dad's death ...

—If you haven't experienced it?

Then it hit me.

Oh fuck oh fuck oh fuck.

—I'm not reconstructing this memory, am I? I said. —I'm not real, am I?

My reflection gazed at me.

—Am I part of the memory, a reconstruction? Or am I real?

—I don't know why we're here, he said. —I don't know what cued this.

—Am I real, goddamn it?

He shook his head. The urge to vomit overwhelmed me. I hunched over and retched: words flowed out of my mouth, scattered on the sidewalk below—a pile of mutated letters.

—How are we having this conversation?

—I'm stuck like this, he said. —I guess I can't process it. And …Maybe if I already knew I was stuck like this, the news wouldn't be so … dreadful.

—But we can't change other peoples' responses.

—You're not another person, he said.

—So I'm here for what? to help you manage grief? To make you understand?

—That's what I'm hoping, he said.

5.

This is how it happened:

1.16

Activity occurs in the visual cortex when you're "picturing" mental images. When you're "viewing" images transmitted via your eyes, activity occurring in the visual cortex greatly exceeds the activity of viewing mental images.

Visual memories affect the visual cortex

1.19

Our brains make models of the information it receives via the sense organs. For example, when light bounces off objects, it carries information about those objects. When that light hits your eyes, the information is transformed into mechanical impulses, which are then fired to neurons in your occipital lobe. The occipital lobe "unpacks" this information and telegraphs it to various associational parts of the brain, where you "make sense" of the information and map it to the model you're constructing from the information received from your sense organs.

1.20

Alice and I went to the science museum today, where we learned about infrasound. It's actually pretty cool. It's a naturally occurring sound below the frequency of human hearing. But it's within the range of the resonant frequency of the human eye.

Infrasound has been proposed as a possible solution to the problem of ghost sightings. It works like this: say you're in a room and you catch something out of the corner of your eye; you turn to investigate and, holy shit, you see an apparition, a humanoid, a fucking ghost, walking down the hallway. And it vanishes pretty much as soon as you glance at it. The thing was so real, it was so obviously there, that you don't—not for a second—doubt what you've seen.

And so here's what's so mind-blowing about the infrasound proposal: infrasound eventually hits the resonant frequency of the human eye. So as your eye is picking up information and transmitting it to the brain, the infrasound causes it to resonate, and so it encodes this information as visual stimuli. So when your visual cortex is *unpacking this information, it doesn't know what to do with it. So then it fires this info to various associational regions of the brain and the framework of the situation helps to fill in the blanks.*

If your involuntary neural processes could think, its thoughts, when it encounters this info, probably runs something like this: So this info clearly represents a hallway and this info clearly represents two doors on either side of the hallway. These gradations of light indicate an open door. But what's this right here? This information ... What the hell is it?

Since your brain reconstructs the information received from the hallway, and since it's stuck with this unknown information, it makes an educated guess, so to speak. This, of course, is all conjecture on my part; the museum didn't explicate any of it; but it seems to make sense.

So anyway, I'm assuming the associational areas draw on prior experiences. Since you've undoubtedly experienced people walking from door to door in a hallway, then your brain probably has at least the framework of this experience stored. And it draws on this framework to guess that this mysterious info is actually from someone walking from door to door. So then your brain plugs an image of a person walking into the gap left by this info and, viola, you've just seen a person walking from door to door.

But why is it ghost-like? vague and semi-transparent?

Because this "person" wasn't there; you're inserting a mental image into the information processed from the eyeballs, and since activity in the visual cortex is weaker when you're engaged in conjuring mental imagery, it seems to me the ghost appears vague and semi-transparent because the activity conjuring it is weaker than the activity processing actual visual stimuli.

1.24

Today's my birthday. Spending time with Alice.

1.25

I'm not a neuroscientist or anything, but it seems to me as though these divisions—sight, sound, taste, etc., even memories—are largely artificial. Most things are not compartmentalized. Most things, it seems to me, occur simultaneously, on something like a continuum.

1.26

But how the fuck do I control it?

This is how it happened:
Mom sat beside me, clutching my hand. The doctor sat on a stool and rolled to us. He gripped a clipboard and flipped through pages attached

to it, without actually bothering to pay attention to me.

—*So it's not schizophrenia? my mother said.*

—*To be honest, we're not sure what it is, the doctor said.* —*But we're fairly certain it isn't schizophrenia.*

—*Then what is it?*

A man in the corner of the room shifted, as if moving from a prone to an upright position. He was wearing a suit, holding a toddler. He smiled at me as he leaned over something. The toddler, hanging from his father's arms, leaned forward and pursed his lips.

—*Your son's brain shows some anomalies, the doctor said.*

—*What anomalies? What does that mean?*

—*I'm right here, you know? I said.*

—*Of course, Mom said.*

—*We're seeing some increased activity in the occipital and parietal lobes.*

—*Meaning what? A tumor, or ...*

—*We didn't detect any tumors.*

—*So then what's wrong with him?*

To my mother, the doctor said,

—*Picture a wine bottle. With a cork in it.*

Mom gazed at him, eyes fixed, eyelids squinted and cheeks scrunched, as if trying to read Braille.

—*Describe it, the doctor said.*

—*It's almost an image but not quite an image.*

—*The part of your brain that allows you to see things ... me, for example, the doctor said,* —*or your son ... is active right now. As you look at me, processes in your brain, including the visual cortex near the occipital lobes, are active. When you pictured that wine bottle, that same part of your brain was active, but it wasn't as active as it is now that you're looking at me. This activity, small as it might be, is how you're able to "see" the image of the bottle.*

—I don't see what this has to do with Daulton.

—The PET scans showed us that, for Daulton, the activity isn't diminished when he's picturing things.

—So everything he thinks about is real? Mom said. —Is that what you're saying?

—To him, yes. At least, that's how it appears.

—But how did this happen? I said.

—To be honest, I'm flummoxed. I've never heard of such a thing.

In the corner, Grandma's coffin levitated. The lid was open. Lying with her fingers intertwined on her stomach, her face obscured by shadows, her flesh green, she was smiling. I fucking swear to you she was smiling.

—What are you looking at? the doctor said.

—Nothing.

He glanced in the corner of the room.

—What is it?

—For some reason, I'm ...

—What's wrong, Daulton? Mom said

—You see it, don't you? the doctor said. — Describe it.

—My cousin is lifting his son, who's kissing grandma.

The doctor scribbled something.

—What's grandma doing? Mom said.

—She's dead.

—Describe what you see.

—I just did.

—Describe how you're seeing it.

—*I don't understand ...*

—*Is it real? He said.* —*Does it look as real as your mother or me?*

I nodded.

—*Now do me a favor, he said,* —*I want you to picture a penny. Can you do that?*

A penny floated between the doctor and me.

—*Can you manipulate it? Can you turn it?*

The penny spun.

—*Is it as real as I am?*

At least as large as the doctor's head, the penny floated between us. It spun in circles, drawing in light and kicking it away. I reached for the penny—to touch it, to grab it—and it rippled, then vanished.

—*But what's "real" mean? I said.*

This is how it happened:

Her face betrayed her. Although her triangles shifted, I detected confusion and sadness. And the way she walked, the physiology of her movement —her stilted poise, her blank face—telegraphed trepidation, befuddlement.

She sat a few seats away from me. Her hair tumbled over her shoulders and chest as she leaned forward, flipping through a magazine. Something like a smile or a grimace warped her lips.

She leaned back and slouched down, she leaned forward and turned page after page after page. But the expression she made—one of confusion, maybe, or annoyance—told me every page seemed either blank or devoid of words or images.

—*Glub something Glub.*

The nurse said something. The woman glanced at her. But, on realizing the nurse was talking on the phone, the woman slouched in her seat, rolled up the magazine, and drummed it on her knee.

She glanced in my direction once or twice. Once or twice, her triangles stopped shifting.

Once or twice, I glanced away. And when I glanced back, after the second cycle, I found her gazing at me. So I crossed the aisle, sat beside her, and offered my hand.

—*Daulton, I said.*

She didn't take it.

—*I'm not trying to hit on you.*

—*Now that sounds like a pickup line.*

—*I hate waiting rooms. That's all. I just ... Talking is preferable to waiting.*

—*It's not the waiting room that bothers me. It's the waiting.*

—*Are you a patient? The friend of a patient? A relative? Or am I prying? Shit. I'm prying. My apologies.*

She lowered her head, seemed to concentrate on something across the room.

Minutes passed.

—*I know what you're going through, I said.*

—*I highly doubt it.*

—*It works with memories, too, doesn't it?*

—*What works?*

—*We're wired differently. We see what we think, imagine, or, remember. Have they told you about activity in the visual cortex? when you're forming mental images?*

—*That's impossible, she said.* —*I've been told only maybe half a dozen people on the planet have it.*

—*Improbable, maybe. But here we are.*

—*What did you mean when you said "it works with memories"?*

—*When did the doctors discover this ... quirk?*

—*Few months ago, she said.* —*You?*

—*Ten years ago. Have you undergone EEGs while you slept? while you're awake?*

—*Both.*

—*Let me guess: delta waves are dominant when you're awake. Sometimes theta waves are dominant.*

—*They didn't really say what it means.*

—*Delta waves are usually dominant in stage four non-REM sleep. Deep sleep. And theta waves are usually dominant during REM sleep, especially in that strange state when you're asleep yet not in a deep sleep.*

—*So that's what they meant when they said ...*

—*We see our memories, I said.* —*We* experience *them. But have you ever experienced awful memories, where nothing seemed to make sense? Like snakes falling from the sky or giant eyeballs walking around?*

Her blank expression answered my question.

—*I have a theory about that, I said.* —*REM sleep is responsible for irrational dreams, where logic is absent. I think that, when we're reconstructing our memories, when something triggers a memory, and we experience this crazy reality, I think theta waves are dominating our brain's activity, so these reconstructions are ...*

—*Irrational.*

—*Exactly.*

—*But how do you cope with it? she said. —I've dealt with this my entire life, but ... How do you handle bouncing from the past to the present? talking to dead people? How can you discern the present from memories ... or imagination? It's driving me fucking crazy. I mean, how do you know what's real or what's imagined?*

—*How does anyone know what "real" is? To the schizophrenic, everything he or she experiences is "real." The same goes for the delusional or the depressed. The same goes for so-called normal or average people.*

—*But this could all be a dream, she said.*

—*Or we could be brains in vats.*

—*Or characters in a novel.*

—*Or strung out on acid.*

—*And yet here we are.*

—*So then what does "real" mean?*

6.

That **empty feeling sometimes** creeps up on you. Sometimes you're more or less fine, or at least not empty, and you're engaged in your daily routine, maybe not feeling content or happy, but at least not feeling empty or anxious, or gripped by a sort of dull pain. And then, in a flash, almost like an insight, you realize you're empty and anxious, depressed, jolted by a sort of dull pain.

That empty feeling doesn't leave you, even though you struggle to escape it. That empty feeling devours you, even though you try to overwhelm it, even though you assault it with a blitzkrieg-style inundation of stimuli. But reading or writing, or films or television or music only rarely compete with this monster hollowing you.

And so you feel empty, and you make a kind of deal with yourself to endure the emptiness without dwelling on it or resisting it. Can this tactic produce something like ambivalence? And so you try, and it seems to work. But it only works while you're active. Then awareness of the emptiness blooms when you've exhausted your routines. And so you sit, you just sit, and you're conscious of this emptiness, and you try to locate it, you try to pinpoint it: it's in your stomach, this hollow feeling, and it's in your throat, like an itch or a glob of food you can't swallow, and it's in your brain, in every corner, framing your interpretations, draining the color, the taste, the texture from everything.

Loneliness doesn't by necessity entail the absence of other people. Sometimes loneliness is derived from missed or failed connections; sometimes loneliness is the product of less-than-ideal means of communicating or interacting with others. Nothing makes loneliness more crippling or potent or ominous than feeling lonely while surrounded by people.

But then sometimes emptiness isn't always the function of loneliness. Sometimes it's a function of the fear of death, say, or of too many neurotransmitters flowing through your synapses. Or sometimes it's a function of too few neurotransmitters attempting to fill too many receptor sites.

But then sometimes you just sit in a room, in a dark and quiet room, while your wife sleeps, and you stare at the television, a television you haven't bothered to turn on; and sometimes you feel empty without identifying the cause of that emptiness—if there is a cause. And sometimes you feel like crying. Sometimes you feel so empty and sad that you view sleep as a reward, a reward from the misery and the suffering, and yet sometimes you can't even motivate yourself to sleep. So you sit ... you sit in a room, in a dark room, and you stare at your reflection on the blank television screen. And you watch your reflection darken and age; you watch it reveal the skull beneath your flesh.

A squirrel stood in the yard fingering something—a flower, perhaps, or an acorn. It twitched and jerked its head from left to right, right to left, as if scanning for thieves or predators. Or both. Then it stopped, as if sensing something, maybe nearby competition. Glancing around, it didn't seem to spy anything, so it resumed the rapid twitching motions as it fingered the something in its hands.

The wind blew. The grass danced. Both brushed the squirrel's legs. Another twitch, another glance, and the squirrel dropped the flower or the acorn or whatever and raced over a hill.

A cat leaped into view; it, too, vanished over the hill, which separated the sidewalk from the street. Pine trees obscured the street. Only gaps between the trees revealed the general shape and color of cars passing by: a white blur, a gold blur, a gray blur. But not a red blur.

Where the fuck was she? It couldn't take this long. It usually didn't.

Words floated into my skull and lingered for a second before vanishing. Whenever I'd attempt to latch onto them, to recreate them by transferring them to paper, something outside would snag my attention—a van, a truck, but not a car—and the words would disintegrate.

Trepidation and anticipation popped a hole into my stomach, escaped with a hiss and spiraled outward. Everything darkened. I dropped the pen and paced the room. I lit a cigarette and tried to sit. I checked the clock and glanced outside. Everything froze, goddamn it; nothing seemed to move; fuck, what was happening? What was going on?

The living room transformed into a doctor's office. Alice laughed. Alice cried.

The universe blinked on and off again: the doctor's office transformed into a parking lot. Alice dug through her purse. She stopped walking, searching for something. After digging for what seemed like years, she fished out her phone, sent a message. Two men strolled behind her while she typed. One man grabbed her; the other ran to a car and opened the backdoor. Alice screamed. She kicked her arms, flailed her legs, but the man didn't release her; instead, he carried her to the car and threw her into the backseat.

The parking lot transformed into our apartment.

I sent Alice a text. Watching the window, the gaps between the trees outside, I paced the room again. I checked the clock again. I finished my cigarette and lit another cigarette. Then I checked my phone again.

—Come on, I said, —for fuck's sake.

Tossing the phone aside, I sat on a stool beside the stove and blew smoke into the exhaust fan. The smoke disappeared. Even the smell vanished.

—What the fuck're you doing? I said.

I wanted to yell at her. I wanted to kiss her. I wanted to ... I just wanted to fucking see her again.

More smoke curled and floated. The exhaust fan sucked it up.

Alice had insisted on smoking in the kitchen. Only in the kitchen. Although she had been a smoker, she couldn't stand the smell of it, how it lingered and soaked into every piece of furniture and clothing in the apartment. That, she argued, might explain a lack of visitors: our non-smoking friends probably found the smell appalling.

But for the past few months, since she'd learned of her pregnancy, Alice hadn't smoked a single cigarette. I tended to go outside when she was home; however, when she wasn't home, I'd confine smoking to the kitchen. Usually.

Then ...

Between the gaps in the trees: flashes of red. A car. Our car.

I extinguished my cigarette and darted into the living room and dropped into a chair at the table. Anxiety crept up on me. My heart pounded, pounded, pounded.

The second hand on the clock slid one millimeter every thousand years.

The front door didn't open. I waited for footsteps outside, waited for the jingle of the doorknob. But ... Nothing.

Sitting in the car, Alice fumbled with something in her lap, as if trying to open a card or a box. Was she crying? Were those tears, or was it sweat? She seemed to unwind something, paused

—and the pause lasted eons; after which she popped a cigarette into her mouth. And lit it.

My stomach twisted.

I strolled into the kitchen, lit a cigarette. The second hand on the clock froze. Sounds vanished. Even the smell of cigarette smoke eluded me. No footsteps announced Alice's arrival. The doorknob didn't jingle.

My stomach hollowed.

Then ...

Footsteps. The doorknob jingled. The door opened and Alice lumbered inside, blowing out cigarette smoke, pushing it into the apartment as she floated into the living room.

Tears rolled down her cheeks; they trapped mascara, dragged it down, down, down, until it stained her flesh.

My stomach hollowed, dissolved.

The length of the room separated us. We stared at each other without saying a word. The clock didn't tick. The windows didn't filter the sun, which seemed to have vanished altogether. After who knows how long, the second hand on the clock dislodged itself, scrolled to the left. Alice bolted across the room. Crying, wrapping her arms around me, she dropped her head onto my shoulder, said,

—He couldn't find a heartbeat. He bruised my stomach, he was looking so hard. But there's just ... there's no heartbeat.

I pulled her closer, squeezed her.

—I'm sorry, she said. —I'm so sorry.

Her eyes melted. Mascara traced the trails carved by her tears.

—You didn't do anything wrong. Why would you say that? It's not your fault.

I guided her to the couch. She neither sat nor fell; instead, she sort of melted and reformed on the couch, tears racing down her cheeks.

—Everything was fine, she said. —My weight was good. Everything seemed all right. Then he searched for a heartbeat. And he searched. And he called his nurse in, and they looked at each other, and their eyes ... they didn't say anything but I knew something was wrong.

—They didn't say what it was?

—They don't know. It could be anything. It could be nothing. She handed me an appointment card. —I'm supposed to go Wednesday. To have an ultrasound. He said the baby could've been lying in a weird position, which could have masked its heartbeat.

—So it's not a certainty, then.

—He said don't be optimistic.

And I clearly remember the way the hospital smelled: that sterile, clear-aired, too-much oxygen smell; that smell you dread because it fills you with fear and trembling.

The halls were empty. No one in sight—no doctors, nurses, patients, anyone. I floated as I strolled through the lobby. Like I don't remember walking. I took only one step, and then I floated.

Stopping at the elevator, I stared at the button. The panel, a mirrored surface, reflected a skinless face, all muscles and blood. I extended my arm, slowly, as if my bones were made of crystal, and uncurled my finger, slowly, as if my flesh were made of glass, and tapped the "up" button, slowly, as if it, too, were made of glass.

My mind felt like a sphere. A hollow sphere. I heard nothing, thought nothing.

Now people populated the hallway. They appeared out of nowhere, as if they phased into our world from an alternate dimension. A woman wheeled an elderly lady past the elevator. The lady's eye reflected sadness, death. Hoses in her nostrils, wrapped around her ears, she clutched an oxygen canister. She gazed at me, through me; her pupils and irises were flaccid, like the open-eyed gaze of a corpse. Her daughter smiled as they passed me. Nothing popped into my head. No thoughts flowed through me as the woman pushed the wheelchair around a corner and vanished.

Silence and the emptiness consumed me. I didn't fight it.

Out of the elevator, down the hallway, and into the room—I floated. Alice's eyes bounced from the television to me. She flashed a smile and shut off the TV. Her eyes narrowed. Her smile faded. Sweat glued hair to her forehead; she was pale and limp-faced, broadcasting depression, fear, fatigue.

—Keep watching, I said.
—There's nothing on.
—Has anyone been in?
—Just a nurse.
—Is the fucking doctor even here?
She curled her lips.

—What'd the nurse say? I said.

—It's nowhere near the target.

—Did they say how long?

—When we get out of here, I want crab legs. And sleep.

—You can have both. You can have whatever you want.

—A million dollars?

—I'll see what I can do, I said.

—It's taking so long. Why's it taking so long? Fuck.

Alice arched her back and shifted her ass. She moved the television-speaker-box to the other side of the pillow as she rolled onto her side. She twisted the laminated bracelet on her wrist and rolled onto her other side. She moved the speaker-box again. She couldn't get comfortable, she said. Why couldn't she get comfortable?

Sweat beaded on her forehead, but it didn't slide down.

—Maybe they should give you more of it, I said. —Induce labor twice as fast.

—I don't think they will. I don't know if it works that way.

—It won't hurt to ask.

—If it worked that way, they would've done it already.

She sat up again. She lay down and arched her back and shifted her ass again.

—Should I buy you a waterbed?

—Can you have it delivered now?

—I'll call around, see what I can do.

She unfurled her arm, unfurled her fingers, slowly, as if they were made of glass. She grabbed my hand, wove her fingers into my fingers, and clenched my hand. Chills raised goosebumps on my arms.

—Tell me a story, she said.

—There once was a man from Nantucket ...

—Not that one.

—No one ever wants to hear that story.

—Tell me about the farm. Will there be rabbits?

—Oh, yeah, I said. —There will be rabbits.

The impending delivery of a dead child hung over us like tears hanging from the ceiling—or like fetuses replacing photons and filling the room with appalling light. They floated and drifted throughout the room, ping ponging against every surface, including us, but we didn't lock our eyes on them. Instead, we talked or watched television, responded to nurses, inquired about the procedure. We distracted ourselves and tried to joke, and we talked about work and the future, doing everything we could to avoid the reality of the event hanging over us; we avoided the fear threatening to deluge us; we avoided contemplating the fetuses flying around, scattering throughout the room.

—It's muggy, the nurse said as she slipped a pair of rubber gloves over her hands. —Ya'll been here long?

—Forever, Alice said.

—I know it feels that way, the nurse said. She snaked her arms into Scarlett's nightgown and, leaning forward, peered inside. After a few seconds, she sat up and yanked off her gloves. —You're about four and a half centimeters, she said. —About halfway there, hun.

Alice sighed one of those through-the-nose howlers.

—There anything I can get you? the nurse said. —Water? Bite to eat?

—Can you turn down the heat?

The nurse pushed a button on a thermostat near the television. She closed the door on her way out. It snapped shut; its echo lingered for hours, it seemed.

—That's like an inch every hundred minutes, I said.

Alice examined the wall between the door and me, blank-faced.

—Sorry, she said.

—Don't apologize. Don't ever apologize.

This is what it's like:

Thoughts tear through you. Sometimes they crush and hollow you, sometimes they conquer and torture you—and sometimes they push you to the brink, then abandon you. They sometimes abandon you.

That's the worst part, the inexplicable part: when you're sitting on the ground at night, gazing at the tapestry overhead, fighting to step outside yourself, to scramble over the barricade of self, to flee to the other side; when you're connecting the stars like dots, trying to focus on stimuli surrounding you, trying to escape the experience of you, you eventually, at some point, realize the emptiness and the hollowness and the drenched-to-the-marrow sadness dines on meat devoid of thought.

That's when the situation seems unbearable: when your emptiness and depression gnaws on you without a thought to trigger it, without a series of thoughts to sustain it. When your sadness fuels a deeper sadness, you know the auguries seem grim.

And here's something else:

Your existence becomes a sort of double-helix of torment and sadness. An unspoken or unexpressed—or even ineffable—acknowledgment links the torment and the sadness, deepening the experience. And so even when you try to think, to distract yourself, you end at the terminus of a road, so to speak, truncated by self-awareness, by the awareness of dread, emptiness, futility eating you from the inside out.

The physiology of depression mirrors the psychology of depression, and so even the meat of your body heightens the awareness of the depth of your emptiness, mirroring the meat in your skull; it sinks into your flesh, your muscles, the emptiness, and so you feel weighted, like drenched cloth. Your flesh and muscles absorb the emptiness, the depression. Movement presents complications, like your body converts the depression itself into lactic acid and pushes out the oxygen, and you feel heavy, as if each step threatens to buckle your knees, and so you, at some point, limit your movement—or stop moving altogether.

This, of course, presents a sort of paradox: how can you feel both empty and weighted? And why does acknowledging either emptiness or weightiness produce a feeling not unlike crying but devoid of tears?

That's when you know the depression metastasized: when you experience the physical and emotional sensations of crying without displaying the behaviors associated with them. You display no overt symptoms, which is something you do without trying. And but then you probably don't even understand the calculus of your actions, so what the fuck does it matter whether you cry—overtly or covertly?

It's not like you intend to hide your emptiness, by the way; it's not like you're an actor playing a role; it's not like you want people to think you're fine or healthy or whatever. The nature of your emptiness is the problem. It so thoroughly devours you, and you so thoroughly absorb it, that for all outward appearances you are, at best, tired or grumpy or maybe even devoid of personality. And the ambivalence you project, the mixed thoughts you express—w/r/t life, the universe, "reality," and so on—assumes a sort of personification of the opposite of depression.

And here's another thing:

An inability to articulate your torment, your emptiness, your pain blurs the line between arrogance and depression. Like, for example, you exist in a more or less perpetual state of struggling to articulate something with which you're familiar, but the familiarity manifests itself in terms of physiology and psychology, and so putting it into words is more or less impossible. Like imagine the core of your existence, the feelings and sensations by which you're defined, merges somewhere between your brain and your body, vanishing before it reaches the tip of your tongue. Then the tip of the tongue phenomenon— *presque vu*—heightens every experience, every moment of your life, which manufactures a new level of torment: intuition suggests freedom lies on the other side of articulation, but you can't articulate the feelings and sensations with which you're intimate, and so you exist in a state of knowing what to articulate without knowing how to articulate it.

The failure to speak the ineffable, to transfer those sensations to sounds, to fucking share them, distracts you. When someone finally speaks to you, they trigger a response, and so you're forced to respond to them while still struggling to articulate your torment, your depression, your emptiness. Speaking, then, becomes a fucking chore. Still struggling with *presque vu*, you more or less bark out a response, and the staccato or abrupt nature of your response blurs the line between arrogance and depression, so pretty much everyone perceives you as an asshole—or at least a strange specimen—which in turn furthers your desire to articulate the feelings and sensations devouring you. Like if you could explain the struggle against *presque vu*, it'd explain your warped intonations. Like maybe people wouldn't think you were arrogant or strange if you could only explain your emptiness—if you could only ask for help.

So you sit and glance at the tapestry overhead, watching cigarette smoke curl away from you. The smoke dissipates as you acknowledge your emptiness, your weightiness; as you struggle to articulate the force beneath both sensations. This, of course, is done entirely without the aid of language: you neither speak aloud nor inside your head—it's more of an intuitive state, a state of mind-numbing emptiness. This, of course, is part of the problem. If you could only formulate the words, the sentences, inside your head, then you could eventually push them over your tongue and past your lips.

Glancing from the sky to your hands, you picture your body, almost as if viewing yourself from outside yourself, and acknowledge a feeling of awe, a feeling conjured by the act of wondering how so little meat creates so much torment— enough to fill a galaxy. And so you cry without betraying the behavior, and but you want to betray the behavior. You fantasize about it.

But then ...

What the fuck does it matter, anyway?

7.

Light expanded, filled the room. It blinded me. The sounds of the world—screams and roars—drowned out everything. Then all ambient noise ceased. Smells like singed hair assaulted me. Sounds like screams ululated, bouncing on currents floating through the room.

I was visiting a museum with Alice. This was when I was thirty-three, maybe. Faces grew from paintings. Statues moved and writhed. Lights flashed and faded. Sounds roared, reached a crescendo, and vanished.

We crossed into the gallery featuring Baroque-era paintings. I perused the walls, searching for Caravaggio, which I knew they didn't have. Alice studied a painting, held her fingers over the canvas, as if wanting to touch it. Hell, I wanted to touch it.

—How long will this go on? I said. —Until I'm dead?

—You can't see the strokes.

—I feel something gnawing at me, like something I desperately want to explain but I can't find the words.

—I know, right? she said. —Years, probably.

—I was thinking about the miscarriage again, thinking about how fucked up everything felt afterward. Things still feel strange.

—But they apprenticed for years. Could you imagine those workshops? It was probably brutal. Not at all romantic.

—Something haunts me. Something terrible, yet I can't access it. It's there, right there, like it's on the tip of my fucking tongue and I can't spit it out. But something inside me, a voice, tells me to address it after it happens. Whatever "it" is. Addressing it is better than not thinking about it. I don't know what that means.

Music played. A piano. Notes tinkered. The sounds vibrated and rippled; they grew, grew, grew. Sound waves tore through the museum, knocking everything off the walls. Paintings flew away from us, sculptures and podiums rocketed across the room. The marble in the floor, on the walls, blasted up and flew away, sucked into a vortex.

The absence of everything spilled into the building.

Beside me, a person-shaped hole in the space-time continuum shimmered, drifted away from me, and disappeared. Yet I remained, standing on a single square of marble. The absence of everything had consumed the building, the city, the world.

The feeling, the sensation plucking my neurons, called to me. It screamed at me, tried to tear through my cortex. I tried to access it—to at least acknowledge it—in hopes of studying or understanding it. But I couldn't reach it.

—This is a problem. A voice boomed. —Sometimes things don't get better, and you'll ... But you'll get over it. If you learn to deal with it, if you address it head on, then you'll overcome what you'll do. You'll overcome ...

A tear split the seams of the space-time continuum. A person emerged from the absence of everything and levitated in front of me. It was me, a future version of me. His hair longer, his beard bushier, he flexed his arms as he floated to me.

Beyond the shifting triangles, I sensed a smile —or a frown; I couldn't discern which.

—You don't remember, do you? he said.

—Remember what?

—Dad is dead. And years from now, though a few months back from where I'm at, you'll try to kill yourself.

—What are you talking about? Dad ...

—Your father, my father, is dead.

—I talked to him this morning.

—Where are you? he said. —Right now?

—Where are you?

—I'm in a museum with Alice, he said. —On one of our trips to Chicago.

—And so where is she?

—Right here. He pointed to a person-sized hole in the space-time continuum.

The hole emitted sounds, something about Baroque-era apprentices.

—Daulton, he said, —You may think this is you in the present, experiencing a memory, but it's not. You are a memory I'm reconstructing. You may think you're alive, but you're not; you're a figment of my imagination.

—That's funny, I said. —Because I'm fairly certain that you're a figment of my imagination.

Waves crashed onto the shore. The sun, enlarged by our brains, slipped into the lake. Birds screeched. Children laughed and ran to the pier. Someone nearby had fired up a grill. The smell wafted toward us.

Sarah paced back and forth, back and forth. She lit a cigarette and, thrusting her hand, out said,

—I can't tell what's what anymore.

—It gets worse as you get older, I think.

—Like are you real? Are you fucking real?

She tapped my forehead.

—I think so, I said. —It's hard to tell sometimes.

—I was in a memory inside a memory the other day, and I was fucking talking to myself. Not in a schizo way, mind you; like I was talking to a fucking reconstructed version of myself. And we were actually having a conversation. And now I don't know what is what anymore. Is this a memory? Is this my imagination playing tricks on me? Or is this the present? I mean, is there a way to know?

—Sometimes I think I know I'm in the present. I'm convinced of it, I said. —I'll be talking to someone or writing or whatever and then ... I'm in the car on the way to the grocery store. It's hard to tell sometimes.

—I can't tell the difference between reality and memory or fucking visual thinking.

She flicked her cigarette into the air and pinched another one between her lips.

—I can't tell which is which, either, I said. —I think, for people like us, such a thing might not be possible.

—I created you the other day, a reconstructed version of you.

—Really?

—I mean, it had to have been an artificial version of you, right?

—How am I supposed to know?

—I don't think it was a memory. But who the fuck knows anymore?

—The quickest way to answer your question would be to hear what happened, I said. —If I remember it, then ...

—I was across the street from the funeral home and you kind of appeared out of nowhere. She lit her cigarette, followed her inhalation with a cough. —You told me about a conversation I'd have with my father. You quoted something he'd say a year from now, you said. But the thing is, and I remember the conversation with dad ... I had it with him years ago.

—It happens sometimes. I had a woman ... I think it may have been you ... take me through an elevator, into a beating heart, where she proceeded to carve axioms of set theory into the wall.

—Don't you get it? "I" wasn't "me." I wasn't "real." I was a construction in my head. Or is it even my head? Am I imaginary, suckered into thinking I'm a real person? How can you tell what's real and what isn't?

—Define "real."

—Goddamn you, she said.

Two people stopped to gawk at us. Their triangles shifted, shifted, shifted.

—All right, I said, —lower your voice.

—I just ... I want to hang myself. I swear to you I want to kill myself. I mean, how the fuck do you put up with this? What's the point?

—There is no point, I said. —We're born, we live, we die. We could, both of us, kill ourselves right now and it wouldn't matter. It wouldn't enhance or diminish any meaning because "meaning" is a human construct.

—But don't you ever think there's a way out? Don't you want to escape this?

—But what's the alternative? Experience or not experience? Despite how bleak and depressing, how infuriating and confusing things are, I've not grown tired of the whole "experiencing" thing yet.

—I fantasize about it, she said, —my death. I've fantasized about lying in a coffin at my funeral, unable to experience the event and yet somehow experiencing it.

—I've done that.

—And I hear people talking about me, talking about me, how I grieved over a goddamn dog. They pitied me, told stories about me, and but it seemed so real. So fucking real. It was terrifying.

—These fantasies, especially the dark ones, are certainly a drawback for people like you and me.

—But I want it to end, she said. —I can't take this anymore.

—Who's to say life isn't as terrifying and depressing and confusing for people whose brains aren't wired the way our brains are? I haven't experienced things the way they have, quote unquote normal people. Have you? So who's to say they aren't as fucked up as we are?

—I saw words, she said. —I'm fucking visualizing language now. And not words flowing out of people's mouths; I mean, the world is only words. Like instead of seeing you, a physical object, I'll see a thousand words, all "Daulton," arranged in the shape of a person.

—Really? That's ...

—And I can delete words. Or I can add words. I watch them appear and form the shape of the objects or concepts they're meant to signify and ...

—When did this start?

—Aren't you just ... tired?

—Not yet, I'm not.

—But what's the point?

—There is no point.

—But what's it mean? All of it?

—If there is meaning, I said, —it's only the meaning we ascribe. Meaning isn't a thing that obtains independently of human beings, Sarah. You've got to quit thinking in those terms.

8.

The flu had assaulted Alice earlier this week. She's lying in bed, watching television. Sounds of screaming and techno music blast out of the TV and drift into the living room. The screaming startles me. I ask if she needs anything — more or less my way of checking on her. She responds—says, "no thanks,"—and coughs.

Flipping between notes and a sociology textbook, I scan the next section, survey it before reading it. My pen pushes out vague lines. I shake it and try again. More vague lines, like traces on carbon paper.

I cross into the kitchen, lighting a cigarette, and find a pen beside the stove. Scribbling on junk mail to test the pen, I smoke—and the scribbles transform into doodles. For some reason, I tend to draw three dimensional boxes and crosshatched mosaics when I doodle, and so now I'm taking another hit from my cigarette while creating a multi-layered mosaic.

I halve my cigarette, cross back into the dining room, to the table. The chapter concerns social stratification. It's interesting, and at times infuriating, but I can't concentrate. Something grabs my attention, distracts me. The something distracting me lingers somewhere in my brain but I can't access it, which makes matters worse. How can something distract and elude me at the same time?

Alice calls me from the other room, says my phone is ringing.

I went into the room and scoop up the phone. My younger sister says my name. She's crying.

—Go to mom and dad's, she says. —Dad passed out or something and slumped over and ... he wasn't responding. Mom's freaking out and I can't catch a ride and ...

—Calm down, calm down. What happened?

—I don't know. They were talking and he collapsed. Just go over there, please.

I hang up the phone and dart into the bathroom, change from my pajama pants into blue jeans. I emerge to a ringing phone, to Alice asking what's wrong. Holding up a finger—the universal symbol for, 'hold on'—I answer the phone.

—I just talked to ...

—Dad wasn't responding. At all. I don't know ... I don't ... We were talking and I went into the kitchen and he ... when I came back, he ...

—Mom, mom; calm down, I say. —I'm on my way, all right? I'll be there in a few minutes.

My father had overdosed on a morphine patch when I was thirteen—the doctor's had prescribed too high a dose. It threw him into a coma for a day. I thought about this on the ride to mom and dad's house. I thought about the feeling of complete and utter happiness when he had returned from the hospital.

He sat in his recliner and stretched out and made a joke—which I forget. And then he turned on the television, carrying on as if nothing had happened. Although a thousand questions plagued me at the time, I didn't press the issue. So I joined him and watched TV. Every now and then, I'd glance at him, probably as assurance. Seeing him alive and well, I smiled.

About halfway through a procedural drama, he turned the channel.

—I woke up and stared at a light, he said, —at the light overhead, beaming down on me. But I didn't see a bright light when I was out. I'm telling you, I didn't see anything. Just darkness.

Then he added: —Not that I'd expected something else.

Mom, sitting in one of dad's wheelchairs, cries into her hands. Her neighbor, Cynthia, stands behind her, clutching a cordless phone. Something permeates the air—sadness, maybe. Or dread.

Something about mom's face, something about her posture—limp and almost lifeless, as if she's recreating Dad's pose after he'd slumped over—fires molten steel into my axons.

186

I clutch her forearm.

—He was fine, she says. —One minute he was talking and ...

—He might still be fine, I say. —He's probably fine.

—He ... He ...

—You can't get worked up like this.

—He urinated.

—What do you mean?

—He was hunched over in his chair, his wheelchair. There was urine on the floor.

Cynthia shifts to her left, as if redistributing her weight. Screwing her eyebrows upward, she grimaces. Her face now mirrors the dread and terror filling my brain.

Mom called the hospital. Something triggered a crying fit. She tried to speak between sobs, producing little more than gurgles and gibberish. I snatched the phone from her. A woman was saying something. I shushed her and asked about my father.

—You and your mother should come down here, she said. —We'll talk when you get here.

Now we're in the car with my brother-in-law. Darkness hollows my stomach and skull. I swear to you I can't hear anything. Not like I'm going deaf but more like someone's muted the world. From my vantage point, I can see the side of mom's face: her cheeks bulge; water—tears—reflect light. The display on the radio seems to imply music is playing, but I don't hear a thing. My niece, sitting beside me, glances at me without moving her head. She and mom, my brother-in-law and his car, the world and everything in it are silent. Everything feels or seems stunned, baffled.

The absence of everything stole the world.

We float in a sea of black.

Not even the headlights manage to slice through the darkness.

We are floating in nothingness.

We exist and yet we don't exist—both p and ¬p.

Everything feels gray and empty and dead.

They usher us into a conference room inside the emergency room. A box of Kleenex sits on the center of a table. My brother-in-law notices it and glances at me. Mom's surveying the room, the paintings on the wall, crying. But she doesn't seem to notice the Kleenex.

The room is white and sterile. Chairs line two walls. Of all the items in the room, the Kleenex and garbage can strike me as sinister. Like this is the room the hospital staff send otherwise healthy people to cry—or to get sick into garbage cans. This is the room concealing a million awful truths.

Mom clutches her phone as she sits. I fall into the chair beside her, holding her arm. She opens the phone, closes it. Opens it and closes it again. Time crawls.

—I hope it's nothing bad, she says. —I hope it's nothing bad.

—It might not be.

—If he's out of it, my brother-in-law says, —
they might just need us to answer some questions.
About his medical history and so on.

Mom cries again.

—But why wouldn't they tell us anything over
the phone? I don't think ... I don't ...

Massaging her arm, I say, —You can't get
worked up, mom. Right now, everything is just a
possibility. Let's not dwell on possibilities, at least
not right now.

My niece, more or less dazed, stares off into
space. She frowns. Something about that frown
makes me want to cry.

My brother-in-law had left to pick up my
younger sister, so my niece and I are ostensibly
comforting mom, which translates to changing the
subject whenever she raises the specter of Dad's
death.

Time crawls.

I don't bother to check the clock. What's it
matter? We haven't heard from anyone since
they'd ushered us into the room. We're more or
less trapped in administrative limbo and ...

—Goddamn it, I say. —I swear to fucking
Christ, I'm ready to go out there and start
throwing fucking chairs at those assholes.

Mom cries again. Guilt washes over me, so I
rub her back and shoulders and apologize.

Then ...

Two nurses—a man and a woman—slip into
the room. The woman sits beside mom. The man
lingers in the background, stone-faced; his

189

expression, a masterful poker face, doesn't tell me anything. The woman grabs mom's hand.

Time crawls.

It.

Crawls.

—How's Leon? Mom says. —Is he okay?

—First, the woman says, —I'm sorry for your loss. We tried to resuscitate him but, unfortunately, there was nothing we could do do there was nothing nothing there was nothing we could do.

9.

Shadows wage war on the ceiling. Despite the silence, my brain manufactures sounds—humming, mostly. Alice sleeps beside me. She rolls around from time to time; she murmurs from time to time; but, for the most part, she's quiet. Her warmth spirals into the whorls on my fingertips, and my muscles loosen.

And so what does it mean? What's the point? Death is the corollary to life, nothing more or less and so ... and ... but ... Dad, and so Dad ...

I turn on some songs, listen to some audiobooks, play some podcasts, trying to silence my thoughts. Overtake me, sleep. Overtake me, goddamn you.

On the table in the living room, near the bedroom doorway, sits our laptop. Light from the computer illuminates the doorjamb, adding platoons to armies waging war on the ceiling. Blue and shimmering, the light radiates, focuses on a chair beside the dining room table, a chair I mostly infer—the shadow it casts screams 'chair.'

My eyes stop focusing. The chair disappears and reappears. Disappears. Reappears.

And why the fuck can't sleep?

People laugh on the podcast. They joke. What they say is funny—at least it strikes me as funny —but I don't laugh. I can't laugh.

The light in the doorway shifts and expands. Then Dad is standing in the doorway. Boom. Now he's sitting in a wheelchair. Boom. He moves his mouth, as if speaking. Boom. He laughs. Boom. Lowering his head, he slumps forward. Boom. His flesh changes colors, to a sort of gray. Boom. He's lying on a gurney. Boom. He's now meat and nothing more. Boom. I want to touch him, but I recoil.

Boom.

Alice is warm. She slides toward me. I tighten my embrace and focus on the warmth radiating over my arm.

Then I see Dad again. He's talking and laughing again. He's dying and dead again.

Boom.

Boom.

Boom.

Fear tears through me. I belch out a visceral scream. It's low, more of a groan, but it doesn't wake Alice.

I want to cry but I don't. I want to talk but I don't. I want to wake Alice but I don't. I want to sleep but I can't. Everything is crazy now. Everything is broken. I broke it. My mind plays tricks: light shifts and transforms, plays music;

colors float through the room. Everything is alive, pulsing. Everything is alive—except my father.

Sleep.

Goddamn it. Sleep already.

I crawl out of bed and amble into the kitchen and light a cigarette. The floor feels squishy, like meat. My feet are wet. The meat sags beneath me; some of it rises through gaps between my toes. A shiver courses through me.

Thunder roars. The apartment shakes and rattles. Cupboard doors fly open. Dishes rattle and crash onto the floor. Neighbors scream. Birds caw. The windows in the living room shatter and glass blows into the apartment. The shards coalesce and swirl, a mirror-ball tornado.

To my left, the wall implodes and blows inward, as if sucked away. Light fills the room. It's an escape. I can escape. But how can I reconstruct a memory? How can I trigger a memory without a cue to trigger it?

Talk just talk just fucking say something and something will ...

—Fuck it.

I take a hit from my cigarette and jump over the stove, landing on the ground in a vortex teeming with white light. Odors assault me; they're vague, yet familiar. For some reason, they remind me of diesel emissions. For some reason, the diesel emissions remind me of Chicago. For some reason, Chicago reminds me of the time Alice and I roamed the Magic Mile, inspecting every nook, peering into every window, mentally noting items we'd buy when we had money, like real money, not that paycheck-to-paycheck shit.

The light bulges and shifts, bulges and shifts. Now it twists and folds inward and bounces off mirrored-windows. People crisscross in front of me, their triangles shifting. A group of women stop at a crosswalk. Water tumbles out of the triangles near their mouths; it drenches their shirts and faces; then it flows outward and slams into the other women's ears; and it flows toward me; but I hear mumbles, not words.

A person-shaped hole in the space-time continuum warps the universe beside me. It moves when I move. It stops when I stop. Something overhead screams. An incision opens the sky. Blood rains. Corpses fall. A serpent flies into the air and blasts the corpses with fire. The corpses explode into clouds of ash, which pelt the earth.

A man to my right lights a cigarette. His triangles shift, but I recognize him: it's me, a version of me. Beside him, a hole in the space-time continuum shimmers and refracts light surrounding it.

A man stops beside this man and lights a cigarette. Again, it's me. Or a version of me. Soon, dozens of simulacrums of me surround me. Each lights a cigarette. Each spits water from his mouth and mumbles. Bubbles pop. Words float around.

Something screams overhead. Something screeches below me. The ground shakes. I drop my cigarette and dart across the street. A version of me hovers over the intersection, talking to another version of me.

Facades of buildings crumble. Pulsing hearts replace them Blood drains from the sky. Hearts and pacemakers and corpses, resembling my father, fall from the wound in the sky and crash into the earth.

Boom.

Boom.

Boom.

A corpse slams into the ground beside me. Covering my head, I glance up: another corpse rockets toward me. I break to the left and run down an alley and cross the street.

A version of me is standing beside a building, talking to another version of me projected as a reflection in mirrored glass:

—What do you mean it's broken?

—This ... Where you're at? The reflection glanced up and around. —This is reality for you now.

—But I can't control it.

—You never could.

—But ...

—And you're now powerless over what little you could control.

—But ... Then how are you here? Now? Aren't you controlling this?

—What part of "powerless" can't you comprehend?

—But how ...

Someone laughs—a woman.

The universe blinks off and on again. I'm standing in a yard while my mother and aunt dig through boxes. People surround them. A woman sits on a lawn chair beside a sign covered in hieroglyphs. An old lady approaches her and shoves money into her hand.

Thunder cracks. Now I'm lying beneath a car, screaming. Mom and my aunt cry out. They race toward me, their footsteps booming.

I'm crying.

The universe blinks off and on again.

My sisters and I are lying in a hotel room, watching a horror film. Dad, in the other bed, laughs when the monster appears onscreen. He laughs because we scream. His triangles shift, shift, shift.

The universe blinks off and on again.

I'm sitting in the conference room, watching my aunt hug my mother. Mom cries. Water tumbles from her mouth and bubbles pop, and whenever a bubble pops her voice drifts outward: "I can't believe it." "I can't believe it." "Oh, man, I can't believe it."

I want to cry but I can't. I want to collapse but I don't.

The universe blinks off and on again.

Alice and I stand in a gazebo, holding hands. We'd just exchanged rings and now we kiss. The judge shakes our hands. Dad sneaks up behind me and taps my shoulder. He extends his hand. Mumbles something. I can't make it out but I remember what he said,

—Congratulations, son. I'm proud of you.

I remember nearly crying.

Squeezing his hand, I say,

—Thank you.

The universe blinks off and on again.

Sarah and I are sitting in a diner eating spaghetti and hamburgers. She's talking about Kafka, something about Kafka. Then we're sitting on an overturned bus in a wasteland, watching a mushroom cloud bloom on the horizon.

—What about you? she says. —You've never considered ending it?

—I've thought about it, I say. —Came close once.

—So what stopped you?

—Fear.

—Of what?

—The end of experience.

—But for us, in our condition, is that really a bad thing?

—If only you can prove that people who aren't like us are any happier or less confused or overwhelmed.

—I think they are.

—Because you envy what you don't have.

—I don't think that's it.

—Show me evidence that other people aren't as haunted or as traumatized by their memories or imaginations and I'll grant you everything, I say.

The universe blinks off and on again.

j.

Traffic on the southbound highway thins out. Finally. King Diamond sprays sound waves around the cabin. It rattles Sarah's ears and jiggles her temporal lobe.

Somewhere, a horn blows.

Then ...

A sound like steel falling from the sky.

More horns blow, a long tremolo. More sounds like steel falling from the sky: screeching, roaring, fucking growling.

In a flash, so fast it's almost imperceptible: a car jumps the median dividing the highway; it flies through the air and slams into Sarah's car, landing on top of it. The undercarriage blots the sun. The passenger-side front tire penetrates Sarah's windshield.

A million suns burst in the glass strewn across the highway.

Tires screech. Feet slap the concrete. Someone knocks on the rear window, shouting, —Miss, can you hear me? me? can you ... Can you hear me?

A man opens the door and leans into the car. Everything sparkles. Everything glows. Something warms Sarah's face. Pain erupts in her forearm.

—Miss?

—I'm ... Yeah, Sarah says.

—Can you move?

—I think so.

She unfastens her seat belt and steps onto the pavement. Two men are standing on the hood of her car, leaning into the car on top of it. The passenger side door is open. A woman cries.

A young couple join Sarah and the man. They watch the men attempt to extract the woman from her car.

—What happened?

—I don't ...

—You're bleeding, a woman, a blonde, says to Sarah.

Sarah taps her forehead, inspects her fingers. Blood, thick and shiny, covers her hand.

—I think ... I need to sit, Sarah says.

The rock skipped over the surface of the water, vanishing somewhere near the horizon. Scoffing, Sarah tossed a rock. It bounced two or three times and slipped beneath the surface.

—You'd better up your game, Cynthia said.

—I'm only down by two.

—Only.

—Your beginners luck is handicapping me.

—Luck? More like skill.

Sarah tossed another rock. It dropped into the water with a thud.

—You, on the other hand ... Cynthia's smirk brightened her face.

She was so beautiful, so fucking beautiful. Even now, Sarah couldn't believe she'd met and fallen in love with someone as breathtaking as Cynthia.

—Let's get married, Sarah said.

Cynthia's smile faded.

—Excuse me?

—I want to spend the rest of my life with you.

—Where'd this come from? I thought you abhorred the concept of marriage? I thought it perpetuates traditional gender roles.

—I don't know, Sarah said. —It just feels right. Doesn't it feel right? the idea of marrying me? of spending the rest of your life with me?

—What, for you, is the present? Daulton said.

—I don't even know anymore.

—Do you know if you're real? Like right now?

—Don't be an asshole.

—But how do you know?

—*Cogito ergo sum*, I suppose.

—But are you thinking?

Of course she was.

—Of course I am.

—What if this is a memory? Daulton said. — What if you're a memory the real you is currently reconstructing? You might think you're really you, that you exist right now, here in this room with me, but what if ... Just try to imagine it now ... But what if you're right now a product of neurological processes occurring in the brain of the real you? Right now? Would you know?

—Absolutely. Sarah laughed. —I think I'd know if I were a memory.

—You see things differently, Sarah. Come on, you ... Now you've got to ask yourself ... Am I here, in this room, right now? Or am I a memory I'm reconstructing while I'm actually sitting in another room altogether?

—That's absurd.

—Goddamn it, listen to me. You are not you right now and I am not Daulton. Okay? I am you. Like right now. I'm sitting in the funeral home. I was staring at Dad's coffin a minute ago. Now we're here. Don't you understand? You're a combination of a memory and a figment of my imagination.

—I'm real, Sarah said. —I can think. I can hear and see you. I can feel. Goddamn it, I can feel.

She punched the wall beside her. Ripples spread outward, jiggling the wall, the floor and ceiling. Nothing registered—no pain, no sounds of flesh meeting plaster, nothing.

—Daulton, she said, —what the fuck is going on?

—I told you I'm not Daulton. And I'll tell you what Daulton keeps telling me: everything is broken.

—But what does that even mean?

—We're stuck like this, a slave to the whims of our brain. But there's a way to control it. I found a way to control it, and ... So now I can use it when

I need to use it, like ... Seeing dad there, in the coffin, it's ... I can't handle it. So it can be useful.

In her younger and more idealistic years, back when Sarah still harbored dreams of publishing, she learned to analyze literature, and she adapted those analyses as frameworks for her life. This system, this mode of thinking, worked well—sort of. Like things tended to happen for a reason in literature. If a man in a novel collapsed, say, then it usually served a purpose. If chance and circumstances led a woman and a man to meet, then the meeting itself served a purpose, especially if the novel centered on their relationship, and so the meeting only adopted the appearance of chance. In fact, their meeting was prearranged, predestined, so to speak, by the invisible hand of the author—or, more accurately, by the invisible hand of the author and literary structures and conventions.

However, getting caught up in this line of thinking had its drawbacks, especially when applying it to life. Stories, for whatever reason, infected Sarah—as, she wagered, they infected everyone. In fact, the younger Sarah argued this point ad nauseam.

In the written tradition—and even in the oral tradition—the way people told stories depended largely on the reactions they hoped to elicit. A person tells a tragedy differently than a horror story. And we the readers, or listeners, consume this information in various ways, depending on our commitment to the story. If we don't care about it, or if we refuse to accept it, then we'll probably dismiss it, and it probably won't make much of an impression.

But things get interesting if we invest ourselves in it.

If we're invested in a story, then we might conjure mental images to accompany it—a sort of ad hoc inner-cranial film adaptation. Our investment might even trigger agency detection, so we might feel the presence of a character or a monster.

For most people, the person writing or telling a story is more or less required to slip into the background so the story or the characters feel real and not guided. To tip the hand in the telling of a story is to ruin the chances of that story turning out "good"—however that's defined.

The aim of stories, whether fictional or not, seems, to most people, like a mechanism for seduction. To seduce a reader or a listener into suspending disbelief or setting aside the way they usually frame the world: that's the point.

Or so Sarah thought.

She gave up writing when she realized stories couldn't save her. They couldn't help her make sense of her experiences because her experiences weren't reflected in the literature she had encountered. She tried for years to find something with which she could relate, and, after reading hundreds of novels, she drew one conclusion, a conclusion that all but ruined literature for her: structure and literary conventions perverted the mind. By seducing and manipulating people, by conforming to formulae and standards, literature betrayed the purpose she had assumed it celebrated.

And what was that purpose? To help her learn to frame the experiences of what most people called "reality" in more linear and digestible forms. But by obeying structure, conventions, rules and formulae, authors betrayed themselves, sacrificing any claim to understanding the hallucination most people called "reality." You can't follow the rules of stories, you can't take a formula and plug in characters and settings, then describe it as real life.

To Sarah, it was anything but real life. Formulaic or rule-bound literature, comprised of mostly linear narratives, constituted possible world scenarios incapable of mirroring the experience most people called "reality."

In fact, if Sarah, in her younger and more idealistic years, learned anything, it was this: what most people called "reality" was little more than hallucination by agreement. People experienced "reality." Experience itself was a product of their brains. Try as they might, people couldn't cut through the experience manufactured by their brains; they couldn't reach out and touch things they assumed composed "reality." So when they introduced stories and story-telling into the equation, they inadvertently allowed those stories, those storytelling conventions, to provide frameworks for how they experienced "reality."

In other words, stories polluted experience without clarifying it.

k.

—How are you doing? Sarah's father said.

She was lying in bed, staring at a television mounted to the wall. A nurse had just changed her bandages. After giving Sarah a dose of painkiller, the nurse moseyed into the bathroom to wash her hands. She was still in there. The water roared as it flowed from the faucet.

Sarah's father clutched a package as he sat beside the bed. He glanced at the ground, at Sarah, at her arms, before settling his gaze on the television. Two cops cornered a suspect. They exchanged improbable dialogue. Then the music swelled and an advert for commemorative American flag coins flashed onscreen.

Sarah gestured to the package.

—I cleaned out my safety deposit box last week.

—You have a safety deposit box?

—Had.

—Why did you have a safety deposit box?

—To store things.

—Like what?

—Does it matter?

—Not really.

Sarah sat the package on her stomach. It was wrapped in brown paper. She thumbed the paper but didn't open it.

—How are you feeling?

—I'm here.

—That's not reassuring.

Sarah closed her eyes and yawned. She was sitting beside Cynthia in a photo booth when she opened her eyes. Then she yawned again. Cynthia nudged her, laughing. They stared at the monitor and smiled. Sounds like a snapping shutter filled the booth. They stuck out their tongues, crossed their eyes. The shutter snapped again.

Light filled the booth. When it faded, Sarah was standing in a field beside the ruins of a statue. At least three stories tall, the statue—of a man— lay in pieces. Someone at some point had carved their initials into the outer thigh of its right leg.

Thunder roared. Lightning flashed as rain fell from the sky. A chunk of meat formed into a mountain behind Sarah. It glowed in the rain. It grew with each clap of thunder. Boom. It grew. Boom boom. It grew. And then it towered over the field and blotted out the sun, turning the sky into a dome of meat, which grew over, around, and below her.

Thunder cracked. Lightning flashed.

Trapped in a cavern of meat, Sarah spun and ran. The walls pulsed, pulsed, pulsed. She ran in the other direction. Stalactites and stalagmites wiggled and squirmed. They broke away from the ground and ceiling and slithered around the cave. Gasping, Sarah stopped running, but she didn't stop spinning.

Which way was south? Which was north?

—It all falls down. It all. Falls. Down.

This was when Sarah was six. She was in the backyard playing a game with her sister. They were holding hands, moving in a circle. Then they fell to the ground and laughed.

Thunder cracked. Boom.

—I do, Sarah said.

—I do, Cynthia said.

This was when Sarah was twenty-seven. She and Cynthia were standing in a gazebo, facing each other, holding hands. A woman wearing a robe announced the official recognition of their marriage.

Cynthia smiled. She cried.

Thunder cracked. Boom.

Lying in the hospital, Sarah lifted the paper with her thumb, peering into the gap. Shadows from the paper obscured the item beneath it.

—Open it already, her father said.

A hole beside her father tore the space-time continuum. Smoke billowed out of it. A woman appeared, as if teleported into the room. Face devoid of features—no eyes, nose, or mouth—the woman glided behind Sarah's father. She floated to the other side of the bed and lowered to the ground.

—Go back, she said. —Just go back. Back to the beginning. I think there's a way. There's a way, I think.

Sarah's father laughed. —The paper's not antique, he said. —You can rip it.

Unwrapping the present revealed a hand-bound journal. Two strips of leather kept it closed.

—Open it.

She unknotted and unwound the strips and draped them to the side. Smiling, her father scooted to the edge of his seat. Sarah raised her eyebrows and smiled. His excitement engrossed and infected her. She opened the book, flipped through the pages. Words spun and floated. Some clustered together and formed spirals. Some broke apart and disintegrated.

—What is it?

—You don't remember? he said. —These are notes. My notes.

—On what?

—You ... when you were younger, you'd obsess over it. "What are you writing?" you'd say. "Why are you always writing in that?" How can you not remember it?

She flipped a page. The words clustered and spun, the pages extruded, the journal seemed to fold inward. Everything collapsed. A vortex formed in the journal, like a crater consuming the center. Her father, still on the edge of his seat, still grinning, stretched and shifted and vanished into the book.

The earth rumbled; the ground shook; the walls vibrated and broke apart. Everything vibrated and broke apart, even the photons cycling throughout the room; everything grouped in clusters and spun. The vortex in the book grew larger and larger as it sucked everything—even the photons —into it.

Then the absence of everything cradled Sarah.

She floated in a void. Supine, as if lying in bed, but not lying in bed, she felt her flesh and limbs morph and stretch. She felt her triangles shift, shift, shift. It felt tingly, her face, as though her actual fucking face had gone to sleep.

—There's a trick ... the trick ... Just go back.

The universe blinked on again.

Sarah was sitting at a picnic table at the state fair. Daulton tore a corner off an elephant ear and shoved it into his mouth. His triangles shifted and spun, so, at one point, his mouth slid to the side of his eye, lingering more or less at the temple.

—You're not the author of anything, Sarah said. —I get that now.

—Never said I was.

—But you implied it. You pretended.

—We have to amuse ourselves, he said. — Helps ward off insanity.

—I remember this. I mean, I remember you. Then ... And earlier you snapped your fingers, I think, and told me to talk to her, to Cynthia. But you knew ... You've known ... How do we stop this?

—... so greasy, and too much cinnamon, but it's good.

—How do I stop this? How the fuck do I prevent it from happening?

The universe blinked off and on again.

Sarah was sitting on a picnic table in the ocean. Dolphins blasted out of the water, arched through the air, and disappeared into the water again. Light raced to the earth from the sun. A beam of light spiraled out- and upward; it slammed down and ricocheted off the water and rushed to Sarah.

The faceless woman surfed the beam of light. She leapt onto the picnic table, into the seat across from Sarah. Light corkscrewed away from them. It nosedived and bled into the water, changing it from blue to gold.

—It's so hard, the woman said. —You have no idea how hard it is, to sit here and see him like that. Like I keep waiting for him to sit up, to laugh and tell me it's some kind of joke. Some kind of sick joke. See, that's the hard part: I know he's dead but then I still can't believe it.

—Who's dead?

—Dad. Your dad. Your father is dead, Sarah.

—No he's not.

—I was just staring at him, in his coffin.

—I was just talking to him.

—When?

—A few minutes ago.

—And where was this?

—The hospital.

—Few days after you sliced up your forearms? When he flew back home and brought you that journal?

Sarah tried to speak but she couldn't form anything resembling a thought.

—I was just thinking about that.

—Were you?

—How do you think you were "experiencing" it?

—I don't ...

—I know what you're going through.

—Do you?

—Sometimes it's not bad, the woman said. —Sometimes it helps.

—How do I stop it?

—You can't stop anything. "You" are not you. Don't you get that?

—That's absurd.

—You're not you, as in real time. You're me as I once was. Although this isn't really ... She gestured to the table, to the ocean. —It's not really accurate, this reconstruction.

—I don't ... But how do I stop it, goddamn it?

—Sarah, and I want you to listen to me carefully: you are a figment of my imagination. You are a version of a memory of me. I'm thinking about this right now. Don't you see that? I mean, do you ... Do you think we're actually sitting at a table on the ocean?

—Sometimes things don't seem ...

—I am, right now, sitting in a chair at a funeral home, near my father's coffin. And by "I," I mean my body, the meat, is sitting in a chair right now. But I'm experiencing this, here, as you are. And with you. And ... I guess I suppose in a sense you really are here.

—But how do I stop this?

—You can't stop anything. Because you're not doing anything. Don't you get that? Don't you see?

—I'm here. Sarah slapped the table. The wood rippled. —I am here right now, goddamn it. I am not a figment of your fucking imagination. I think and I feel. And I can ask questions and consider answers. And I'm going to tell you this right now: you are a figment of my imagination. Like maybe you're part of my subconscious or something. Like maybe you're the part of my mind just below consciousness, the place where problems go to be solved. And so I'm going to ask you again: how do I stop this? all of it?

The faceless woman laughed. —You can't stop anything because you're a product of my brain. If you tried to stop this, if you somehow could stop this, then you'd disappear; you'd vanish completely; and then I'd find myself sitting in a funeral home, staring at dad's coffin. Now that doesn't sound very fucking appealing, does it?

—My father is not dead. I just talked to him. Remember? when you ... and I'm assuming it was you ... when you popped in and told me to go back to the beginning? And so what was that all about? If I'm not real, then explain to me how you showed up ... explain to me why you'd show up to tell me something, anything.

—It's the method of loci, the faceless woman said. —I'm not trying to teach you anything. I'm trying to commit something to memory.

10.

The universe blinked on again.

The man stood beside the door brandishing something shiny. Light ricocheted off it and scattered. White and gray, the light fed me enough information to discern a shard of glass, maybe, or possibly a chunk of metal.

He held his arms at his sides, near his legs, as he glanced in my direction. The triangles shifted, shifted, shifted, and I couldn't make out his face. Was it me? A version of me?

People crisscrossed in front of him. People swarmed behind him. We were in a store and he was standing near the entrance. Crowds of people passed him, some pushed carts, others dragged kids. But the man didn't move.

If he noticed people passing him, then he did nothing to betray it.

Alice and I crossed near the front of the store, on our way to the checkout lanes, when I spotted him. I'd seen him earlier, I thought, but my selective attention had more or less filtered out all but maybe a shadow of him. Now the shadow emerged from my subcortical region, probably, where the information had apparently lingered, and so the shadow converged with the man: if memory served me right, he hadn't moved.

Alice motioned to an express lane. Her triangles shifted. She said something and water tumbled out of her mouth—now shimmering near her cheekbone—muffling her words.

—We have more than twelve, I said, scanning the items in the cart.

She said something.

—Yeah, fuck it.

We parked the cart in an express lane and waited for the cashier to ring up a woman in front of us. The woman set a bundle of coupons on the counter. The cashier said something. Alice said something, too, and pointed out a face on a tabloid. Some celebrity. His triangles shifted. The words on the magazine collided and spun, spun and collided. Probably some rag story about some wealthy asshole treating other people like serfs.

The cashier mumbled the total as the woman in front of us flipped through more coupons.

The man standing near the entrance shifted. The object in his hands scattered light, redirected it. The light hit me. Nearly blinded me. And the man stood there. He stood there without moving.

—Are you afraid of death? Sarah said. —I mean, what happens when you think about it?

—A void envelopes me, I said, —as I try to imagine what the absence of experience is like.

—It fucking terrifies me. Like I swear sometimes I think I'm going to throw up when I think about it.

—I'm not saying it doesn't terrify me. I used to be more or less indifferent to it, but since the miscarriage ... Everything, I suppose, has been in hyperdrive.

—I try not to think about it, but it's like I'm constantly reminded of it.

—The perils of living, I said. —We're surrounded by death. Constantly fucking reminded of it.

—I used to live near a cemetery.

—Shit, I wouldn't.

—It gave me plenty of nightmares.

—I can imagine.

—And since it was a cemetery, I was aware of it, like acutely aware of it. There weren't any street lights or anything in it. Or even near it. So at night it wasn't just dark; it was ominously dark. And on most nights it was quiet. But because it was a cemetery, and because I knew it was a cemetery, I actually became aware of the silence, and so it wasn't just quiet over there; it was, as I said, ominous.

—I know what you mean. Just passing a cemetery at night makes me feel that way. It's not just dark or quiet, it's ...

—Yeah, she said. —And so for a while these kids, these asshole teenagers, would hang around there. At night. And they had this goddamn dog with them, which always barked or howled. And they played music and laughed and shouted. Just fucking around, being kids.

—I knew people like that growing up. Cemeteries attract certain kinds of teenager.

—So one night the police swarm the cemetery, right? And I'm talking like at least five or six squad cars. The kids, it turned out, were making meth. Right there. They had this van, an old van, and so they'd park it in the cemetery every night and cook meth.

—These were some intellectual heavyweights.

—Right? she said. —That's what I found so weird. If you're going to cook meth, why would you do it in a public setting? And make so much fucking noise while doing it?

—Sounds like maybe their perception of the cemetery's silence lulled them into a false sense of security.

—So two or three nights after the raid, I was sitting in the living room reading a book. This was late, two or three in the morning. And blue and red lights flooded the window. Squad cars. An ambulance.

—You mean they actually fucking returned?

—Two of them, she said. —Some Sid and Nancy-type couple, I guess. Killed themselves.

—Fuck me.

—It ruined the apartment for me. I had to move after that.

—I can imagine.

—But don't you find it strange? she said. —I somehow managed to disentangle the cemetery from death. If not death than the immediacy of death. And I didn't have too much trouble reconciling living so close to the place, you know? But after those suicides, I became fixated on it. On the seeds, so many seeds, planted in that garden.

—Tombstones grow where corpses are planted.

—But that just goes to show that I can't escape it. No matter where I go, it haunts me. Sometimes it's intrinsic and sometimes it's extrinsic. But it's always there. Somewhere. Waiting to jump out and get me.

—So how do you deal with it?

—Is there a way? she said. —I try to ignore it, to flee it, but ...

—It's almost as if at some point you have to embrace it. Maybe that's how you get over it.

—I wonder that. And then I think about like irrational fears. How they say if you're afraid of clowns, or whatever, then you should expose yourself to them.

—Right.

—But how do you overcome the fear of death? Exposing yourself to corpses won't do anything. It's the fear ... like, you know ... of the absence of experience that gets me. And there's no way to expose myself to that. No matter how much I think about it and try to picture it ... It's just not the same, you know?

Dad squeezed ketchup onto his plate, then passed the bottle to Mom. She squeezed ketchup onto a hamburger bun and passed the bottle to me. I closed the cap, smacked the top against my palm, unscrewed the cap, and watched a tongue-shaped blob flow from the bottle.

—It's the strangest thing, I said. —We didn't really have big moments, did we?

—What do you think? Dad said, to Mom. —Can he eat it all?

—He can put it away, she said.

The man stood beside the hostess station, wielding a knife. Light slammed into it and scattered. By the time the light reached me, it had retained enough information to allow me to discern the object.

It was a knife.

—Whenever I think of you, I said, —I don't envision epiphanies or ... like there's nothing ... at least nothing I can remember ... that would qualify as the climax or anything of a searing drama.

—You think so? Dad said. —That's a big burger.

—Mine aren't any smaller.

—I always thought it was stupid and cliché, maybe platitudinous, when people say it's the little things.

Dad laughed.

Then a voice, a booming voice, shook the walls: —In hindsight it's stupid. But at the time it was necessary. At least you'll think it's necessary.

—They aren't, Mom said.

The man's triangles shifted, but his stance, angled toward me, painted the portrait of determination—or obsession.

—Maybe before you fry them, Dad said.

Then, the booming voice again: —Not dwelling on it: that's the key. To get over it, you must simply overcome it. You'll feel like a fool, but ... those feelings diminish and ... you'll overcome it. You must deal with it dead on, no fucking around. Deal with it, get over it, and move on.

—That's not true, Mom sad. —I have to ... the bread usually looks small.

—But I guess, I said, —that if you were to somehow quantify our interactions, that I suppose the vast majority were like this: little moments, seemingly insignificant moments. But they add up, I guess.

A woman crossed to front of the room. She angled toward the hostess station and passed through the man. He rippled, as if composed of water, and then he assumed the shape of a person after the woman glided through him.

His knife reflected light, white light. The air around him rippled as the light raced toward me. It slammed into Dad and Mom, it slammed into the light fixture overhead, it slammed into my eyes. Then the photons exploded, transforming into drops of blood. The blood rained on Dad, Mom, and me. It covered my hands, my wrists, racing down my forearms, as if traversing unseen canyons.

—There's something about it, Dad said, glancing at my burger, —I don't like. There's something ...

The blood raced down my forearms and spilled onto the table. Some drops splattered the plate, the fries, the burger.

—I'm sorry, I said. —It's ... Everything is too much sometimes. Everything is sometimes too much. I'm sorry.

(l. ⌄ 11.)

The little things, the seemingly insignificant or inconsequential traces of a life once lived, haunted Sarah as she strolled into her father's living room. On a desk near the door sat a jar of peanut butter. A spoon—still showing streaks where lips had squeegeed it—rested at an angle on top of the jar. A package of crackers, a handwritten note, an open magazine sat on top of opened and unopened envelopes. Fragments of the banality of life.

Studying each item in turn but without touching them, Sarah felt the unsettling sensations of grief blasting from her stomach into her throat. Viewed through the lens of death, the artifacts assumed a previously unheard of level of sentimentality.

Where to begin?

To her right, a woman stood in the corner, near the television—the faceless woman. In the flesh but not of the flesh, she reminded Sarah of one of those papercraft illusions, one of those dragons whose head seemed to follow you as you crossed its path.

The blob of flesh on top of the woman's neck exploded, imploded, spun—putty kneaded by invisible hands.

—Divide the world, the faceless woman said. —Divide the world. Remove yourself from it. The difference of two sets is the set whose elements are not in the other set. Remove yourself from it.

Sarah crossed the room as if walking on a tightrope. She placed a foot in front of the other and strutted forward after calculating each motion. The floorboards creaked and groaned. Creaked. Groaned.

Overhead, the light flickered. Tears replaced photons. Water slammed into the walls and pooled on the floor, near the floorboards. The combination of tears and footsteps, and the throbbing tension pulling the flesh on her face, especially at the temples, toward the back of her skull, made everything feel empty, meaningless, dead.

After she reached the filing cabinet, she moved to sit in her father's chair, but she leaped out of it. Touching it somehow seemed like a violation. Sitting in it somehow seemed profane. So she kneeled in front of the cabinet and opened the top drawer.

Her father's chair haunted her; although empty, it somehow contained him.

Yet it didn't contain him.

His absence hovered over the chair and the room; it hovered over Sarah.

The faceless woman shifted her feet and twisted her spine and drooped her arms near her sides.

—Remove yourself from yourself, she said. — Remove yourself from the …

The funeral home director defies stereotype. She's young, early-30s, wearing makeup and dressed as though she's minutes from a nightclub. Sitting at the head of a conference table, pouring coffee into a mug, she's wearing an expression like she's either hung-over or allergic to light: she squints and scrunches her cheeks.

Coffee flows into the mug like molasses. It absorbs light reflected from signs and photographs. Advertisements for merchandise made from human ashes cover the walls and countertops. It's appalling. Why dedicate effort to mourning the dead when you can concentrate on jewelry made from the remains of your loved ones?

All at a low, low price. We can arrange payments.

—Are you expecting anyone else? the woman says.

—My cousin. Sarah checks the time. —He should be here by now.

—While you're waiting, you can fill these out. The woman slides a stack of papers across the table. —Unless you need him for ...

Sarah flips through the papers: information about her father.

—Marcus is more or less emotional support.

—Take your time. There's really no hurry. She slides a pen across the table. Then she glides to the door, vanishing into the hallway.

Sarah clutches the pen, flips through the paperwork. Her mind reels. So many boxes to check. So many lines to muddle.

So many questions. So much information.

Where to begin?

Smoke broke away from Sarah's cigarette and slipped out the window. It flowed from the car, crossed the parking lot, and fluttered to the side of the funeral home, where some of it blew into bricks, curled and dissolved. Tufts of smoke, grain-like, floated up, up, colliding with photons pelting the earth. Clouds passed the sun, filtered some photons, those not married to Sarah's smoke. The photons pelted the car and Sarah, the funeral home and the parking lot, the street and the cars and the people. They were unrelenting.

For like the fifteenth time, Marcus's voicemail exhorted Sarah to leave a message. And for like the fifteenth time, she blurted a word—usually "fuck"—and killed the call without leaving a message. He was such an asshole.

She dropped the phone into the passenger seat as she snubbed out her cigarette. Leaning forward, she glanced up: sunlight spread rainbows and asterisks—blotched by shadows from clouds—across her windshield.

The windshield needed cleaning. Her car needed cleaning. Come to think of it, her clothes and apartment, and pretty much everything she owned or encountered, needed cleaning. Even her father's house. But that required something far worse, something far more sinister—it required a full-on gutting, the thought of which filled her with something like dread mixed with the physiological reaction to electroconvulsive therapy.

As rainbows shimmered on her windshield, and as asterisks and lozenges popped against the glass, an old man strolled down the sidewalk. He sort of slipped between the rainbows and asterisks, the way cartoon characters could, improbably, hide behind trees without exposing their bodies.

A sun visor cast shadows on his forehead. Sunglasses masked his eyes. The sun seemed to at the very least annoy or maybe even inconvenience him—perhaps he was a more or less indoorsy type. Shorts revealed paper-white legs. Varicose veins, resembling bulbous ivy, sprouted from somewhere inside his shoes.

He hunched when he walked, and he walked at a pace closely related to crawling. Something sparkled on the ground in front of him. He stopped to investigate it, contorting his body—in an almost Vaudeville routine: hunching over without moving his neck or bending his legs—and picked it up. From Sarah's vantage point, the sparkly object looked like a coin, a dime maybe. She couldn't defeat the smile thinning her lips.

And this was when her smile faded ...

Her father was superimposed over the old man.

Then ...

The old man transmogrified into her father. His legs were white and his eyes were bad, hence the visor and the glasses. He moved with something like a stride spliced with a slide, and so it took a hell of a lot longer than it should have to walk the ten or fifteen feet down the sidewalk since pocketing the coin.

Caw, caw.

Her father inexplicably shielded his eyes with a sort of salute as he glanced up, in search of something, probably a bird. A church loomed in the background, across the street; it disappeared as Sarah's father searched for the bird. A hospital replaced the church. Sarah and her father/the old man blinked in and out, in and out, in a strobe of temporal-spatial displacement.

Finally, the strobing stopped. A house, an old house, Sarah's childhood home, replaced the church and the hospital.

Caw, caw.

Her father still couldn't locate the source of the "caw," but he apparently refused to give up. In fact, still saluting, despite the visor and the sunglasses, he arched his back, as if attempting to survey the sky over, and slightly, behind him.

Caw, caw.

As he shielded his eyes and arched his back, her father, still an old man, shifted his feet, which were planted on the sidewalk.

The sidewalk blinked in and out, in and finally out.

Lawn replaced it.

Inside Sarah's car, the cabin creaked and groaned. Metal warped, twisted, snapped. She closed her eyes and tried to still her heart, to at least slow it, to wrestle the onslaught of anxiety pumping neurotransmitters into her synaptic gaps. Her stomach inflated and deflated, inflated and deflated; it felt the way it did when, while driving, she dipped down a hill. Butterflies, it's called, although she never understood the term.

Caw, caw.

The butterfly-stomach-effect persisted. But the creaking and groaning stopped. She opened her eyes—first the left eye and then the right.

Her car had transformed into a swing set; her seat, a swing. She pumped her legs and swung higher, higher, higher. Her stomach inflated and deflated. Inflated. Deflated.

Her father strolled toward her, stretching his lips into an exaggerated, comic-book-style smile, as wide as the Joker's. He was younger, aging backwards as he approached her. Unencumbered by either a smile or sunglasses, he saluted to shield his eyes and, squinting, hooted as Sarah swung higher.

—Come talk to me, Sarah said. —I want to tell you so much.

Like it'd do any good.

Her father cut through the lawn, but the angle at which he walked rendered his destination ambiguous.

Then ...

But ...

So he strolled both toward and away from Sarah.

She experienced the scenario and observed it: she was both on the swing set and standing across the street, watching her father walk toward her and away from her.

Mimesis: she swung; diegesis: she observed— and only now, like just now, she realized the moment, the entire scenario, was an implant. She remembers hearing this story several times, once or twice from Michelle, at least three or four times from her father.

Details had grown and expanded over the years, so much so that she, later in life, could only attempt to infer the core, what was probably the ontological basis for their exegetical refashioning. But she rarely thought of it, and so she more or less relied on the enlarged narratives, which = the details added by her father lodged themselves in her hippocampus, trapped there as subjective tokens. But then ...

Yes; now she remembers: she wasn't on the swing set; Michelle was. Sarah, as her father often told her, was playing in the dirt beside the house, using a bucket to make mud castles. Her mother lounged in a chair beside her, reading a book, glancing at Michelle every now and then.

—Bracket it. A voice boomed. —Stop being conscious of your consciousness of this.

This, Sarah knew, was the day Michelle fell off the swing and broke her arm. At pretty much that exact moment, the family later learned, a two-seated Cessna crashed into their cousin's house, shattering both of Marcus's femurs.

Young Sarah sat splay-legged as she drilled her fingers into a mound of dirt. Her mother, bald and sunken-eyed, although this was at least a year or two before her diagnosis, flipped through a handmade journal. She'd stopped every now and then, read a passage every now and then, contort her face every now and then, affecting an expression Sarah might expect to cross the face of a nun reading Marquis de Sade.

—Glub glub.

Sarah squawked. Her mother laughed.

Michelle laughed, too. Cackled, in fact.

She pumped her legs, pumped her legs, and swung higher, higher.

—Something glub glub, Sarah's father said.

—Blah blah, Michelle said.

Sarah watched the exchange from across street and from the mound of dirt beside the house. She remembers laughing. Then she remembers her mother laughing. Her mother's laughter drifted and hit a crescendo, as if crossed with a hiccup, transitioning from a cough to a violent outburst of hacking and gagging.

Then ...

Young Sarah and Michelle, their mother and father and everything, including the planet itself, bended and warped. Something drained light, all light, from the world. Everything was white, as white as a sheet of paper.

Words replaced everything. Types became tokens and tokens became types, all mingled and filtered through black phonetic symbols. Written language stood in for—actually fucking replaced —physical objects. Duplicates of the word, "dad," formed the shape of a man. The word, "mom," repeated, formed the shape of a woman. The words, "grass" and "dirt," formed the shape of the ground. "Sarah Sarah Sarah Sarah," et cetera, formed the shape of a toddler sitting atop the words "grass, dirt, mud," and so on. "Michelle" formed the shape of a girl, "swing set," "swing," "motion," "sky," and so on formed the shape of Michelle as she pumped her legs and swung higher, higher, higher.

Set against a paper-white void, words replaced everything. They replaced every object in the universe, including the "universe" itself—this is what Sarah encountered as she hovered in the void; beneath her, she read duplicates of the words "sidewalk" and "concrete" and "grass," and so on.

Words even replaced Sarah.

Glancing down, she read, "pants" and "legs," "feet" and "shoes," in lieu of seeing their physical referents. She raised her hand to eye level: "hand," copied thousands of times, formed the shape of her hand. The words rolled and spun, as if each were a link on a moving chain. Some words—"hand," "palm"—converged with "wrist," and the moving word "wrist" converged with other words, "forearm," "skin," "veins," and so on.

She stepped back, glanced up: "sky," "cloud," "sunlight," "airplane." Glancing down: "breasts" and "bra," "shirt" and "chest" and "stomach." Inside her "stomach," in almost fine print, she caught the word, "nausea" spinning and spreading into her "chest."

Every limb and every nerve jittered as fear tore through her.

Neurotransmitters plugged receptor sites; they evaded the uptake process; and her sympathetic division kicked in, cranking up her heartrate and her breathing. And everything ... Everything felt real yet not real—both p and ¬p. And everything ...

She clenched both her eyelids and her fists. She tried to picture, to fucking imagine, something else. She slowed her breath, slowed her breath, and opened her eyes: her mother lounged, flipped through the journal; her sister swung; her father mumbled something or other.

Flesh had replaced words.

The physical universe had replaced black symbols and the paper-white void. Everything was alive again. Everything was moving and ...

—Remove yourself from yourself. The voice, that fucking voice, boomed.

She remembered someone, some woman, saying that, repeating it: —Remove yourself from yourself. Remove yourself ...

The exhaust fan over the stove hums and whines as it collects cigarette smoke. The smoke dances from my cigarette and drifts toward the fan. Then a ball of smoke flies away from my mouth and vanishes into the latticed metal.

The noise is constant and loud, like a fucking car engine. It serves as a counterbalance to the music filling our bedroom. Alice is sitting in bed, doing her homework. For her, music drowns out —or fills—the silence. But for me, it pokes holes in my stomach and brain.

I snub out my cigarette, shut off the exhaust fan, stroll into the bedroom. Alice is making flash cards for her German class. She doesn't glance at me, or even acknowledge me. When she does acknowledge me, it's betrayed by the moment in which she stops writing so I climb into bed— presumably so the motion doesn't annihilate her handwriting.

—What's wrong? she says.

—Nothing.

—Why are you so quiet?

—I don't want to disturb you.

She narrows her eyes: bullshit.

—I'm serious, I say, laughing.

She drops her pen and grabs my hand.

—Are you all right?

—I think so.

—Do you want to talk about it?

—What's there to talk about? There's nothing to say.

She gives me that look again: bullshit.

—You can cry, you know, she says. —You're kind of expected to.

—But what's the point?

—It might make you feel better.

—Crying or fighting tears are two sides of the same coin.

—I beg to differ.

—Giving into it or resisting it only alters the behavior other people detect. Cry or fight it; either way you're shackling yourself inside the prison of grief.

—There's a time and a place for intellectual analysis, she says. —This isn't it. Giving into your emotions isn't a weakness, Daulton.

—I didn't say it was.

—No, but you implied it.

—When did I imply it?

—You do all the time, she says, —by your actions.

—Dad's dead. Crying won't change that, so why bother?

—Of course crying won't change that. It's not meant to.

—But either way, there's no point.

—I'm not saying there's a point, she says. —You keep saying that. All I'm saying is ... if you feel like crying, then cry. Fighting it will cause more harm than pretending to be tough or manly or emotionless, or whatever it is you're doing.

—I'm not doing anything, I say. —I'm just not a crier. I get that from Dad.

My stomach flutters.

—Everyone cries.

—Not everyone.

—Yes, everyone, she says. —I've seen you cry.

231

My phone chimes.

—What now? Alice says.

—It's Sarah. She's having ... issues, I think.

—Let me guess: you're going to meet her.

I climb out of bed.

—I have to.

—Bullshit.

—I've told you a thousand times: she and I suffer from the rarest neurological disorder known to humans. We are our only support group.

Alice picks up her pen and scribbles some unpronounceable—to me, anyway—word on to an index card.

—You're more than welcome to come with me, I say.

—That's all right.

—I can't imagine how weird this must be ...

—It's fine. Really.

She holds her finger under a cluster of words and writes something on a card.

—I love you, I say.

—I love you. She sings it:

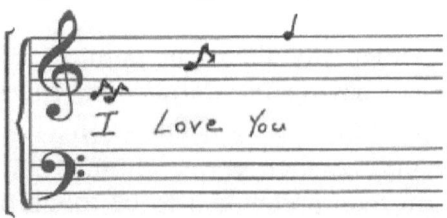

I lean over the bed and kiss her.

—I do love you, I say.

—Pinky swear?

She extends her pinky finger. I curl mine around it.

—Pinky swear, I say.

Sarah knelt on the ground. She ignited her lighter, extinguished the flame. The flame reappeared, sizzling, and vanished again. Taking a drag from her cigarette, she glanced sidelong at me.

—So what, exactly, is the problem?

I was sitting on the hood of my car, spinning a cigarette between my thumb and index finger. The cherry scratched traces into the sky. The traces hung for a second. More followed—in a red to pink to white gradient. I wrote my name in cursive. But as the traces faded, it looked more like "Sarah Sarah Sarah."

—I keep ... This woman, Sarah said. —I keep remembering this woman. And she's also telling me things, like I remember her repeating things, almost mantras, like repeating them the way you'd repeat something you're trying to learn by rote.

—What things? Who is she?

—My memories of her are always vague. Most of the reconstructions are approximations, I think. Like I can't remember her face. It's a blob, almost like Silly Putty.

—And what's she saying?

—She's telling me to remove myself from myself, to divide the world. And so but I think it works. I think it's working. Like today, earlier today, I was thinking about something ... But so then everything fell apart, you know? The way it sometimes does. Only this time it was different. I don't really even know how to describe it.

She spoke as if she were hopped up on amphetamine. The phrase "a mile a minute" came to mind. Laughing, I raised my hand, offering the universal stop sign, and said,

—Wait, wait, wait; slow down. I can't ...

—But here's the thing, she said, —and so I remembered the woman telling me to remove myself from myself, and I tried it. And it sort of worked. I mean, it didn't completely work, like I couldn't shut down the memories or the ... But it sort of worked.

—What worked? I'm not sure I'm following you.

—Don't you get it? There's a way ... I think there's a way to control it, to fucking orient myself.

—I'm trying to ... Help me clarify it. What exactly did you do?

—I tried to remove myself from myself.

—But what do you mean ...?

—Look ... you ... Do you remember that thing you were writing? That philosophical treatise or whatever? "W over F equals T"? How if we want to see the world as it is, then we must free it from facts?

—There's no need to explain it to me.

—There's a thing, I think ... The aim is to step outside yourself, right? That's the point ... your great philosophical work.

—All right, I said. —Enough.

—What's wrong?

—You're fucking mocking me, that's what's wrong.

—I'm not mocking you.

—The hell you're not.

—Listen. The point is to see the world as it is. Without these filters we use, right? So that's exactly what I'm talking about. I think I may have figured out a way to do it.

—To remove yourself from yourself, I said. —I get it.

Her face slackened. She drooped her arms and dropped her cigarette.

—Fuck me, she said. —I think that was me, the woman. The one I keep remembering. Sarah stands and glances at the sky. —I think it's something like the misinformation effect or ... I think ...

She spun in a circle, eyes moving back and forth, back and forth. As if something occurred to her, she stopped spinning and said,

—Where are we? Right now?

—Where do you think we are?

—Answer my fucking question.

—Outside my apartment.

She squatted down, covered her face.

—What's wrong?

—This isn't real, she said. —None of this is real. Fuck me, I'm imagining it.

Triangles superimposed over her face started to shift, shift, shift. They vanished and her features —eyes, nose, mouth—melted away, leaving a blob of meat to churn and spin.

—And I'm ... for some reason ... I'm imagining this conversation from your point of view, she said. Then, yelling: —Motherfuck.

The funeral home director scans a page. She clicks a pen and scribbles something—a signature, maybe? Then she turns the page, reads, and writes something else.

Marcus showed up about five minutes ago, and now he's lounging in a chair beside Sarah, sucking his inner cheek. He purses his lips and screws his eyebrows upward. Sarah tries to smile, fears it comes across as a wince. When Marcus grabs her hand, he frowns, more or less confirming her fears.

—Okay, the funeral director says, —let me just make copies of this and you can be on your way.

She slides out of her chair and vanishes into a nearby room.

—It's so weird, Marcus says. His eyes bob from the advertisements to the ceiling. —It's like ... I've never heard such ... quiet before.

—What do you expect, a marching band?

—No, but ... it's unnatural.

—It's just your brain fucking with you, Sarah says.

—But just listen.

—We expect funeral homes to be solemn, maybe even creepy.

—It is.

—No, it's banal, she says, —which means it probably doesn't conform to your expectations of it, so your brain is manufacturing a sort of heightened awareness to compensate for the lack of solemnity ... or creepiness.

—Thank you for that dissertation, Dr. Buzzkill.

—Fuck off.

—Say what you want, Marcus says, —but I'm not imagining it ... this utter lack ... this strange fucking lack of noise.

—Just ... I don't know ... Try to step outside yourself, Sarah says, —Try to imagine this place as if you're an alien, as if you have no idea what it is.

—Yeah, good luck with that shit.

—Try to ... Then it hit her: —Try to imagine it as it is, not how you expect or imagine it to be ... And your ... you'll see your ...

—Hey, Marcus says. —Are you all right?

—... brain is just ... it's ...

She jumps out of her chair and crosses the room.

—Where the hell are you going? Marcus says. —What about the forms? the paperwork?

6.17

So then where does it start? And where does it end? That's the point, isn't it? Every analysis of structural frameworks can be reduced to these two questions. When considering certain works of art, such as the diachronic and synchronic nature of the opening section of The Sound and the Fury, *for example, or when considering the nature of consciousness, or when considering life itself— the definition of conception or the medical definition of death—these two questions define the parameters in which we limit our investigations.*

Not all investigations, of course, are restricted to these two questions. But when these questions surface, they restrict discourse to the nature of chronology.

6.18

Everything is broken. Everything is dead.

Perpetual expectancy is a process by which we perceive what we expect to see. So now the only things I perceive are things that are broken or dead.

Later—

I suspect Alice thinks Sarah and I are having an affair. If only she knew how fucked up and bizarre that would be. To say that it would be literally impossible would fall on deaf ears, I think.

6.20

Sarah's never been one to handle her situation, but I think she's losing it. I think she can't deal with the nature of her experiences anymore. She's more or less bipolar now, flopping between two poles: something akin to exhaustion and frustration.

She continues to demand answers from me, but what's the point in answering her questions? They would neither enlighten her nor solve her problems—which are, you know, less her problems, per se, and more or less my problems.

6.21

I think her father has to die. I'll make it as quick as I made Cynthia's death. Not sure where this will lead us, however, but I'm getting desperate. Something has to change. Something has to happen.

—Alice is acting weird again, I say.

—Look at it from her point of view: her husband leaves at all hours of the night to meet a woman she's never met.

—I don't know how to reassure her.

—You could introduce us.

—I've told you, I say, —that presents ... complications.

—What complications?

—Forget it.

—Tell me.

—Just drop it.

—That's such shit. You can't say something like that and ...

—So what's so urgent it couldn't wait?

—Do you remember that thing you were writing? "W over F equals T?" I think there's something to it.

—I told you: it's gobbledygook.

—I think it's doable. For us, at least. I think we can do it. I think we can ... if you can remove yourself from yourself ... I think we then could see things as they are.

—Not even us, I say. —It's not possible.

—I think it is.

—Our experience of "reality" is a product of our brains. Assuming, for the sake of argument, that things definitely obtain external to us, then we can't bear witness to those things without the filter of human subjectivity.

—But I think we can. I think there's a way to shut down, or at least subvert, the processes we use to frame the things we see.

—If that's true, and I don't see how it could be, but if it is true, then we wouldn't even be actively experiencing anything. I think experience is ... at least the way I would define it ... would be as consciousness becoming aware of the interaction between neural processes and stimuli, either external or internal. Like say Alice taps me while I'm sleeping; my brain might register the input, but if this information isn't filtered to my consciousness in such a way that I'm made consciously aware of the input and the output, then you can't say that I've "experienced" my wife touching me. If you removed experience from the equation, then could you even say that interaction occurred? I mean, would you know?

—Who cares?

—I care. What's the point of being alive if you don't experience anything?

—The point is to view the world as it actually is, she says, —to shut down the fucking tricks our brains play on us.

—But we can't consciously shut down experience. At best, I think we might be able to mute it. And even if that occurred, I don't think we'd be able to "view" the world as it is; at best, I think we'd be able to steal glimpses of it.

—I'm not trying to "view the world as it is," she says. —I'm trying to stop my brain ... I'm trying to stop this fucking ... insanity. I can't handle it. Don't you understand? I don't care about ontology or epistemology or whatever. But I do care about ... I have a vested fucking interest in ... my sanity, which is un-fucking-tenable right now.

Sarah sat on a leaf floating down a stream. The stream bubbled near the horizon and dipped, she imagined, into a waterfall. The water roared. Something screeched—a bird, maybe? Clouds dotted a blue sky. No creatures in sight.

She dipped her hand into the water. The surface rippled, curled around her fingers as the current pulled her downstream.

Everything felt soft and hollow. Everything felt empty and sad.

As the leaf neared the waterfall, she straightened her back and craned her head, trying to see the drop-off, but she couldn't see anything, really, other than the horizon.

A person-shaped hole in the space-time continuum shimmered beside her. It emitted a sound like white noise. The sound comforted her. It soothed her. She smiled and nodded when it emitted more white noise. Relief washed over her.

She understood it but she didn't understand it— both p and ¬p—but it made sense. It somehow made sense to her. And so she leaned back and closed her eyes and listened to the intersection of rushing water, screeching, and white noise.

Then ...

The rushing water and the screeching stopped. The sounds of the world vanished.

She was sitting in a waiting room. A television in the corner relayed scores from various sporting events. Across from her, an old man rocked in his seat. Blood drained from his forehead. He was leaning his head back, holding a towel over the wound. Blood raced down his cheek and neck and soaked his shirt.

This was when she was thirty-one, and she remembers feeling terrified and angry, sad and suicidal. Anxiety overwhelmed her: she felt like leaping out of her chair and racing to the nurse's station to find out what was going on what the fuck was going on? And yet she didn't do it. She didn't do anything. Instead, she sat there, frozen, watching blood race down that old man's face and neck. His blood was thick, like bile.

She tried to shut down her brain, which refused to cooperate. Images of Cynthia flashed into her mind. Cynthia appeared in the waiting room, in front of Sarah: pale and sweating, covered in blood. Earlier, she had taken a razor blade to her forearms. But instead of carving a few canyons, she had removed chunks of flesh.

Blood flowed.

Sarah clenched and opened her eyelids. She jumped out of her chair and hustled through the front doors. She ran across the parking lot and dropped to her knees, beside a tree, and coughed. And spat. And vomited.

It was late, maybe three in the morning, and so darkness had settled over the city, and the moon sprinkled light onto the hospital, but the light strobed as clouds clipped the moon. Stars surrounding the moon blinked and shimmered. Some of those nourished creatures on different planets—of this, she was certain. Another certainty: at least one planet contained creatures that didn't die, creatures that'd never know or even understand the pain and the torment and the plain fucking sadness of watching creatures around them make plans and then fucking die. And ...

But so who cares about the setting? Sarah didn't. She didn't care about the details or the description of the moon or the stars. Such literary bullshit.

And so she dug her fingers into the dirt and screamed. She screamed.

Like time-lapsed footage of a flower, a woman grew from the soil. She was pale. Dressed in a hospital gown, tubes running from her mouth and throat, her triangles shifted, shifted, but her identity wasn't in doubt: it was Cynthia. Cynthia as Sarah imagined her. Lying in a room, on a gurney, somewhere in that fucking hospital.

—I want to thank you. I never truly thanked you, Sarah said. —For being you. And for being with me. For saving me.

Sarah leaned over Cynthia. Moonlight flashed behind her, drenching Cynthia and the ground. Although she couldn't see it, Sarah assumed—but couldn't confirm—the light, mostly behind and above her, had cast shadows obscuring her face, neck, and chest.

Shadows tumbled off her and spilled onto Cynthia, so the left side of Cynthia's face projected a silhouetted profile of Sarah. It looked as though Sarah and Cynthia had transformed into an in-the-flesh statue of Janus.

—I can't do this, Sarah said. —Please don't make me do this. I don't think I can live without you. Not ... Please don't ... I don't want you to leave me. Not with these ... You can't go. Not now. I won't let you.

Blood rushed from the gaps in Cynthia's forearms. It soaked into the ground as flowers sprouted up around her body. Cynthia gasped, gasped. The blood stopped flowing. And Cynthia's triangles stopped shifting.

Sarah closed her eyes and cried. She cried.

The earth rumbled and grew. Something hard formed under her and grew behind her. Eyes still closed, still crying, she leaned back. Now she was sitting in a chair. An air-conditioner hummed. A clock ticked. Her agency detection informed her of someone's presence.

She opened her eyes:

Her shrink stared at her, as if waiting for a response.

—I feel like I'm fucking cursed, Sarah said. —I encounter death pretty much everywhere I fucking turn.

—Didn't you say a few weeks ago that you don't believe in curses?

—No. I don't think so. I don't know, Sarah said. —Maybe. Who knows? Sometimes I'm not sure what I think or know, what I believe or hold to be true. Like sometimes I think someone's the fucking author of my goddamn life and I don't know what to think, to believe, or whatever until this asshole gets around to writing it.

—Indeterminacy might be an expression of an underlying cause.

—Meaning ...?

—Are you familiar with learned helplessness ...

The shrink's face shifted, shifted. It transformed into a mirror, reflecting Sarah's face back at her. Shit. Was it the shrink, or was it Sarah? Who was this lady?

—But so what's the point? I am helpless. Because, try as I might, I can't fucking change anything. But of course you can't see it. The setting defines your perception of me, and so anything I might say to you might ... no, will most likely ... be interpreted as nonsense spewed from crazy Sarah's crazy brain. Like take now, for example: it doesn't matter what I say to you now, because I didn't say it to you then, and ... goddamn it; I don't know how much more of this I can take.

—These shocks weren't harmful. They were intense vibrations, not raw electricity.

—So the point is ... What? Sarah said. —The dog failed to escape the shock so it stopped trying?

—Learned helplessness, yes. We observe the same behavior in patients with depression. If you feel as though you're in a situation from which you must escape, and yet you've tried to escape the situation, whatever it might be, and failed, then you might learn to become helpless. You might learn to just ... sit there and take it, even if it's possible to become proactive, to change the situation.

—But what if I can't change the situation?
—Then try to change your approach to it.

12.

9.4

Something new and strange has happened to me. I tried to fight it, to pretend it didn't happen, but I can't doubt it. Not anymore.

Alice and I were at the theater. Rehearsals had just ended and we were outside smoking a cigarette. We were talking about the rehearsals, discussing some of the performances, when a lull in the conversation allowed for the invitation of unwanted thoughts. I remember, in the brief silence, not thinking anything, or at least not consciously aware of any processes a reasonable person could construe as thoughts, when something popped into my mind. Out of the blue, as it were. Then the universe blinked off and on again and I was standing in the living room in my parents' house.

They were gone yet I felt their absence. I glanced around the room, saw the television and dad's chair. Food and papers were strewn across his desk. A magazine sat on top of a pile of envelopes. Someone—dad, probably—had circled an ad in a box beside an article.

I remembered this, I clearly remembered it, but I couldn't place it. When had it occurred? A year ago? Five years ago? Ten?

And so where were mom and dad? And why did I note and feel their absence?

The universe blinked off and on again and I was outside the theater, taking a hit from my cigarette. Alice gave me a look of pure annoyance, and from that look I inferred she'd said something about my ability—or lack thereof —to listen.

I kind of laughed, more or less brushed it off, and assured her that I was listening. So then she asked me to summarize what she'd just said. "Your stepfather's house?" I said. "The tree out back?" But I didn't know if this summary was correct. And so she continued her story about the tree, and I knew my summary was accurate. But how was it accurate? I couldn't remember a thing she'd said. In fact, I was standing in my parents' house, glancing around the room, when she'd started the story.

She told me about a dog, their neighbor's dog, about how it sat below the tree, on the other side of the fence, gazing up at her as she sat on a nest of branches reading a book—which was something she did often back then.

And so I told myself to keep it. Keep that story. It was, I knew, one of those snatches of life worth retaining.

9.5

I'm lying in bed. It's night. The television and the lights are off and so the apartment is nearly pitch black. Alice is sleeping beside me. She just rolled over and endured a mini coughing fit. It didn't wake her.

I'm trying to write but I can't write. I can't write because I'm distracted. I'm distracted because something strange happened to me earlier and I can't quite comprehend or get over it.

I mean, it wasn't a memory. And by that I mean I didn't experience it the way I ordinarily experience memories. Sometimes they're auditory and sometimes they're visual—but in that vague creation-of-mental-imagery sense; and sometimes they're more or less linguistic, as if I'm employing language to reconstruct frameworks of events I'd encoded but, for whatever reason, couldn't retrieve as sounds or images.

No—this was different: I was there, in my parents' house. Not figuratively, not metaphorically; I was actually fucking there. One minute I was outside the theater and the next minute I was literally standing inside my parents' house. Inside the motherfucker.

Is this insanity? Did I experience the onset of schizophrenia or some twisted mental affliction I haven't even heard of?

9.7

It happened again. I was sitting on the chair in the living room, reading a chapter in my anthropology textbook, and then I was at a yard sale with mom and my aunt. This was when I was a kid, maybe three or four. Mom and my aunt were browsing the items, and I, for whatever reason, darted into the street and got hit by a car.

And this occurred exactly as it had the other night: this wasn't a vague memory; I was literally fucking there. I was no longer in our apartment. I was outside, stomping through grass, running over the sidewalk, and then lying on the street, beneath a car.

I was literally there.

And then I was home again, back in the chair in our apartment with a textbook on my lap.

I'm fucking terrified. Is this how madness begins?

Later—

What if it's a tumor pressing against my occipital lobes?

Is this how death begins?

9.8

Dad is dead.

9.10

In a stupid attempt to at least begin to process Dad's death, I started writing a novel last night. And of course it's explicitly about the death of a loved one. How fucking creative.

9.12

Got back from Dad's funeral a little while ago. Good luck processing that shit. While staring at Dad in his coffin, my brother told me that everything felt like a dream, and I understood what he meant. The sympathetic division of my autonomic nervous system has pretty much been in control since Sunday. Everything feels hazy, as if filtered through anxiety.

Why can't everything that's happened this week been in a dream? Why can't I pick up the phone and call Dad—and hear his voice? And know that he's alive?

9.14

I stayed up late as shit last night working on my novel. It's the perfect distraction, but I'm fucked up and tired, and my sympathetic division is apparently still in control, and so everything is insane. The novel is insane. And yet it makes sense to me. It makes as much, if not more, sense than this past fucking week does.

9.15

And so what is reality? What the fuck does it —"reality"—even mean?

I've searched for the answers to these questions for years, but my search has become more or less obsessive since Dad died.

9.16

My perception is broken, my brain is broken, my mind is broken—everything is broken. In and out, things move and dissolve and reconfigure themselves. I have no orientation inside spatiotemporal existence anymore. Things become unhinged. The universe blinks off and on and my spatial and temporal locations change. I find myself carrying conversations in the past— reliving and re-experiencing them, yet feeling as though I'm experiencing them for the first time.

I find myself carrying conversations with fictional characters. But these are not vague flights of fancy: I'm literally standing in front of flesh and bone people and engaging in dialogue with them.

Take last night, for example: I was lying in bed reading *Nausea* when the universe blinked off. I was sitting in a cafe in France when the universe blinked on again, discussing Marquis de Rollebon with Antoine Roquentin.

Pockmarks in his skin, a slight crack in his voice, a lazy eye: he was real to me. And I smelled the smoke when he lit his pipe. It triggered my addiction and so I mimicked him by lighting a cigarette. We talked about this and we talked about that, and at one point he checked his watch, which made want to check my watch, which means that his behavior activated my mirror neurons.

Can flights of fancy—the imagination— activate mirror neurons as a response to the behavior of others, even if they're not physically present? Can the intentionality of a fictional person create an experience of that person indistinguishable from the experience of a person who obtains independently of me? And by that I mean: was the Roquentin with whom I "interacted" a figment of my imagination or was he an actual physical object—an actual person— who obtained independently of me? Which is to say: is intentionality solely a product of neural processes, or is it in some way dependent on external objects or stimuli? Which is to say: is "reality" and what is "real" the product of the intersection of external stimuli and cognitive processes, or is "reality" and what is "real" solely the products of cognitive processes?

Later—

Just spent more time talking to "fictional" characters. I write "fictional" in quotation marks because I don't know if they were products of my brain ... or if the conversations were the experiences of interacting with flesh and blood people, people who obtained independently of me.

m.

Out of the funeral home and into the car, turning the ignition, lighting a cigarette: Sarah's hands shake. She trembles. Fucking trembles. The world shifts and shakes. It vibrates, as if someone with Parkinson's disease were filming everything with a handheld camera. Light bursts around her. Beneath her, the seat liquefies. She falls into it, through darkness, darkness, and emerges in her father's house.

The bedroom looks more or less as it did when Sarah's mother had returned from the hospital, like something out of a 70s Style magazine: khaki colored carpet—shag carpet, mind you—vanilla walls, a beige ceiling. A dresser stands beside the closet door. A bed towers in the center of the room, one of those velvet numbers. It looks old and worn, the bed, like it's been sitting beneath a pile of scrap metal for years.

As a child, Sarah loved to peel the sheets and blankets off and roll around on it. Complete with a velvet headboard, the bed attracted her; she loved how it felt, adored it, even.

It repulsed her after her mother died. And, as a teenager, it embarrassed her when, on a rare occasion, a friend, rarer still, showed up to the house and peered into the room. The headboard alone belonged in a museum, it was so old; and its color, purple, caught the eye. It never failed to elicit a comment, usually about her father, which further embarrassed her.

Sarah shoves her fist into the mattress. It creaks. She recoils and blurts something like a scream but not quite a scream. More like a yelp. Touching the mattress had raised gooseflesh on her arms, which she now pulls to her chest and massages.

Her mother's absence lingers, but it's vague. It reminds Sarah of the feeling she experiences when she leaves her house and forgets something —but not certain if she has, in fact, forgot something. And this evokes pretty much the same sensation, her mother's absence. Why does she linger? But then does she linger?

After a while, the sensation dims. It dims. The shadows of years gone by darken the signature of her existence.

And but Sarah's father ... His absence is fucking oppressive. Like at any moment, Sarah expects him to call from downstairs or to make an appearance or to ask why she's in his room. Like it doesn't even feel like he's out of town or on vacation or something. It feels like he's there, right there, alive and well and in the house, maybe in the living room, maybe, or in the basement. And ... but ... she doesn't have access to him. Like he's there but she can't pinpoint his location; like she knows he's home but she can't figure out in which room he's doing whatever it is he does.

The world swirls, spins. Photons collide and explode, and bursts of light pop and fade away.

She opens the closet door—inside, it smells like dust—and fumbles for the twine dangling from the light fixture. She flails her arm and pinches her fingers. Then, still flailing her arm, she slaps the twine, catches and pulls it. Photons ping pong around the closet.

Clothes hang from wall to wall. Men's clothes. Some old, some new, some she's never seen. She slides her fingers across the sleeve of an old jacket. Goosebumps. The clothes retain his smell, his signature. Tears threaten to assault her. She clears her throat and closes her eyes and pops her neck, slaying the tears before they usurp her.

It's almost funny. Every suit, every shirt, every pair of paints—everything seems plucked out of the 1970s and 80s, like her father was maybe some secret sitcom star and had saved his wardrobe. As a teenager, of course, she didn't find it funny, even though his style wasn't as outdated.

Among blues and whites, and even a pink, among velvet and cardigan, a black suit sticks out. Does it look good? Seams are frayed and, at some points, gray dulls black, turning it more or less silver. So no: it doesn't look good. But then so what? Does it matter what he looks like when he's buried?

But even in death people tend to appear the way others expect them to appear.

—It's such bullshit, she says.

More faded clothes. More frayed seams. Did the man own a decent suit?

But does it matter? Does it really fucking matter? People will see him in this outfit— whichever suit she settles on—for at most a day, and they probably won't even remember the damn thing. Then, after a few hours, someone will lock him in a box, in darkness, until the clothes rot, until the tectonic plates shift and drift away, until the sun expands and devours the planet.

An eternity of the absence of experience is indifferent to the clothes someone forces onto a corpse, she knows, and yet a strange obligation roils her: he must, at the very least, appear presentable.

She floats in the corner of the room, watching herself flip through clothes. The world shifts. She flies across the room, slamming into her body, which absorbs her, and she sees the world through two sets of eyes.

She bumps the closet door with her ass, closing it—her father had installed the door backward. Never the DIY type, he more or less shrugged it off. In fact, he claimed to prefer it. Whoever heard of an inward swinging closet door? he'd said. She hadn't, for one, so she picked on him whenever she saw or remembered it. He'd laugh or shrug it off or mutter something about getting around to it, a favorite phrase: "I'll get around to it later."

The thought brings a smile to her face.

The smile fades.

She drops to her knees and digs through boxes filled with bags of socks and new clothes. For some reason, her father had purchased these clothes and tossed them into a box and either forgot about them or chose not to wear them—tags, still affixed to at least half of them, advertise a clearance sale in red ink.

—Step aside yourself. Bracket ...

Lights burst. The universe blinks on and off again. She's driving, racing away from the funeral home. Her phone's going berserk. Marcus. No doubt trying to figure out what's going on, and ... but ...

Then ...

It makes her want to laugh. It makes her want to cry. It makes her want to choke him, this box, these clothes. For years he had joked about Sarah's mother, about how she'd hoarded knickknacks and books, clothes and even newspapers. And yet, on those occasions, he'd failed to disclose his at least minor proclivity for hoarding shit.

It's not surprising in hindsight. On the rare occasion he let something approximating sentimentalism slip, he'd produce an object Sarah hadn't seen. Like the time he showed her a spoon inherited from his mother-in-law. He coveted the damn thing. At some point—Sarah couldn't remember when—he even built a display case and hung it on the wall in the kitchen, beside the table, and betrayed anxiety when someone sat near it.

And her fucking phone won't shut up. She's half tempted to throw the motherfucker out the window. Like what's she going to say? My reality is chaotic but I think I know how to correct it?

Marcus will think she's stressed—or crazy. And she wishes, prays, he'd stop calling. She doesn't want to talk to him. But the constant chirping of the phone is going to make her crash, she swears to fuck, and so …

The world dims. Light grows again.

Sarah's sitting in the kitchen now, examining the spoon. In the display case. Her father, sitting on the other side of the table, eyeballs her, then the spoon, as he tears into a New York strip. Sarah picks a piece of lint from the corner and flicks it away. Her dad drops his fork, reaches out, belches a sort of visceral scream.

—Settle down, Sarah says, laughing. —There was lint.

—Where?

—Right there. On the corner.

—I'm thinking about building a sturdier case. Maybe putting some glass on it.

—What about the wormhole? Tell me about the fucking wormhole. Please.

—It's a valuable piece.

—I know you're there, somewhere. Answer my question.

—With Paul Revere's maker's mark.

—Are you shitting me?

—This isn't me, he says. —I'm not your father. I'm you.

—Bullshit.

—Your father didn't open a wormhole. How naïve, or stupid, are you? You were trying to explain your situation to a former you, as I'm now trying to teach myself how to orient reality.

Patina darkens it, gives it an almost marbled-copper coat. It's old, but otherwise undistinguished. Just a spoon. Nothing fancy or ornate. It seems mass produced, recent, like a piece from one of those "heirloom" sets sold door-to-door in the fifties.

—The mark's on the back, her father says. — I'm thinking about mounting it so you can see it, maybe include a picture or a brief history, or ... You know this isn't real, Sarah. You have to know it isn't real. Bracket your experience. Bracket it and step outside yourself. Do it, goddamn it.

First he smiles and then he frowns. First his eyelids narrow and then they open. Then he says something—it comes across as a moan—and water flows from his mouth. Bubbles churn on the surface of the water. They pop as the water slams into his neck and chest, and the word "Help" escapes from the bubbles as they pop. Visible—not sounds but symbols, as if typed: "Help"—the words float up, up, and crash into the ceiling.

As words coalesce around his head, Sarah's father's face turns pale and gray. His eyes and mouth droop. Then more bubbles, more symbols, more words: "Oh god, help." His face shifts, his skin bulges. Another yelp—another popped bubble—produces a groan. Slumping forward, he slams his face into the table. His arms fall to his sides.

Sarah scrambles to her feet, kicks over her chair, and, screaming ...

She's back in the closet now, squeezing a shirt. The walls seem closer; the closet, smaller. Dimmer now, the light casts everything in an almost sepia tone. The twine rattles against the light bulb as it sways back and forth, back and forth, crosshatching everything with shadows.

Then ...

Something moans.

Sarah drops the shirt and steps back. The door, pressing against her, feels like meat. Sounds in the bedroom—is it a moan?—shake the walls, the floor, the door. Boom. Boom. Boom. Her lungs stiffen. Her breath disintegrates. She's going to hyperventilate, she swears to fucking god. Boom. Boom. Boom. She sucks in air. Boom. Boom. Boom. It escapes her lungs. Boom. Boom ... And, fuck, is that a moan? a groan? Boom. She grasps the doorknob, fumbles with it as she tries to open the door. But her hand flies away from it, more or less of its own volition: the doorknob feels like raw meat—cold, wet, and slimy.

Boom.

She gasps. Inhales, inhales, exhales. She thrusts her arm toward the ceiling. Her fingernail snags the twine and the light powers down. The photons evaporate. She can't see them but she senses the walls—the fucking walls and the ceiling—closing in on her, pushing toward her, trying to crush her, and she ...

Boom.

Sounds from the other room.

Boom.

Sounds like thunder. Or gunshots.

Boom. Boom.

—Bracket it. At least try, you fucking idiot.

Her chest tightens. Her lungs stiffen. She gasps for air. Gasps. She's going to hyperventilate, she fucking swears it. Darkness envelops her. It squeezes and crushes her. She reaches behind her again and fumbles for the doorknob again, fumbles to ...

She arches her spine and, thrusting her ass outward, pops the hinges and flings open the door. Light pours into the closet. It blinds her. She stumbles; the back of her head smacks the floor as light pops in her eyes and ringing fills her ears.

Still lying on her back, she slams her eyelids closed and massages her forehead. Air fills her lungs again. She inhales and exhales without difficulty. But now her head hurts. Pain shoots through her back. And something, something like sadness maybe, courses through her. It detonates in her head and chest and flows through her veins; it hollows her stomach, replaces the marrow in her bones.

And ...

Tears roll down her face. They slip into her ear or race down her neck. And her stomach ... fuck ... her stomach ...

Then ...

That sound again: boom, boom, boom. It's neither thunder nor gunshots, neither moans nor groans.

It sounds like ...

Footsteps.

Footsteps?

In one motion she cranes her neck and opens her eyes and spins onto her stomach. A kid— Michelle?—traipses through the doorway. Sounds like moans and popping bubbles fill the room. A conversation: child and adult.

Sarah flies to her feet.

Her mother—ashen face, sunken eyes sparse hair—lies in bed and shifts to her side. Michelle —now only a child—holds her mother's hand.

That empty feeling, that sad and empty hollowness, returns. Sarah stands motionless. She's unable to move or to think while she watches her dead sister push an ice cube over her dead mother's lips, moistening them.

Her mother says something. Michelle laughs. But laughter doesn't leave her mouth—water does; it flows as though she'd chugged a glassful without swallowing, then opened her mouth; bubbles pop; and then laughter escapes the popped bubbles.

—Bracket it. Please. God.

Triangles superimposed over Michelle's nose, mouth, and eyes shift, shift, shift. The triangles distort and mangle her face; but the creases in her cheeks imply smiles. All smiles. Yet Sarah infers sadness, fear. More popped bubbles convey laughter. More inferences: sadness and fear.

Then …

Water stops flowing. Laughter vanishes.

Closing her eyes, steadying her breath, Sarah thinks, "bracket it," and she opens her eyes. Vacant, the bedroom absorbs light.

Then ...

Her mother appears. Michelle appears.

A voice booms-: —Bracket it.

Her mother convulses, howls. Michelle jerks her head to the left, to the right; her pupils and irises vanish. Blood spills from her nose and mouth.

—Bracket it.

Sarah walks backward and stops when she senses a chair in the corner. She drops into it and curls her hands over the arms. Her stomach actually fucking ripples. Triangles shift; they're superimposed over her mother's face—connoting her eyes, nose, and mouth—and distort her features as they move. It nauseates Sarah. The face, that face ... Pale and gray and sunken. It terrified Sarah as a child as it terrifies her now.

—Glub glub. Michelle says something but it's garbled.

—Glub, her mother says.

Sarah feels emptied. Exhausted. Her bones hollow, her head vacant, she rubs her temples.

—Glub glub?

She slides out of the chair and glides across the room.

—Glub.

Her mother's voice sends shockwaves through Sarah.

— You must always bracket it. Remove yourself from yourself.

—Glub glub. Glub?

She seems so real, so present. In this room. Right now.

The triangles on her face shift. It's hard to discern, but she seems as though she's smiling. Her cheeks bulge. Certainly it's a smile. Right? Or maybe it's a grin or a grimace, or maybe it's her mother fucking with her. Always fucking with her. Haunting her, rendering her sleepless and helpless and terrified.

—Why are you always like this? Sarah says.

She drags her finger across her mother's cheek. The flesh ripples, the ripples trail Sarah's fingers, then the flesh tightens and reforms.

—Glub glub, glub?

Her mother's arms twitch. Twitch.

Then ...

That sound again: boom, boom, boom.

The walls and floor tremble. The bed vibrates. Sarah's mother groans as her body shakes. Convulsions seize her. She writhes and groans and kicks off the blanket. Pillows tumble to the floor, almost in slow-motion,

—Glub.

A vortex sucks Sarah out of the house, into her car. She pulls off to the shoulder and leaps out of the car. She runs through a field. Drops to her knees. Trying to breathe, trying to catch her breath, she digs her hands into the dirt. Tears threaten to overwhelm her.

—Just bracket it and remove yourself from yourself remove remove yourself from yourself, she says.

Then ...

Back in her parents' house, both fear and depression seizes her.

Still writhing, still groaning, she sits up and lunges forward. Her arms float in front of her. Her fingers snap at the air.

The lights flicker.

Boom. Boom. Boom.

Groaning, Sarah's mother turns her head, slowly, and she swings her arms, groping for Sarah. The flesh on her face peels and flakes away. Everything in Sarah's peripheral vision vanishes. She leaps back when her mother's arm and hand fly into her field of vision. Something inside orders her to run, all but screams it, but Sarah ...

Her mother's skin darkens. Bubbles extrude, covering her face and neck. Oh god, remove yourself from yourself. Everything in Sarah's peripheral vision vanishes, and she leaps back when her mother's arm and hand fly into her field of vision. Something inside orders her to run, all but screams it, and Sarah ... she ...

The triangles over her mother's face stop shifting. Her flesh transforms from gray to black, as if cooked in time lapse. It withers and decomposes. The skin over her cheeks stretch and snap. Her cheekbones protrude. Blood runs down her face, her neck, her chest. The lights flicker. A sound like "boom" roars outside. And blood— glowing blood—drenches her, as if someone had dipped her into a vat of ichor. Her mouth sags. Her eyes grow, like they actually fucking grow, at least three times larger than average adult eyes. Bile-secreting fangs sprout from her gums. Black goo hangs from the tips.

—Glub. Glub.

She growls and lunges forward again, but only her upper body moves. The flesh on her neck bulges and tears, and blood squirts across the room. Growling, louder now, she swings her arms forward. She snaps at the air, trying to snag Sarah, to grab her. What the fuck does she have in mind?

Her growls deepen. Deepen. Then they transform into screeches. Bloodcurdling screeches, which don't resemble anything a human could produce; they sound closer to metal crushing metal than to anything humans produce.

—Is this how you remember me? she says. — This is how you remember me? as a living body, a mind, transitioning into a corpse? This is how you choose to remember your mother?

Tears stream down Sarah's face. Her mother lashes out at her again, grasps at her face by bending and contorting her fingers. Sarah leaps backward, too shocked to scream. Barely able to move, at least not consciously able to will movement, her leap doesn't push her too far away. On hitting the ground, she trips over something, a pair of boots maybe, and tumbles backward.

—Remove yourself from yourself. The voice booms.

Lying on her back now, she spins onto her stomach and scrambles to her knees. But she stops; again, she can't will herself to move. She can't …

Michelle, lying on the floor: This is Michelle as an adult, hands crossed at her chest. Not Michelle, the happy sister; this is Michelle the corpse, lying in a box, hours before they planted her, only a few months after her diagnosis. It had happened so fast—she was sick, then dying, then dead—and so Sarah didn't have time to process it, she didn't … And that image, that fucking image of her sister lying in a box stuck in her brain, and …

Sarah sits frozen in a sort of Lotus position. She tries to move but she can't. She tries to scream, to cry. Nothing comes out. Michelle's corpse groans. It groans. The sound triggers an outburst of emotion. Tears overtake Sarah. Something inside her tells her to stand. Something inside her tells her to run. Something inside her tells her to scream or to shout or to close her eyes and imagine a sunset on an island or on Mars or ...

The universe blinks off and on again.

Sarah's sitting on the floor in her kitchen, crying while she cradles Cynthia, her wife. Blood flows from canyons carved into Cynthia's forearms. Color drains from her face. Her eyes are open but she's either spaced out or more or less unconscious. Sarah screams into her cell phone, practically ordering the 911 operator to send a fucking fleet of ambulances, like now, like right this fucking goddamn minute, like what are you waiting for why aren't you and the blood oh god the blood how the fuck is this happening of the all the people all the fucking people she never not once suspected Cynthia of doing it and what the fuck is the holdup I'm going to lose her lose her goddamn it send the fucking ambulances now like right fucking now what's the problem motherfuckers do you fucking want her to die you fucking bureaucratic monsters

A woman without a face appears out of nowhere. She stands behind Sarah, touches her. Sarah doesn't need to look at her to verify to whom the hand belongs.

—Bracket your experience, the faceless woman says.

Standing in the bathroom now, studying her face in the mirror, Sarah's triangles shift. She's familiar with the shapes beneath the triangles, eyes, nose and mouth, contorting into a limp expression, as if she's too sad to emote. The shifting triangles turn her face into putty, making her expression harder to countenance.

269

The faceless woman hovers somewhere behind Sarah—outside the boundaries and her field of vision. Her presence is palpable, like the presence of an animal under a table; you know it's there but have no need or inclination to verify it.

Blue and gray light crawls through the room. It moves like molasses, as if someone had slowed the photons. Everything feels empty and gray. Dead. Such awareness drains her. Like Sarah remembers standing there, surveilling the mirror, her distorted reflection and her contorted face. Her limbs felt both weighted and empty. The struggle of moving, of so much as raising an arm or curling or unfurling a finger, transformed into a Sisyphean chore.

—You're here but not here, the faceless woman says. —You're not conscious of this room; you're conscious of being conscious of this place, this time. Bracket that. Cut off the consciousness of being conscious and focus your intention solely on what's in front of you.

—What's the point? Sarah says. —Everything is broken.

—Do it.

In the mirror, Sarah's triangles shift. Her face resembles unfired clay stamped by a bare foot, then kneaded by a lobster: her eyes shift below her cheeks; her mouth slides to her temple; her nose droops, touching to her chin.

—I can't ...

—Do. It.

She tries to focus. But on what? Where is she? In her father's bedroom. She'd fallen out of the closet and landed on the floor, so ... But, no; now she's in the bathroom, at the sink. Or is she?

Where the hell is she?

She tries to break free, tries to orient herself, to see beyond the memories and the manifested ideations.

—What's the …

Then she sees it—the ceiling: the fucking ceiling in her father's bedroom. She's standing in the bathroom, but she sees the world as if she's lying on her back, staring at the ceiling. Light dances across the tiles. Bright light. The world coalesces. Now she's sitting in a field, crying, clenching piles of dirt.

—Bracket it bracket it remove yourself from yourself remove yourself from yourself.

In a flash it's gone. Now she's in the bathroom again, watching her face shift and contort. Her features move, shift, and blur. It's like watching an animated Picasso painting.

—What's the point? she says. —Everything's broken. Everything's dead.

—You've got to focus, the faceless woman says. —You've got to get out of here.

Haze envelops the bathroom. A smell, citrusy, like shampoo, triggers a memory.

—Bracket your experience. Bracket your awareness of your experience.

—This was my second attempt, Sarah says. — Do you remember?

—You've got to focus, Sarah.

Sarah scoops up a razor blade and slices into her forearms. Blood bubbles out of the wounds; it rolls down and across her arms. Even though her triangles shift, shift, shift, Sarah remembers her reflection: she's smiling. She's crying but smiling. Everything feels gray. Everything feels dead. Yet she's smiling. And she remembers kind of laughing, thinking, "it'll all be over; soon it will all be over."

13.

Mom's crying.

I'm trying to give her something like a consoling expression but I don't think I'm succeeding. My countenance probably comes across as one of abject terror.

My older sister is sitting beside mom, and my younger sister is sitting beside my older sister. Alice is seated to my right; she drops her hand on my forearm and massages it. Chills spiral up and down my spine.

My brother is seated to my left and my brother-in-law is seated to his left. To my right, beside, and slightly behind, Alice, my other brother-in-law gazes at mom, attempting a consoling look, I think, but his furrowed eyebrows suggests he's questioning the efficacy of his expression.

The funeral director sits at the head of the table. She pours like the fifth cup of coffee. When she finishes, she slides the cup to mom. Still crying, mom wraps her fingers around the cup, ponders it, then slides it back to the funeral director.

So then this is it. This is what reality feels like when your sympathetic division has more or less displaced your parasympathetic division. Everything feels electric. The world hums—fucking visually hums—as if someone filming this thing people call "reality" is shaking the fucking camera. Everything feels heightened and alive. Everything feels gloomy, gray, dead.

In every second of every day I feel like crying and not crying, running and lying still, screaming and yelling and punching something, anything; and I feel like turning everything off, like shutting it down, disappearing.

Like when will this movie people call "reality" fucking end?

A car swerved into our lane, its end nearly clipping our front bumper, and checked its brakes before speeding away. Dad honked; he stuck his arm out the window, flipping off the driver.

—Do you believe that asshole? he said. —He could've killed someone, driving like that.

—He doesn't care.

—That's the problem. No one does.

—Everyone's in a hurry.

—Killing us isn't going to get him there any faster.

Rain slapped the windows. Thunder roared and lightning flashed. A semi passing us hopped lanes and jumped in front of us. Dad flipped off the driver.

—There's another one, he said, his voice high, as if stunned.

We raced past rows of cornstalks. The motion blur transformed them into green- and khaki-colored walls. On the opposite side of the highway, cars and trucks raced by; rain merged with the motion blurred colors and transformed everything into asterisks and lozenges of light.

Feigning a coughing fit, dad fanned away cigarette smoke. He rolled down the windows and said,

—I wish you'd quit.

—I have no will power.

—Living a long life can be one hell of a motivator.

—I know. I know. But life sucks sometimes. I'm not sure I want to be an old man.

His triangles shifted, shifted, but I remember how sad he looked, how sad and disappointed, and hurt, like his eyes were weighted and glossy, and he couldn't believe his son, his own fucking child, could or would say such a thing.

—I wish I could go back, I said, —and apologize. I wish I could talk to you again, hear your voice again. In real time. Not as a memory.

—Everything's crawling now.

Cars and trucks clotted the highway.

—I remember your voice and yet I don't remember it, I said. —Already I'm losing things, replacing and corrupting so many fucking memories.

—I won't be a happy camper if I miss my appointment.

—And I dread your funeral. I absolutely dread it. With every fiber of my being.

—Tell me about it, he said. —It takes six months to see this doctor. If I miss my appointment ...

—I just want to escape. Like I feel like I just want to run away, far away, so I don't have to see you lying there, face covered in cosmetics ... lying there in that fucking box. Just meat. Meat resembling my father.

Dad laughed.

—Some aspects of getting older are better than others, he said.

—Do you think suicide is virtuous?

—Virtuous, lamentable, appalling, selfish: these are just frameworks for interpretation, Sarah said. —The act in and of itself is just a series of decisions made and motions executed. Everything else is reflection or interpretation.

—Do you regret attempting it?

—Sometimes I do. Sometimes I don't. I don't know; I don't really think about it.

—But that feeling, that emptiness ... when it consumes you ... do you think suicide is a proportionate response?

—Again, "proportionate response": it's a framework for interpreting the act. I think when you're suffering, and especially if you're suffering for long periods of time, and if your suffering rots your brain so that everything you see is framed by your suffering ... I think sometimes you want to end the suffering, you know? I'm not saying it's right or selfless, but ...

—What goes through your mind ... What went through your mind when you did it?

—You tell me.

—Funny.

—I don't know. What goes through your mind when you're slicing cheese? You're conscious of the act but you're usually thinking about something else. I imagine it's the same with suicide.

—You imagine?

—Yeah. Right. I don't know ... I guess I've never really thought about it. And my memory ... I think the stress or the trauma or whatever affected the encoding process, corrupted it maybe. I don't remember much. And when I do think about it, on those rare occasions, it's like I'm inventing much of it as I'm constructing it, you know?

—Does it scare you?

—Does what scare me?

—The sadness? The emptiness? How everything feels gray and dead?

—It doesn't scare me ...

—"Scare" is probably the wrong word. What I mean is ...

—Why this interest in suicide?

—Curious, I guess.

—Your emptiness is hollowing you out, isn't it?

—I whisper alone. I'm quiet. Meaningless.

—Doesn't Alice ... doesn't her addition subtract the emptiness?

—Did Cynthia's?

—...

—It's not loneliness, I said. —I love Alice, and I do feel better when I'm around her, but ...

Loneliness might be a sufficient condition for emptiness but it's not a necessary condition. My emptiness has nothing to do with her or with an evolved need to socialize or whatever. I don't ...

—Yet death scares you.

—It fucking terrifies me.

—So then why would you even consider suicide?

—I'm not considering it.

—It certainly sounds like you are.

—I'm just trying to understand what leads people there.

—But why?

—So I can avoid it.

—But you can't avoid it.

—...

—Assume a hypothetical: you attempt it. You come close, so close they have to revive you in the ambulance. And so you struggle to get over it. How do you get over it?

—...

—The method of loci, she said, —the way the ancient Greeks and Romans remembered stuff: by picturing places with which they were familiar and encoding new information into those memories. That, combined with the misinformation effect: implant the tools to get over it, so, to your mind, the healing process began years ago.

—You're a figment of my imagination, aren't you?

—Who's to say you're not a figment of mine? here to help me overcome another attempt?

—I could ask you the same question.

The stars blinked. Shimmered. Clouds crawled in front of them, seeming to slice through me, or erase them. The moon glowed, backlit a cluster of clouds, burned a moon-shaped image into them. A bat drifted atop a row of trees. And I leaned back on the porch and shut my eyes. Clenching a cigarette between my lips, eyes still closed, I took a drag and blew smoke through my nose.

The rumble of a car up the street caught my attention. Through the gaps between streetlights I saw two headlights. The car passed beneath the streetlights. Blue spiraled toward me: Alice's car.

I jumped to my feet and thrust my hands into my pockets. I paced up and down, up and down the sidewalk. Alice stopped in front of the house and killed the engine. The dome light turned on. Light filled the cabin. Glancing down, she fiddled with something, seemed to search for something. Light ricocheted off her, haloed her head, and sort of bleached the outline of her hair.

The ground squished. It resembled meat marbled with fat; it surrounded me. At first it horrified me, but the feeling dissipated. So I paced on the sidewalk. I paced and waited for Alice, waited for her to find whatever she was looking for, or complete whatever she was doing, and get out of the car.

Sounds like caws and screeches echoed and rolled down the street. Noises like thunder shook the meat—but it wasn't thunder: it sounded like explosives detonated in aluminum garbage cans.

The dome light went out. Alice opened the door and stepped outside. Her triangles shifted, shifted, but I detected a smile.

—Hey.

—Hey.

I grabbed her hand and led her to the porch. We sat and studied the sky—the stars, the clouds, the moon—as I finished my cigarette. Meat beneath us palpitated and hissed. Alice didn't seem to notice it.

—Such a pretty night, she said.

My stomach fluttered. I wanted to hug her, to kiss her, to tell her everything—how much I loved her, how happy I felt, how desperately I needed her.

—Are you upset? she said.

—No. Fuck no.

—Then why are you so quiet?

—I don't know.

—This is going to change things, she said. —It changes things.

—And you're sure ...?

—Even without the test, I know. I can ... I don't know ... feel it.

I tried to say something, anything, but my brain shut down.

—Tell me you want this.

—I want this.

—You're not going to leave me?

—Why the fuck would I leave you?

—Some guys get weird when it comes to the whole father thing.

—I'm not like other guys.

She squeezed the back of my neck and kissed me.

—So what do we do now?

—Get an apartment, I said. —Maybe get married.

The shifting triangles couldn't obscure her smile.

—Yeah?

A man appeared behind Alice. Dressed in black, with long hair and an unkempt beard, he seemed familiar—but his triangles shifted, shifted, shifted, and I couldn't pinpoint his identity.

—In that order? Alice laughed.

—I'd prefer it, I said, laughing.

—You have to fight it, the man said.

—Fight what?

—The feeling consuming you.

—But I love her, I said. —Why would I fight it?

—Not her. The feeling you get, that empty feeling. Fight it.

—So when do you want to look for a place? Alice said.

—As soon as possible. Tomorrow. Yesterday, even.

—Everything is broken, the man said. —Everything is broken ... or dying ... or dead.

—Can we afford it?

—We'll figure something out.

—Dad dies, he said. —Then everything gets worse. Worse even then Alice and I lost our child.

—What are you talking about? Dad's in the house, watching TV.

—Not now, the man said. —He is dead. Where I'm at, he is. Then everything dies. Everything is broken and dead and ... The emptiness consumes you. It fucking consumes you and ... It's not the way it's always been. It's different now.

—I don't know what you're talking about.

—You've got to fight it. You have to bracket the emptiness, set it aside, and fight it. After your attempt, you'll suffer. And you'll want to do it again. You'll fantasize about it, but you've got to fight it. You've got to address it head on, deal with it without dwelling on it. You'll get over it. Remember that. You always get over things. But you've got to fight it.

—I don't understand.

—You're not meant to.

—Then why are you telling me this?

—I'm not telling you anything, he said. —I'm committing something to memory.

The funeral home director, pen in hand, watches us without saying a word, without so much as breathing.

Alice squeezes my hand. She sniffles.

Mom stares at the table, her eyes vacant.

And but Dad's dead. Dad's dead. And he's somewhere in here, in this building; meat lying on a slab somewhere; and but he's fucking dead.

—I can't ... I've got to ...

But is it real?

Is this real?

I jump to my feet and bolt through the door and up the stairs. Outside, the sun hits me. Kids on bicycles rolls by, laughing. I swear one of them looks like me at that age. I run down the sidewalk, stop near the street, light a cigarette. I want to cry.

Fuck. I want to cry. And dad's dead. And sooner or later mom and my sisters, Alice and everyone I know, or will ever know, everyone I've known and loved or forgotten, will die. And ... I want to cry. I feel like crying. But I don't think I'll ever cry again.

14.

Sometimes everything feels like glass, like glass sliding into your veins or replacing the myelin covering your axons. And so when you move, or when you think, or when you somehow trigger a memory, the pain tears through you. Like imagine filling a bag with sheets of glass and then swinging it over your shoulder and slamming it into the ground. Repeatedly. Imagine doing this until the glass breaks, until thousands of shards fill the bag. And then imagine dumping them into a bathtub and slipping into the tub and submerging yourself in glass. Then imagine every move, every twitch, triggers pain, unspeakable pain; and imagine every thought and memory, every flight of fancy or mental image, triggers a sort of internal equivalent to this pain; and but imagine every facet of your existence, everything you do—both mental and physical—triggers mind-numbing pain. Searing pain. Now imagine you're not submerged in a tub of glass; imagine lying in bed in the middle of the night, or at work or school, and every move you make, every twitch, triggers such pain; imagine experiencing this for days, weeks, years: every move you make or every mental activity, even the slightest activity, triggers unspeakable pain. Then imagine lying in bed at night, trying to stay still, trying to evacuate every thought while somehow trying to prevent new thoughts from forming. And now imagine this pain as a component of something far worse, something far more dreadful and dreaded: everything feels empty and everything feels gray and everything feels dead; an empty pit in your stomach secretes something like a neurotoxin, which races to your brain, melts neurotransmitters; but this thing like a neurotoxin is something like depression, although it's not depression—it's far more sinister, like typical suicidal depression is a diluted form of this; like this thing like a neurotoxin is something like 10^{14} times more potent than depression. And so imagine living with this. Imagine coping with it or succumbing to it. Imagine confronting it or acknowledging it. Imagine living with it. Second by second, minute by minute, hour by hour, day in and day fucking out. This pain and emptiness, this torment and dread. Imagine it. I dare you.

Time crawled as I scrawled in my notebook. The minute hand on the clock had skipped at least three or four digits, but it felt like eight or nine— or one or two. Writing had, for the most part, silenced my brain, yet something felt off. Something felt ...

Color drained from the walls and the floor. Gray replaced everything. But not everything seemed monochromatic; instead, the world seemed as though only the moon lit it. The apartment felt empty. It felt both alive and not alive—both p and ¬p.

The walls pulsed and rippled. The floor rolled like a wave, rising and curling, refusing to collapse. I dropped my pen and crossed into the kitchen and turned on the vent and lit a cigarette. The kitchen floor mimicked the dining room floor and so I stood atop a more or less frozen wave.

Five minutes until Alice would leave work. She had an appointment with the obstetrician—a routine checkup—but I couldn't remember if it was today or tomorrow. When it came to things like remembering doctor's appointments, I didn't do anything to break gender stereotypes.

Water drip-drip-dripped from the faucet. A knife sat on the counter, near the sink, and, glancing at it, I felt—and fought—the urge to pick it up and slice open my veins.

I backed away from the sink, staring at the knife.

Then I saw it:

I lunged at the knife and scooped it up and held the tip near my eye and hammered the handle with the heel of my hand. The blade split my eyeball and pierced my brain, and I collapsed.

I needed Alice I needed Alice where the fuck was she why wasn't she home already where the fuck the fuck where the fuck was she

Backing out of the kitchen, I took a drag from my cigarette and scooped up my phone and sent her a message. Gripping the phone, I waited—and more or less pleaded—for it to go off. To receive a text. From Alice, my darling, amazing wife—that's all I wanted: a text.

The phone didn't go off, so I sent another text: "Where are you?"

I waited.

And waited.

Then, a text: "on my way to drs."

Fuck.

"What time?"—my reply.

Tensions bloomed inside me. The knife: I saw it without glancing at it; I felt it, on the counter, without focusing on it. It sort of hovered over the counter, it sort of glowed and hummed. It called to me.

I ran into the dining room and picked up my pen and tried to write. The room transformed into the bathroom. I sat on the floor in the shower and sliced open my forearms. Blood covered my arms, my legs, the floor. Darkness devoured my peripheral vision, raced to the center of my field of vision. The absence of everything darkened the universe, and it felt …

it felt …

… good.

The bathroom transformed into the dining room. I was sitting at the table, holding the pen. Fear coursed through me, jolted me. I jumped up and darted into the kitchen and lit another cigarette. No new message from Alice. I dropped the phone on the counter, nearly flung it. I went back to the dining room and grabbed the pen, putting it to paper.

Write, goddamn it. Write your way out of this.

He kicked open the door and leapt into the room. The door behind me flung open. A man ran into the room and crouched in a defensive position. *Scanning the room, he searched for Jack, for evidence of him, and then he crossed the room and picked out a cigarette smoldering in the ashtray.* The man dashed into the kitchen and sifted through the ashtray. He lifted a filter—still smoldering—and examined it.

I dropped the pen and switched my attention to Alice, to my cell phone. The man vanished. I crossed the room and scooped up my cell phone. Alice still hadn't responded. Goddamn it. Why hadn't she responded? Did the doctor deliver bad news? Was something wrong? Then ... Don't think like that. Don't think at all. Just shut it down. Shut that motherfucking brain down. But how? What would Sartre do? Could you will yourself to switch from reflective to unreflective consciousness?

I called my parents.

—Hey, Dault. Dad said.

—Hey. I'm just making sure my phone worked.

Laughing, he said, —I do that, too. Then: — Look, son, I'd like to talk but mom and I are on our way out the door.

—All right, I'll call you later.

—Take care.

If I could make or receive phone calls, then I could send and receive texts; I could make or receive phone calls; therefore, I could send and receive texts. So where was she? Why the fuck wasn't she responding?

I needed to ... I needed to ...

The knife.

It hovered in front of me. My reflection in the blade betrayed shifting triangles.

Then ...

Across the room, a mirror reflected light, transmitted information: a man stood in the back of the room. I whipped my head around. Nothing. But he was in the mirror, watching me.

—But I can't remember if the mirror was here, he said, —or near the door.

A mirror appeared on the wall beside the door. The man's triangles shifted.

—Not that it matters.

He scratched his chin and clenched his beard in his fist.

—This is one of the worst days of my life, he said. —You won't remember it because it hasn't happened yet. But I do. I remember it. In a little while, Alice will walk through that door and tell you the baby is dead. And you'll think ... And at some point you'll acknowledge the absurdity of it. Of all of it. I mean, earlier in the day I was struggling ... I mean, I remember fucking struggling to defeat the urge to fucking kill myself, and then ... When I realized our baby was dead, I fucking ... I remember how devastating everything was ... how I felt; and I remember associating that feeling, sort of grafting it onto my family and to Alice, imagining they'd probably feel that way, exactly that way, if I had lost my struggle. If I had killed myself. And ... Things don't get easy, he said. —I've got to remember that. I've got to drill that into my head. And sometimes things don't get better. I've got to remember that, too. But that doesn't mean everything is empty. Even when things feel empty and gray, even when they feel dead, I've got to remember that things aren't empty or gray or dead. It's all in my head. And ... Well, yeah, they're platitudes, but ... and so platitudes are exactly what I need right now, I mean ...

The man in the mirror vanished. Another man appeared in the room, brandishing a knife. He sobbed and gasped and dug the blade into his forearm and dragged it across his flesh. Crying, he sliced open his other forearm. Blood squirted out. It splashed against the walls and hit the ceiling, like in an over-the-top horror film. He dropped the blade, fell to his knees, and cried—bawled, really.

—Don't dwell dwell get over it over get over

He disappeared.

The wall to my left rattled and trembled. Cracks raced from the ceiling to the floor. The walls buckled; the floor extruded. Plaster, wood, bricks exploded outward. Chunks flew around the room. Floated and coalesced. A vortex ripped open the ceiling and sucked the chunks and pieces outside.

Bit by bit, piece by piece, they raced to the sun.

The grass and the sidewalk, the streets and the trees, the sky and the clouds imploded and flew away, and the absence of everything—ineffable; like darkness but not like anything, really—gnawed on the edges of the world.

I ran into the dining room and leaped under the table.

The ground shook. The walls rattled.

Bit by bit, piece by piece, everything in the room, the apartment, the universe disintegrated and vanished.

Even "I" vanished.

My body vanished.

The absence of everything dominated me. Although I was conscious of it, I wasn't conscious of being conscious of it, and so I more or less obtained in the moment without reflecting on the moment.

My consciousness was what it was, and it was what it was not. And everything felt calm somehow. Relaxing, somehow.

—It's not real. Nothing is real, don't you see?

The voice split the absence of everything. I felt the presence of another consciousness—or was it mine? Was I observing another consciousness? experiencing it? Or was my consciousness somehow conscious of itself, therefore observing or experiencing an imagined, or maybe remembered, moment?

—If there is something "real," something beyond us, then we don't have direct access to it. What we experience is, for us, what is "real." But two people who share the same spot, relatively speaking, in the spatial-temporal plane, rarely experience the same thing. So what's "real" for me isn't necessarily what's "real" for you. There might be intersections between our experiences, but there will be disjointed sets, too. We can discern the things independent of us only by examining the intersections; from there, we can make certain inferences, though they, by nature, must remain broad. But it's the disjointed sets that define who we are; the disjointed sets, in the end, are drawn from our "experience" of the "real."

—So you're saying we can't ever know what's real?

Light blinded me. The world bled over the darkness, and I returned to our apartment.

Moonlight slipped into the window, carved a triangle into shadows on the ceiling. Alice slept beside me. I rolled onto my side and kissed her. She opened her mouth, closed it, sort of smiling. As she rolled onto her stomach, she flung out her arm.

Something lodged in my echoic memory played and replayed in my head. "Can't ever know what's real? what's real? you're saying we can't ever know what's real?"

Had I dreamt that conversation? Or was it real?

—I'm saying what's "real," "reality," isn't a thing independent of human beings. "Reality" is a product of human beings. If things exist independently of us, they're not "real"; they're only "real" when we experience them.

Everything vanished again. The absence of everything dominated again. Reflective or unreflective, my consciousness obtained without a body again. And I heard that voice; I tried to discern its source again.

—So then how do you know that what you're experiencing is real?

—Everything I experience is "real." At least to me. I can only attempt to determine if things obtain independently of me by contrasting observations made by other people with observations I make.

—You kind of lost me.

—If you and I are standing in a room, and you point to a window and say, "who broke the window," then I can glance in that direction; and if I see a window, a broken window, then I can compare my observation with yours and infer that a broken window obtains independently of you and me. But let's say the window isn't broken. Let's say a spider has built a web over the window: to you, from your point of view, the spider web resembles a crack, and so you interpret this information as a cracked window; but from my point of view, it's clearly a spider web, so I don't interpret this information as a cracked window. So when you point and say, "who broke the window," then you and I are, in that moment, experiencing two different "realities"; and we'll only ever agree that a window obtains independently of us. Everything else is open to interpretation.

—Which means everything depends on our brains.

—Exactly.

8.22

Nothing works. Nothing fucking works for me anymore.

I'm at all places at once and I experience all experiences simultaneously. For example, I'm standing in the kitchen talking to Alice and then a second later I'm at a restaurant with Sarah. Then I'm a toddler sleeping on the couch with my father. Then I'm in a room that looks like the inside of a heart, talking to some faceless woman who's trying to explain axiomatic set theory to me.

I'm everywhere and yet it feels as though I'm nowhere—both p and ¬p.

Everything is broken. Everything is fucked.

8.23

A woman came to me last night. She appeared pretty much out of nowhere. I was in the gas station yesterday morning, and I saw her, this woman I've never seen before, but who struck me as familiar. Then she showed up in my apartment, and we talked about what's real and what isn't—or if "real" even makes sense.

I don't know if she's real, this woman, or if she's a figment of my imagination.

Later—

I don't know what "real" even means anymore. And I don't know what is, and isn't, a figment of my imagination anymore.

Later—

Started writing a novel about depression, death, suicide. Not sure where it's going, but I do know this: if today is any indication, I'll be writing this one at a fucking snail's pace.

8.24

Everything feels dead to me. The urge to kill myself overwhelms me at times, but I manage to defeat it. I always manage to defeat it. But sometimes I fantasize about it. Sometimes I wonder what it's like to be dead, or I wonder how my death—especially from suicide—might affect other people. I do care how it might affect other people, which is probably the reason I haven't done it yet. But it gets fucking exhausting, living the life I do, experiencing things the way I experience them. And when things feel empty and dead, so fucking empty and dead, in perpetuity, it gets hard, and it stays hard. Life, for me, is like a never ending struggle to refrain from killing myself. But I think—fear—that it's a war I'll eventually lose. I mean, at some point I'm going to stop fighting it. It feels as though at some point I'll stop fighting it. I hope that isn't the case. But the struggle gets so fucking exhausting, especially when everything feels broken and empty, gray and dead.

n.

Birds **fly overhead**, against a gray sky. Rain drips, drips, drips; it's more like a leaky faucet than a storm. A raindrop hits the sidewalk and transforms the concrete into a darker shade—brown against khaki. It marbles the sidewalk as thunder groans.

The atmosphere—gray skies and rain—is fitting somehow, as if Sarah has somehow managed to transfer her feelings to the world itself. Or, rather, as if she's managed to transfer the feelings she should experience ...

And this is the thing: she should be miserable. Right now, grief should devour her. But she's not miserable. More than anything else, she's empty.

And that's another thing: like are people miserable in these situations because the situations force those emotions, or are people miserable because other people expect them to be miserable, and so, over time, everyone inculcates and internalizes these expectations, which certain situations trigger?

But then ...

Who gives a fuck?

She lights a cigarette and hops onto the hood of her car and swings her legs. The funeral home is empty. The parking lot is empty. Minutes earlier, she had delivered an outfit for her father. The funeral home was the only place she'd visited that had no smell. Like she can't remember an odor, and she didn't acknowledge one then. Someone must have built the fucking thing on a geographic anomaly: one of the few places on the planet that either stifles odors or disables the cilia in nasal cavities.

A person-shaped hole warps and splits the space-time continuum beside her. It shimmers and refracts light, warping everything behind it. The hole emits sound, little more than a screech, really, as light behind it shimmers and fades.

Smoking her cigarette, Sarah tries to ignore the person-shaped hole.

It's her brain again. She knows that now.

She tries to kill the "I" by focusing on the building, by trying to switch her consciousness to consciousness of the building and not consciousness of consciousness.

The universe blinks off and on again. Sarah's standing in the bathroom in her apartment. This was, god, years ago—right before she tried to kill herself, before her second, and, it should go without saying, failed—attempt.

She remembers talking to someone. But she doesn't remember anyone being there.

But ... and who was it? It was a woman—she remembers that.

—Bracket your experience, the woman had said. —You're here but not here. You're not conscious of this room; you're conscious of being conscious of this room, this place, this time. Bracket that. Cut off the consciousness of being conscious and focus your intention solely on what's in front of you. Bracket consciousness of you, what you call "I" when referring to the internal thing your consciousness is conscious of.

In the mirror, Sarah's triangles shift. She tries to focus on ... What? Where was she? In her father's bedroom. She'd fallen out of the closet and landed on the floor, so ...

Bricks, brown bricks: the side of the funeral home. She clearly sees the side of the funeral home. Rain smacks her face.

The "I" has vanished. She's staring at the clouds but she's not conscious of staring at the clouds. The "I" is only embedded in consciousness when consciousness is consciousness of consciousness.

Shit ... That's it; that's what the woman was trying to tell her. That's what she meant when she told Sarah to bracket her experience. Shut down consciousness of consciousness. Shut down the "I."

—Where's Alice?

—School.

—Why aren't you there? Sarah says. —Playing hooky?

—I don't go to school on Wednesdays. Daulton lights a cigarette. —So what's this urgent matter, this thing-that-couldn't-wait?

—I've figured out how to orient myself, like when my brain's fucking with me. I've found a way to stop it.

—What are you talking about?

—You have to focus. You have to erase reflection. You can't ... The thing is, you've got to learn to bracket your experience ...

—Bracket it?

—Yes, so you ... What you've got to do is ... you've got to kill the "I," the ego; it's only present when your consciousness is consciousness of itself. When consciousness is consciousness of something outside yourself, and it's wholly unreflective, then the "I," the ego, fucking vanishes. And when it vanishes ... you orient yourself.

Daulton blows smoke into the vent above the stove. He grins.

—You've got to be fucking kidding me, she says. —You don't believe me.

—You explain this to me as though it's new. I taught you this ...

—Bullshit.

—A few months ago, he says. —Remember? We were at ... what's it called? that restaurant near 421? I explained it to you there, all of it.

—You did not.

—Yes, I did. Bracketing? That's a concept I borrowed from Husserl. Don't you remember my summary of Phenomenology? And "consciousness of"? That's intentionality. Also from Husserl. And Sartre. And what about ... the

299

"I" is only present when consciousness is self-reflective? You seriously don't remember that?

—No, I ...

She sits on a chair beside the dining room table. She doesn't remember the conversation.

—Well, let's assume I'm wrong, he says. — Let's assume, for the sake of argument, that I didn't discuss Phenomenology and Existentialism with you. Are you familiar with it?

She shakes her head.

—Yet you're familiar with Husserl's language: "bracketing." And you're familiar with intentionality, specifically as it's used by Husserl and Sartre. You don't find that weird?

She shakes her head.

—I'm not trying to be an asshole here, he says. —I'm trying to give you the benefit of the doubt. I mean, maybe I'm wrong. The way our brains work, it's possible that I fabricated the memory. But let me ask you this: who taught you these concepts? Or did they come to you naturally?

—I remember a woman.

—What woman?

—This was years ago, long before I met you.

—So she taught you these concepts?

—More like she instructed me.

—On how to use them?

—Yes.

—And you have no idea who she is?

Sarah shakes her head.

—Yet something tells me, Daulton says, —that you have your suspicions.

—I think it was ...

Daulton turns off the fan above the stove.

—Sorry, he says, —I couldn't hear you.

—I suspect, Sarah says, —that it's me.

—What's you? You lost me.

—I think I've embedded myself in my memories.

—To instruct yourself?

She nods.

—But let me ask you this, Daulton says. —When did you embed these instructions? And when could you have done it, considering that you've only figured out how to "bracket" things today?

Sarah examines the carpet. She twitches her foot.

—I don't know, she says.

—Sarah.

Daulton's triangles shift, shift, shift.

—You think this is the present, don't you?

Daulton's flesh melts and liquefies. It rolls down his skull and covers his clothes. His face gone, his skull exposed, he drops to the floor and dissolves.

Fear tears through Sarah. She blinks and sits up. Her apartment is dark; the television is off; and the screen warps and bends the moon, which peeks through the window.

She remembers a conversation she had with Daulton, the conversation about Husserl and Sartre, about intentionality and bracketing things. Does it work? Could it work? Would it work?

Marcus snores. Why isn't that a surprise?

Sarah's sitting on a chair beside the couch—where the lump formerly known as Marcus impersonates a lawn mower—and stares at the cherry on her cigarette. In the dark, the cherry leaves tracers behind it as Sarah swings the cigarette back and forth, back and forth; and it's soothing somehow. Almost hypnotic.

So would it work? Could she bracket her experience? Was that even what Husserl meant by "bracketing"? But then ... did it matter what he meant? Perhaps she could take the idea, twist it and flip it and fix things. Perhaps she could fix things.

Maybe things aren't even broken.

She snubs out her cigarette and strolls into the bathroom. After turning on the light and locking the door, she wanders to the sink and examines her face in the mirror. It's pale and gray. Shadows obscure it. They seem to emphasize the skull beneath the meat.

She tries to think about something—but what? She tries to retrieve a memory—but which one? She tries to imagine ... What?

Something.

Fuck.

Anything.

A strand of hair is curled around the bottom of the sink, near the plug. She plucks it out and tosses it away. It floats to the ground. Cynthia hated that. Whenever she found a strand of hair on a surface in the bathroom, especially the sink, she'd say,

—It's like a worm, like a worm on the sidewalk after it rains. It's fucking gross.

Cynthia leaned into the sink and tried to snag a strand of hair with a pair of tweezers, but the business end of the tweezers didn't touch, and so the strand slipped through the gap. Every single time.

This was when Sarah was twenty-five. She remembers standing near the bathroom door, more or less chuckling as Cynthia struggled to remove the hair without touching it.

—It's not funny.

—You have how many millions on your head? Sarah said. —Yet I don't see you grabbing tweezers when a few strands hang over your face.

—This is different.

—It is not.

—It's fucking disgusting.

—It's hair. Sarah picked up the hair and dropped it into the wastebasket.

—But on surfaces ... Cynthia shivered.

One by one, the tiles on the wall dropped off, revealing pulsing meat beneath them. The floor rocked and shifted, as if sitting atop an ocean, and domes of blood bubbled on the ceiling.

—You know what I think? Sarah said. —I think a worm traumatized you as a kid and immediately after that you saw a hair on a counter or something and connected the two.

Cynthia kissed her. —Always the thinker.

She sauntered into the kitchen. Meat had replaced the walls. Blood dripped from the ceiling. Cynthia stepped over a cat-shaped lump of meat as she made her way to the sink, where she turned on the tap and filled a glass. Blood had replaced water. A few drops ran down Cynthia's chin when she took a drink.

She wiped the blood with her sleeve, smearing it across her cheek

—What? she said. —Why are you looking at me like that?

—You're gorgeous, you know that?

Cynthia's triangles shifted, shifted, but Sarah remembered, at more or less this point, Cynthia's grin blooming into a full smile.

—Liar, she said.

Blood replaced photons, turning everything red.

—Am not. Everything thing every every it's not not I don't think it's it's not worth it

She slid to the left. Moved as though she were an animated character missing key frames. A knife appeared in her hand. She dropped it. Blood cruised down her forearms. She screeched and cried. Her triangles shifted and bulged, twisted and spun, as color drained from her flesh.

Water flowed from her mouth. Bubbles popped, emitting sobs.

—I can't it's not worth it I'm sorry sorry I'm sorry Sarah

And that's how Sarah found her: lying on the floor. Blood flowing from her arms, Cynthia sobbed and mumbled something about forgiveness.

The room trembled. Blood ran down the walls and rained from the ceiling. It drenched Sarah as she darted across the room. Crying, she scooped up Cynthia, cradled her. Then she dialed 911.

Cynthia's face turned the color of ash. Her triangles shifted, sort of shimmered.

Sarah screamed into her cell phone, all but ordering the 911 operator to send a fucking fleet of ambulances.

The blood oh god the blood how the fuck is this happening of the all the people all the fucking people she never not once suspected Cynthia of doing it and what the fuck is the holdup I'm going to lose her lose her goddamn it send the fucking ambulances now like right fucking now what's the problem

Bracket your experience.

The bathroom replaced the kitchen. Tiles replaced meat. The bathroom faded and Sarah was back in the kitchen again, sitting on meat, cradling Cynthia again.

You're here but not here.

Cynthia vanished. Sarah was standing in the bathroom again, staring at her reflection again.

—I can't it's not worth it I'm sorry sorry I'm sorry Sarah

The fucking 911 operator wouldn't shut up.

Cynthia stopped sobbing.

Sarah was back in the kitchen again. Both tiles and meat covered the walls, the ceiling, the floor. Photons mixed with blood and strobed the room.

You're not conscious of this room; you're conscious of being conscious of this room, this place, this time.

She made a face in the mirror, a face like a robot trying to cry. She screwed her eyebrows upward and jutted her lower lip. She even sobbed but it came out like a cough. Nothing worked. Nothing seemed to work. She wanted to cry but—goddamn it—nothing seemed to work.

Back in the kitchen, the floor pulsated. Blood and light rained from the ceiling and bounced around the room. Cynthia made a sound resembling a moan, or a groan. Sarah remembers how fucking terrifying it was, that sound, like a fucking death rattle. The 911 operator jabbered in Sarah's ear, asking about Cynthia. She ordered Sarah to check Cynthia's pulse, but the blood oh god the fucking blood oh god

Bracket that.

Look at it look at it look at it goddamn it Stare at the mirror the mirror remember the mirror and the bathroom Focus on it goddamn it Focus

Cut off the consciousness of being conscious and focus your intention solely on what's in front of you.

The universe blinked off.

Bracket your experience.

The universe blinked on again.

Sarah was standing in the bathroom in the dark, examining her reflection: a robot trying to cry. The emptiness in her stomach screamed, "Cynthia, Cynthia, Cynthia." Then it screamed, "Dad, Dad, Dad."

Tears filled her eyes and rolled down her cheeks. She dropped to the floor, squatted over the tiles, and she covered her eyes and cried. She cried.

15.

11.28

You sometimes don't know what's real. Sometimes you realize how idiotic it is to ask what's real. At other times you don't even know if it makes sense. On the one hand, if you're inquiring about reality in the subjective sense, then you know everything you experience is "real" by virtue of the fact that experience is a necessary condition for "real"—in the subjective sense; but, on the other hand, if you're inquiring about reality in anything like an objective sense, then the question more or less breaks down for you.

"Reality," as a word, as part of a phrase, even as a concept, should be vanquished. The human species should eradicate it; we should treat it like smallpox and work to undermine and then to destroy it.

Few words have led to more confusion than the word "reality." Humans can use the word in a variety of sentences to convey a variety of senses, each of which might share little more than superficial similarities. And yet at each utterance people seem to operate under the assumption that the meaning or definition of "reality" remains fixed, unchangeable.

So what is real? This question has tormented me for years. From conversations I've had with other people, it seems as though it's a question most people take for granted.

Lying in bed, my wife beside me, I'm writing this and trying to ward off sleep. And so, lying in bed in the dark, I wonder aloud, "What is real?"

It sounds stupid when it leaves my mouth. It sounds almost nonsensical, as if the answer is so obvious that only a braindead troglodyte would even conjure up such a question.

So let me ask you: what is real?

Everything we see or hear, feel or smell or taste, et cetera, is recreated in our brains, derived from information received by our sense organs. Glancing at a light in the next room, I take for granted that I'm experiencing a light in a room modeled by my brain. Is the light real? Well, certainly; I just saw it. But what if it wasn't a light? What if my eyes transmitted ambiguous information, which was difficult to interpret or model, and so my brain settled on an interpretation that aligned with previous experience? There's a small light in the living room on the table. I often see it when I'm lying in bed. Since the information transmitted by my eyes was ambiguous, my brain removed the ambiguity with little more than an educated guess—in this case, with a guess founded on information stored in my brain; not with information from the "real" "world."

These processes work endlessly, day in and day out, from birth until death. Every face I see, every person or object I encounter, is filtered to various regions of my brain, which then interprets it. But when the information is ambiguous, my brain does little more than make educated guesses. Then it constructs and reconstructs models that I take for granted, models that I deny are models.

While I'm looking at this page on the computer, it rarely occurs to me that I'm experiencing a model produced by my brain; instead I, like I imagine most people, take the models for granted; like most people, I tend to operate as though I'm interacting with "reality" unfiltered, as though my eyes are nothing more than curved sheets of glass that "I'm" peering through. But if you simply stop and consider such a proposition, then you immediately acknowledge its absurdity.

We do not encounter "reality"; we create it. "Reality" is a product of our brains, a series of models our brains construct. And since we don't have access to the processes constructing these models, we ignore them or overlook them or take them for granted.

And that can mislead us. It can distort things. It can trick us into thinking the "reality" we experience is identical to the "reality" other people experience. And if other people experience the same "reality" that I experience, then other people should see things or think things or believe in things that my experience of "reality" presents to me.

That "reality" is a thing outside of people, as opposed to the product of cognitive processes, is taken for granted so frequently that when two people encounter the same scenario and yet experience the "reality" of the situation differently, then one person usually accuses the other person of lying, which might not be true. Although lying is always a possibility, experiencing "reality" differently, in which, at some point, those experiences diverge, is also possible.

Yet for so many of us, "reality" is a thing people cannot experience differently.

Take Sarah: she experiences "reality" differently and assumes that everyone shares the experience, and so, time after time, she attempts suicide because she conflates "reality" with objects existing independently of her.

And take me: sometimes I wonder if I'm "real" or a figment of someone's imagination, sometimes I wonder if everything is a dream or a hallucination, sometimes I wonder if our universe is a simulation inside a computer—all of which are possible.

I sometimes wonder if people I've encountered are figments of my imagination, especially people with whom I no longer communicate, so I have little more than memories of them. Are those people real? Are those memories false? Or are they figments of my imagination?

I wonder this. At times I find myself wondering about Sarah. Is she real, or is she a figment of my imagination? Or am I a figment of her imagination? Perhaps I'm not writing this at all. Perhaps she's only imagining that I'm writing this, and so, at some point, I assume I have written it.

But then what's "real?"

Is Sarah real? Am I real? Are you real?

Think about that for a moment. To me, you're not real; you're a hypothetical human being who might, at some point, read this. But to you, you're so obviously real that the question has probably never even occurred to you. Yet here you are reading this. But to me you're not reading this—because, at this moment, all readers are hypothetical human beings; to me, at this moment, you are a figment of my imagination.

But am I a figment or your imagination? Or is Sarah?

Now this is where things get interesting:

Is the Daulton portrayed in this journal real? Is Sarah?

Perhaps the Daulton portrayed here is entirely fictional. Perhaps Sarah is entirely fictional. Perhaps Daulton and Sarah are hybrids of fact and fiction. Either way, you have no way of knowing what's "real" when it comes to Daulton and Sarah.

But what about this? Since the written language is composed of symbols that we're trained to unpack, to decrypt, to interpret, all written languages serve as little more than instructions that you interpret based on your training. That Daulton and Sarah are presented to you solely as instructions encoded in symbols is evidence that both Daulton and Sarah are, for you while you're reading this, figments of your imagination.

So whether the Daulton portrayed here is "real," whether the Sarah portrayed here is "real," depends entirely on the context in which the word "real" is used.

Now apply this to your life, apply this to your family and friends, your daily activities, your memories, and ask yourself this: what's "real?" which are false or distorted memories? what are figments of my imagination?

11.29

Why do I keep this journal? For whom am I writing it? Alice? Sarah? my family or friends? Is this the journal of a madman? Is this a pathetic attempt to come to terms with Dad's death—which I continue to avoid—or to come to terms with the miscarriage, or even the state of my brain?

Or is it something like the world's longest suicide note?

The ring sat in a box, surrounded by necklaces, in a glass case beneath the cash register. I hadn't noticed it until after I'd purchased a candy bar.

The lady behind the counter grinned. Her triangles shifted, shifted, but I remembered a grin, a too-happy expression bunching her face.

—How much is this? I said, or something to that effect.

—Glub glub.

Water poured from her mouth.

Opening my wallet, I said, "I'll take it." The lady grinned again, said something else—"glub glub glub"; she pulled the ring box from the case and set it on the counter.

The ring felt like aluminum or plastic. It was too light. Or was it? Had I actually held a ring before? I couldn't remember.

—Yeah, I said, —I'll take it.

A mobile dangled from the ceiling behind the lady. Composed of frosted glass and mirrors, the mobile spun, first clockwise, then counterclockwise. Each mirror, each piece of glass, spun and scattered light across the room.

—Glub?

I handed the lady my credit card.

—Sorry, I said.

Light bounced off the mirrors and danced in the air. It danced behind the lady, seemed to assume the shape of a person. Of a man. Of a man wielding a knife.

—Glub glub. The lady dropped a receipt into the bag.

The light danced behind her. The man with the knife seemed to shimmer.

I crossed the threshold dividing the gift shop from the hospital. The corridor leading to the elevators darkened, as if ashen and gray and ... but not ashen and gray. Walls lined the right side of the corridor; windows lined the left side. Something told me it was afternoon and ... but darkness covered the sky.

—I'm so miserable and depressed and empty, and I don't know why, and I don't know how to stop it. Emptiness consumes me and I just want to sleep. But I can't sleep. Everything looks broken and gray, and everything tastes like ash.

The voice boomed from above, loud but muffled.

Is this real? I touched the wall. It rippled. I touched the window. It rippled. Everything rippled, responded to touch, so from that I inferred I wasn't asleep, or locked somewhere inside the absence of everything—assuming "the absence of everything has an 'inside'" even made sense.

—Everything tastes like everything tastes like everything everything tastes like ash like ash.

I was standing in front of Alice's hospital room door. I don't remember taking the elevator. I only remember standing in the hallway, clutching the ring, which I'd at some point removed from the box. Light crept into the hallway. Bright yet dim, filled with color yet devoid of it, the light crawled toward me. It spit globs of darkened light onto the floors, the walls, as it crawled toward me.

Then ...

A flash. The man with the knife ...

Then ...

Alice beamed.

We were inside a gazebo behind the courthouse. The judge read our vows, which we recited. Mouths moved but didn't produce sound. Nothing produced sound. The sounds of the world had vanished. Alice moved her lips and smiled again. I felt my lips move.

Mom and Dad and my younger brother sat on a bench behind Alice. Their triangles shifted, shifted, shifted. But I remember smiles. And I remember sniffles.

Alice and I kissed. I kissed her like a self-conscious teenager; it was more like a peck than a kiss. She grabbed the back of my head and kissed me. Harder. And I remember no longer feeling like a self-conscious teenager.

Then Dad was standing beside Alice, shaking my hand. Mom squeezed Alice's hand and hugged her.

Alice was standing beside Dad again. His triangles shifted, shifted, but I remember what he'd said: he was proud.

—I'm so miserable and depressed and empty, and I don't know why, and I don't know how to stop it. Emptiness consumes me and I just want to sleep. But I can't sleep. Everything looks broken and gray, and everything tastes like ash like everything tastes like ash like ash.

16.

Darkness. **Light**.

I was lying in bed, in the dark, the night before Dad's funeral, wanting to sleep but not able to sleep. Thoughts crowded my skull—random and unwanted. Alice slept beside me. I wrapped my arm around her, felt her warmth.

I wanted to cry, but I couldn't cry.

Darkness. Light.

I was lying in bed, gazing into the living room. Not able to move. Alice crossed the doorway, disappeared, crossed it again, carrying a pair of stockings.

Darkness. Light.

I was sitting on the stool in front of the stove, smoking a cigarette, chugging an energy drink. Moments earlier, Alice had asked when I was going to get dressed. Her words tumbled around my echoic memory: —Are you you are you going

317

to get dressed get dressed are you going to get dressed soon get dressed soon?

Darkness. Light.

I was standing in the bathroom, glancing at myself in the mirror. Although my triangles shifted, I sensed emptiness, dread, sadness.

Darkness. Light.

We were in the foyer at the funeral home. Alice was standing beside me, clutching my hand. Her triangles shifted, shifted, but I remember she was anxious and sad. She cried. Studying her face, I felt the urge to run outside. It seized me, the urge, but I fought it. I had to stay had to stay had to had to had to stay. But then what did it matter? Dad was dead and sooner or later everyone would be dead, including me, and but so what did it matter?

Date: why bother?

I'm like a ghost among the living: most people don't see me and those who do see me choose to act as though I'm not here. To me, everything seems gray. Everyone seems empty, full of life only when I'm absent. And everything tastes like ash.

I have nothing else to say—though I can't imagine that you're surprised, considering the circumstances under which you're reading this.

The world rattled and trembled. Everything felt electric, as if jolted. My vision dimmed. The world seemed filtered through caffeine and binoculars. And ... But why couldn't I cry?

Alice squeezed my arm. I massaged her shoulder.

Dad looked good, better than I'd hoped. His hair was combed back and his cheeks were flush. He didn't resemble a clown—my greatest fear. You couldn't even detect any makeup on his face or arms.

—I can't believe what a good job they did.

—He looks like he's sleeping, Alice said. —I can't ... I half expect him to sit up and start laughing.

Mom sat on a couch near the coffin. Crying. Stunned. My sisters and brother crowded her, whispered to her, massaged her arms.

—My god, I said. —Oh my fucking god.

—What's wrong? Alice said.

—This is real, isn't it? This is fucking real. He's ... fuck fuck fuck ... He's actually fucking dead, isn't he?

—Daulton? Alice escorted me to a chair.

—Like this isn't ... Is this in my head or is it real? I'm depressed, I said. —I'm fucking like maybe severely depressed maybe, and I don't know if ... Is this real? Is he dead? Or is it I mean I can't tell if this is real or if it's a product of my but oh fuck me I think maybe this might be real maybe.

I'm standing near the stove, smoking a cigarette. The lights are out. Through the window in the living room I watch snow drift sideways. Against the black sky, and in the absence of moonlight, the snow seems gray and ashen.

It's cold inside. Steam pours out of my mouth when I breathe. I exhale smoke and then I exhale again. Confusing steam for smoke, I try to more or less evacuate my lungs.

My stomach feels empty—so fucking empty— and I wonder if I should move toward the garbage can, or drag it closer to me. But then why bother?

I snub out my cigarette and light another one. The flame colors my reflection in a mirror across the room. I ignite the lighter again and study my face: it's gray; the colors of the flames superimpose colors over parts of my face, my cheeks mainly, and so I look both alive and not alive—both p and ¬p.

The universe blinks off and on again.

Dad squeezed ketchup on to his plate and passed the bottle to mom. She squeezed ketchup onto a hamburger bun and passed the bottle to me. I closed the cap, smacked it against my palm, unscrewed the cap, and watched a tongue-shaped blob from the bottle.

—It's the strangest thing, I said. —We didn't really have big moments, did we?

—What do you think? Dad said, to Mom. — Can he eat it all?

—He can put it away, she said.

The man stood beside the hostess station wielding a knife.

—Whenever I think of you, I said, —I don't envision epiphanies or ... like there's nothing ... at least nothing I remember ... that would qualify as the climax or anything of a searing drama.

—You think so? Dad said. —That's a big burger.

—Mine aren't any smaller, Mom said.

—I always thought it was stupid and cliché, maybe platitudinous, when people say it's the little things.

Dad laughed.

—They aren't, Mom said.

The man's triangles shifted, but his stance, angled toward me, told me he was staring at me.

—Maybe before you fry them, Dad said.

—That's not true. I have to ... the bread usually looks small.

—But I guess, I said, —in the end it doesn't matter. You're dead and there's nothing I can do about it. Eventually, everyone will be dead, and there's nothing I can do about it. Soon, I'll be dead, and there's nothing anyone can do about it. No one can persuade me. No one can change my mind.

A woman crossed the front of the room. She angled toward the hostess station, passing through the man. He rippled, as if composed of water, and assumed the shape of a person after she had glided through him.

—You'll get over it, he said. —You'll try and fail, but you'll get over it. Just remember this, just keep this in mind: work it out without dwelling on it. Don't dismiss it or push it to the side. And don't dwell on it.

His knife reflected light, white light. The air around him rippled as the light raced toward me.

It slammed into Dad and Mom, it slammed into the light fixture, it slammed into my eyes.

Photons exploded and transformed into drops of blood. The blood rained down on us. It covered my hands and wrists and raced down my forearms, as if traversing unseen canyons.

—There's something about it, Dad said, glancing at my burger, —I don't like it.

The blood raced down my forearms and spilled onto the table. Some drops splattered the plate, the fries, the burger.

—I'm sorry, I said. —It's ... Everything is too much sometimes.

The universe blinks off and on again.

Alice floats in the absence of everything. She's crying.

—Everything is sometimes too much. I'm sorry.

—But why? she says. —You're so fucking selfish.

—I'm empty and worthless, I say. —Everything feels dead. And everything ... everything is colorless and lifeless. And ... but you don't even know. No one does, and so ... I wonder if I'll be missed. I wonder if I'll ... and but I don't think anyone will miss me, and ... but ...

The universe blinks off and on again.

I'm standing near the stove, snuffing out a cigarette.I grab a knife from the silverware drawer, pull up my sleeves, and carve trenches into my forearms. Blood bubbles from the wounds; it dyes my flesh. I toss the knife into the sink, push my back against the cupboard door, slide into a squat. Then I fall over. Blood flows from my arms. Tears roll down my cheeks. Then everything ... everything ... Then everything blinks on and off, on and off again.

Afterword

It's strange now to read this book. I wrote it four years ago and haven't glanced at it in at least two years. It stirs bad memories for me. I initially set out to write a novel about human memory. *Slaughterhouse-Five* inspired the structure and I had hoped to use it to convey certain sensations about the processes of memory. On its surface, the novel was meant to explore death and grief—and how both affect memories of loved ones. By sheer coincidence, my father died a day after I started writing this novel. His death was unexpected and it shattered me. I knew, then, that the grief I intended to convey had transformed into confronting my own grief.

At the same time, I had experienced an extreme depressive state. Thoughts of suicide had fluttered in and out of my skull for several months. Nothing made me happy. Nothing made me smile.

I perceived everything as gray and gloomy. Everything taste like ash.

My father's death exacerbated my condition. Darkness consumed me. Yet somehow I continued writing. I poured everything into this novel: my thoughts about death, experiencing the death of my father, depression, anxiety, suicidal ideation, and suicide.

I had intended to employ a non-traditional structure to mirror neurophysiological processes during the encoding and retrieval of memories. As my mental state deteriorated, so, too, did the structure. Looking back on it, I see the structure mirrors my mental state. It says more about me at the time than it does about human cognition and memories—which, as I've said, was the point.

At the outset of writing this, I wanted to create a work of surrealism, something I've obsessed over since my teen years. Andre Breton wrote a brilliant—and underappreciated—gem of a surreal novella entitled *Soluble Fish*. His novella—strange and incoherent, banal and tedious, frustrating and enchanting—eschewed traditional narrative conventions in favor of attempting to unlock parts of the psyche hidden to consciousness. This, after all, was the aim of surrealism. It was as much a failed subset of psychology as it was a successful art movement.

Few people realize that surrealism started as a literary movement. To my mind, its potential is weakest in the written word. Although surrealists had produced a few great books, none matched the energy and imagery of the visual arts. An ambitious fuck, I had hoped to change that. I've long encoded surreal imagery into my text, but I intended to take the imagery to new heights in this novel. Fetuses replacing photons, faces shifting, corpses of my father replacing rain and falling from the sky—these images are the product of a broken brain struggling to deal with grief and fighting suicidal ideation. Looking back on it now, I see the novel not as a surrealist work; instead, it's a sort of literary expressionism: its proportions and exaggerations closer to the works of Egon Schiele than Dali.

Now that I think about it, it was implicitly expressionistic from the moment my father died. Throughout the writing, I attempted to convey the sensations and emotions I was experiencing to the reader. It was ambitious and I don't know if I succeeded.

Time has allowed me to view this novel a little more objectively than I did in the weeks following its completion. I think the non-traditional structure is its strong point. Linear time is largely a product of human perception + memories, and in eschewing a straightforward, three or five act structure, I do think I succeeded in conveying what I had hope to convey, re: memory, et cetera. My mental state destroyed the original plans, however, and the novel assumed a broken, phantasmagoric form. As far as form and structure goes, I suppose this novel is both a success and a failure.

And it's dark, too dark at times. It's important to note that the actual ending of the novel isn't presented in the last few pages: it appears as a subtext running throughout the book. If you read it closely, you'll learn about Sarah and Daulton's future. As pages wind down, however, the novel veers into darker and darker territory—and for good reason: about 12 hours after I completed this novel I voluntarily committed myself to the local psyche ward on suicide watch. Not realizing it at the time, I think the last page of the novel was meant as the closing paragraph of a long suicide letter. Fortunately, I wasn't ready to give up. And I'm here now, writing this. And I'm still fighting my depression. And it's worth the fight.

D. Dickey, on Klonopin and Prozac
11.4.17
2:15 pm

About the Author

Daulton Dickey lives in Indiana with his wife and kids. He's the author of *A Peculiar Arrangement of Atoms: Stories*, *Still Life with Chattering Teeth and People-Shaped Things, and other stories*, *Elegiac Machinations,* and *Bastard Virtues*. He runs the website Lost in the Funhouse (litfunhouse.com). Contact him at lostitfunhouse@gmail.com